CARALIS

by

REESE GABRIEL

CHIMERA

Caralissa's Conquest first published in 2003 by
Chimera Publishing Ltd
22b Picton House
Hussar Court
Waterlooville
Hants
PO7 7SQ

Printed and bound in Great Britain by
Cox & Wyman Ltd, Reading.

CARALISSA'S CONQUEST

Reese Gabriel

Senelek's eyes glowed a little more hotly. 'Perhaps I am his equal,' he crooned suggestively, his hands thick in her hair. 'In at least one area.'

Caralissa clenched her fists. 'I yield my body to you, Senelek,' she said proudly. 'But my desire is something you will never have.'

'Ah,' he said, feeding himself between her lips in a manner most satisfying to himself. 'But with the taking of your body shall come the possession of your heart, and even your very soul.'

There was no way to respond, the thick manhood of the priest having already pressed itself deep to the back of her throat. As if to enforce the men's dominance over her, hands came down now from behind, one upon each of her naked shoulders. Not forcefully pressing, but resting, possessively, as though enjoying her vicariously.

Chapter One

Caralissa, queen of Orencia, moved through the enemy encampment like a shadow, her lithe body concealed in garments of black leather, the breeches and vest of a man, her green eyes the only light as she darted from tree to tree. What arrogant fools these barbarians were! A mile into her territory and still they'd posted not a single sentry. Not that it would have mattered, for the moon goddess was on her side, conspiring to conceal her silvery rays behind a bank of clouds until the crucial moment when she must enter the warlord's tent.

Caralissa's heart pounded in her chest as she crouched, now at the flap of it. Even here there were no guards. Drawing from her belt the dagger she slipped through the narrow opening, silent as night. She saw him at once, his body framed by moonlight. Varik, chieftain of the Rashal hordes laying on his back, unclothed, a single layer of fur his only protection from the cold ground. The weight of sleep lay heavily upon his bronzed form, the nudity of him barely concealed by a second fur bunched at his waist. The man was larger than she expected, more formidable. Wasting no time she knelt beside him, hoisting the knife overhead, the pearl handle clutched tightly in both hands.

Caralissa had never killed anyone before, and she knew she must not allow herself to see this man as human if she were to complete her mission. She must ignore the mane of black hair spilling over his shoulders, the sculpted chest, the softly breathing lips, the hands large and capable of wielding a heavy sword or axe. It was said the Rashal chieftain could fell a tree, or a company of soldiers in a single swipe.

The moment is now, she thought, now or never. Taking aim above his heart she uttered a final prayer to the goddess, then fell forward against him with all her woman's strength. Eyes clamped tightly shut, teeth clenched she braced herself for the collision of razor-sharp steel on flesh and bone.

It was a collision that never came.

Caralissa cried out in shock as the knife suddenly recoiled and flew from her fingers. There was a flash of pain and then she felt herself hurtling backwards till it was her lying upon the furs and not him. Opening her eyes, blinking in the misty half-light, she saw him: Varik the Invincible, awake, his body lying across hers, his left hand pinning her wrists together above her head, his right clenching the intended murder weapon, the dagger of state her father had left her upon his deathbed.

He regarded her in silence, appraising, evaluating.

'When you seek to kill a man,' Varik told her at last, his voice calm and clear, as though delivering a lesson to a student, 'you must cut across the jugular like so, while holding back the head thusly.'

Pressing the knife to his thickly sinewed neck, arching it towards the ceiling, he offered her a simple demonstration. This accomplished he thrust the dagger into the ground beside him, sinking it to the hilt with an easy thrust.

'Now perhaps you would be so kind as to tell me why you have invaded my tent,' he suggested, fixing her with his deep blue eyes.

Caralissa returned the gaze, unflinching. 'I will,' she replied, determined to avoid staring at even a part of his magnificent body. 'As soon as you explain to me why you have invaded my country.'

He raised an eyebrow. 'Your country? I was not aware kingdoms in this region of the world were being handed out to comely wenches. If memory serves, we invade a place called Orencia in the morning, the king of which goes by the name of Lysanis. Of course we have invaded three kingdoms in this valley already this week, so I may well be confused.'

Caralissa pushed out her chin in fury. This Varik was not only a cruel warlord he was an egotistical blowhard to boot. Besides, he was starting to hurt her, with his muscled chest pressing down on her ribcage and his fingers squeezing her wrists. 'King Lysanis was my father. He has passed from this world and now I, Caralissa, am queen.'

'Queen, you say?' Varik released her, sitting upright so he was on his knees, straddling her midsection, his thighs on either side of hers. 'That is most interesting. You do realise, do you not, Queen Caralissa, that despite your rank you are now my prisoner. My slave, if I so choose.'

Caralissa felt the swell of him against the crotch of her leather breeches, her hunter's garb. 'I demand to be treated as a man,' she declared, attempting to extract herself from under him using her elbows on the soft furs.

Varik pinned her in place, exercising only the slightest tension to his thickly corded legs against her hips. 'I see,' he nodded, folding his arms across his chest, obscuring for the moment his dark brown nipples and hairless pectorals. 'Well, I suppose we could torture you and have you impaled upon a spike as we would any ordinary assassin.'

Caralissa felt the blood drain from her face. 'Good,' she bluffed. 'The sooner the better.'

'Of course, there is an alternative,' he continued, his eyes studying her intently, his emotions unreadable.

'An alternative?' she asked, trying not to sound desperate as she sought to settle herself beneath him in a manner that was dignified and befitting a monarch.

'Yes,' he said. 'An alternative, because you are a female we could treat you as such, making the sentence for your crime entirely different.'

'Different?' She frowned, giving a slight pout to her naturally full lips. 'And just out of curiosity, what would that sentence be – for a female, that is?'

He shrugged. 'Not impalement or torture, certainly. As a mere female, more than likely, you would simply be spanked.'

Caralissa laughed without humour. Though her long, fiery red tresses were currently tied back in a ponytail, and though her body was sheathed in acutely non-feminine clothes, she knew herself to be naturally beautiful, the desire of many a thwarted suitor. As for Varik's so-called sentence, it was a thinly disguised pretext to lay with her, nothing more. 'You would spank me for attempting to kill you? With such deterrents I am surprised you do not have would-be assassins lined up at your door.'

'Am I to assume, then, that you consider the prospect of my hand disciplining your bare buttocks as pleasurable?'

Caralissa regarded him with blatant disgust, even as she fought to keep at bay the strangely troubling image of herself naked before him, helpless under his power. 'Don't flatter yourself. I merely meant that if it were known in Orencia how lightly you punish, there would be thousands of women eager to attempt to finish you off.'

Varik pursed his lips. 'That is a possibility I hadn't considered. Tell me, are all the female killers in Orencia as eager to crawl onto my furs as you?'

Caralissa reddened at the implication. 'I shall see you dead,' she vowed, her eyes narrowing. 'I shall watch the jackals pick over your bones as I host a celebration for the thousands upon thousands of innocent people who have lost everything to your demon hordes and who even now suffer in anguish under your despotic rule! As for your insulting and demeaning punishment, I tell you as a "mere female" that you may take it and thrust it to the bottom of your scabbard!'

Varik shrugged. 'As I said, the choice was yours. I was merely trying to be agreeable.'

'Agreeable?' she cried. 'Well if that isn't rich, coming from a man who has to sit upon a woman to get her attention!'

'I take it a spanking is not to your liking. I could, as an alternative, give you a kiss.'

She screwed up her face in contempt. 'A kiss?' she mocked. 'Are you simpleminded as well as brutal and evil? Do you think we are courting now?'

'That is my offer, take it or leave it. One kiss as punishment and then, if you choose, you may go home.'

'That's it? No strings attached?'

'None,' he agreed. 'However, I must warn you, I am a very effective kisser.'

She bucked her hips, making a futile attempt to escape. 'At kissing pigs, maybe, but not women. Let go of me!' she cried. 'Who are you, anyway? You don't even talk like a barbarian.'

'My brother was raised in a city. He taught me their ways. I shall now kiss you. Resist me if you are able.'

Caralissa's expression dripped venom. 'Good luck, barbarian. You will find it easier to seduce a rock than to…'

Varik moved like lightning, employing the same power as when she'd tried to plunge the dagger into his chest. This time it was her lips he wanted and when she tried to

9

squash them shut, like a flattened strawberry, he reached out instead with his hand, placing it full upon her left breast. The caress was firm, pervasive, even through the thick leather. Opening her mouth in shocked protest Caralissa found it quickly filled with the man's tongue, deep and probing. All along her body she felt him; too late now she realised the folly of wearing the lace-up leather vest and pants with no undergarments.

Pointlessly then, with no power to back them, she put her hands to his chest. She intended to push him away, but all that came from her body was a moan of protest, small and weak emanating from somewhere in the back of her throat. For agonising minutes he worked her mouth and lips, as though she were a forgotten lover or a complicated puzzle from some ancient land to be solved. At one moment gentle, the next brutal, he plucked her senses, her emotions, her memories, systematically, mercilessly.

Piece by piece she felt her body betray her; her arms snaking round his shoulders, her fingers seeking and barely reaching across the broadness of his back, legs spacing themselves in subtle unwitting invitation, breasts straining at leather, pressing to his chest, neck arching, slim and delicately submissive, belly heating, softening, boiling in unknown anticipation. Lungs and nostrils sucking at the scents, the signatories of potent maleness, the musk of his skin, the complex aroma of hair, reeking of smoke and sky and the almost imperceptible odour of victory.

On and on it went – an onslaught, an unspeakable invasion – until finally, eyes shut, muscles collapsing, Caralissa was left no choice but to yield, inviting him as he plumbed from her depths untold secrets, untold possibilities.

'That is enough,' said Varik, removing himself from

her lips. 'I am satisfied now.'

She watched in disbelief as he rose to his feet, walked a short distance to the centre of the bare tent and sat down in a cross-legged position.

'What are you doing?' she demanded, her voice uncomfortably shrill as she sat up on her elbows, still breathing heavily.

'I am meditating,' he told her, reopening his closed eyes, betraying slight annoyance.

'But – but what about me?' she stammered.

'What about you? Your punishment is done. You may go home.'

Caralissa blinked in confusion. 'Home? But the kiss – I mean, I thought…'

'You thought what?' he asked as her sentence trailed off into nothingness.

She lowered her eyes, felt the heat rush to her cheeks. 'I thought you enjoyed kissing me,' she said softly.

'I was punishing you,' he shrugged. 'What was there to enjoy?'

Caralissa felt the bile rise to her throat. 'Bastard,' she hissed. 'You miserable, cruel bastard.'

The knife was within arm's reach. Freeing it from the ground she charged at him, giving little thought to the wisdom of her actions. Varik diverted her easily, landing her on her stomach painfully. Without pausing for breath she picked the weapon up again and stumbled towards him. This time he stood. With a single motion he snapped the blade from the handle and put her on her back, her neck beneath the crush of his heel.

'I think I shall have to impale you after all,' he decided, towering over her, her life hanging in the balance of his whims.

'I choose another kiss!' she exclaimed, reciting the

11

words as though she were countering some move of his in a game of skill.

Varik removed his foot. 'I do not think so. You are male after all; I see this now. I shall summon my guards and we will be done with this. It will take but a short while to fashion a suitable pole for your impalement. I hope you have not eaten recently, because it will make a bit of a mess.'

Caralissa's pulse quickened. The brute was calling her bluff. 'But you said yourself, I was sweetly breasted,' she reminded him, choosing for the moment to remain at his feet in the dirt rather than antagonise him by rising. 'That is not the quality of a man.'

He shook his head as he reached for the hollowed animal horn that hung from a rope upon one of the four wooden poles, the ones which held the four corners of his squared tent. 'There is no point to your words. I should have gathered from your clothes that you are not the sort of woman who desires a man. Perhaps you are of the *Mirax*,' he speculated, referring to the mythical race of forest dwellers said to possess androgynous body parts.

'No!' she protested, sitting up so she could reach for the tie of the strung leather that bound the slick vest across her bosom. 'I have the breasts of a woman, see?' she declared, having parted the halves of the material.

Varik beheld Caralissa's outthrust chest, the twin globes, firm and shapely. They shook visibly from her breathing, which was shallow and irregular.

'A woman's nipples should respond to a man,' he observed, bestowing an idle glance at her before putting the horn to his lips. 'Yours do not. You may wish to cover your ears. The sound is rather loud. Remind me, before your impalement, to allow you to evacuate your bladder. It will simplify matters.'

'Varik, please!' she cried, leaping to her feet, her hands at her nipples. 'Mine do respond, see?'

Caralissa manipulated the rosy pink nubs furiously, her hopes momentarily raised as she saw him lower the horn to his side to observe her. Somewhere in the back of her mind a voice was telling her that he was tricking her, using her own emotions against her to force her self-abasement by terrifying her with images of torture, but she couldn't think quite so clearly – not now, not with her loins still heated and her mind awash in a thousand competing thoughts and fears.

'You see?' she whispered, lowering her hands, revealing the evidence of her work. 'They are much bigger now. I am told they are one of my best features. A man I know has written poems about them, in fact.'

Varik was silently staring and for a moment she entertained the wild hope that she might yet seduce him, bring him to his knees, or even to his back. Would she have the courage, then, to strike him, not with the broken dagger, but with his own sword, the one that rested in its leather scabbard in the corner next to the dragon-painted shield and the axe, the sword that was nearly her height and probably half her weight as well?

'You have proven nothing; those breeches are not those of a woman,' he told her, drawing a deep breath for the horn. 'Who knows what they might conceal?'

'Oh no,' she insisted. 'These were specially made, for my – my mission. I wear dresses at home. Men seek what lies beneath them, though none has yet proven worthy. Please, don't blow the horn! Let me show you more.'

She was at his arm, pulling with all her might to prevent his touching the thing to his lips, and yet she could not move him a millimetre. The horn was midway now,

13

between his scantily clad midsection and his strong lips. Keeping one hand on him she clawed desperately at the opening to her trousers with the other.

'See?' she said, skinning the material down to her knees, revealing her bare sex, a triangle of fine red fleece every bit as vibrant as that on her head. 'I'm not a *Mirax!*'

Varik frowned, looking the part of a man whose patience was being sorely tried. 'What are you telling me, then? Do you wish to be treated as a human female or as a male?'

'Female,' she heard herself say, her mind racing at the various implications, complicated and dark. 'I – I wish to be treated as a female.'

Varik looked her up and down, assessing her in her fevered state of half undress. She blushed, her skin flush and damp with sweat.

'Very well then. Strip off your clothing, female. All of it.'

Caralissa removed her boots and pants, slipped off the open vest. Was it her imagination, or was there a certain edge in Varik's voice now, something subtle but hinting of a distinct change in their relationship? Back straight, arms at her sides, her every nerve on high alert, she stood before him anticipating the worst.

Saying nothing he looked at her, making her wait. In Caralissa's mind the seconds passed like hours, each one a blow to her shattered nerves. If only the light were a little better, so she could read his expression more fully. Then again, even close up this particular man was a mystery. Why was he unlike all the others – the boys and men who panted after her in the court of her father, buffoons and charlatans, a thousand times her inferior, a million miles behind the pace of her racing thoughts?

'Well?' she blurted at last, unable to bear the tension.

'What do you expect me to do?'

'You may kiss me,' he offered. 'If you wish.'

She stiffened. 'And if I do not wish to kiss you?'

'Then it will show me that you are a man who wishes to be flogged and burnt with pokers and then impaled.'

Caralissa went to him at once. Avoiding body contact as much as possible she leaned in, intending to plant on his cheek a single peck. Somehow, however, it was his lips she encountered once more, the rim of his dangerous mouth. Her cry of foul play was dissolved as Varik possessed her anew, regaining all his previous ground and more.

'You have twice more tried to kill me,' he said, pushing her away at last, his hands gripping her forearms, her toes barely grazing the ground. 'What should be done about this, female?'

The mention of her gender sent a chill down her spine. Between her legs she was wet now. 'I should be punished,' she managed weakly, the words emanating from stabbing breaths. 'I should be punished by you – by your hand.'

Caralissa shuddered as Varik placed his palm on her buttock, casually, yet with obvious possessiveness. 'With this hand?' he asked.

'*Yes…*' she replied, drawing the word into several syllables.

'You choose the disgrace of a girl's chastisement over the honourable death bestowed an assassin?'

'I do,' she confessed, her voice an intimate waft of air onto his chest. It wasn't just the horror of death that motivated her – she needed his hand, hard, firm, punishing. 'I choose to be treated as a girl.'

'As a naughty girl,' he corrected. 'One who, while she could be of no actual threat to a man on account of her being a mere female, has nevertheless annoyed him and

15

shown him disrespect.'

'Yes,' she agreed, allowing her attempted act of noble sacrifice for her country to be trivialised, feeling the flood of shame, delicious and hot between her legs as she formulated the words. 'I am a naughty girl. Please, Varik, please punish me.'

Varik's hand cracked loudly upon her firm posterior and Caralissa cried out, clutching him in wide-eyed wonder. 'Again,' she heard herself say.

'Not like this. Your punishment will occur on the furs, across my lap. But first you must relieve the pressure, so I can concentrate properly on your sentence.'

'The pressure?' she repeated numbly.

'Between my legs,' he said. 'Must you be taught everything from scratch?'

Caralissa swallowed hard. Of course she felt it, the man's sword, his natural one, swollen and hard, pressing against her thighs. But how was she to 'relieve' it exactly? 'Varik, there is something I must tell you. I have never before – never before...'

'By the gods,' he grumbled. 'Are you a virgin?'

'Yes,' she admitted, eyes downcast, never imagining such could be a deficit in a man's eyes.

'No matter,' he shrugged. 'It will only make punishing you more fun. For now, however, I shall make use of another part of your anatomy. At least that way I shall be freed of your incessant chattering for a time.'

Caralissa felt the words hit her like a brick. Her mouth. He was referring to her mouth. Did he intend to put his manhood down her throat? Was such a thing possible?

'Will you – I mean how will I...?' she began foolishly, only to find herself trailing off as Varik's hands found her shoulders, sending electric charges down her spine as he pushed her firmly downward till she was on her knees.

16

'There will be a discharge,' he explained. 'I am told it is without flavour, though there may be a large amount. When it begins swallow hard, several times in succession and you will have no problems. I will not expect you to take the length of me this first time, though I expect diligence, and over the course of time, improvement.'

Caralissa's mouth hung open as she beheld the thick rod, inches from her face, bulbous and pulsing, its base crowned with twin sacs, flesh coloured. Improvement, he'd said, over the course of time. Which meant she would do this again, perhaps many times. Her heart thudded in her chest. Did he intend to keep her then, as prisoner, or even as – perish the thought – a slave? He'd said it was his right. If he wished to exercise it, who would stop him come the morrow when he swept aside the pathetic ranks of weaklings who made up her army?

She clenched her fists, imagining for herself the split second luxury of resistance. If only she were a man. If only her father were alive, in his prime, the Lion of Orencia, he and his stalwart guard, the last of the true men of her nation. Then this story would have a different ending.

'Use your tongue on it, as if it were a sweet meat,' he counselled.

A sweet meat her eye! Tentatively, demonstrating duress, she dabbed at the extremities, determined to tinge her obedience with a healthy dose of disgust. If he were any kind of gentleman he would become so ashamed by her performance that he would have no choice but to put a stop to it.

'Not that way, Little Flame. Like this.'

Little Flame? What sort of a name was that?

Varik guided her head, his hand on the back of her neck, moving her into place. Caralissa gagged.

'Mmm, better,' he said, the head of his cock having

17

pressed itself halfway. 'Now use your tongue. Good. You are a natural. Perhaps I should offer your services to my men. What do you think? We would have to have raffles, of course, choosing representatives from each company. Five hundred or so in all. It would only be right. Rashal men share everything, you know.'

'I hate you,' she gurgled onto his shaft, the words dissipating in the warm pool of spittle surging between her cheeks. 'I hate you.'

Varik sighed, running a hand over the top of her head, stroking her like a dog. Humiliated, naked and on her knees, Queen Caralissa continued her ministrations. Apparently her protests meant nothing, nor did her rights as a free sovereign.

Very well, she thought, let me bide my time. He must sleep eventually. Then I will finish what I came here to do.

'Pay attention now, Little Flame,' he lectured. 'It will be soon. In my homeland a man's semen is revered. Were a slave to fail to retrieve every drop of her master's emission, she would be whipped.'

Caralissa longed to spit out the foul liquid when it came. In his face, in fact, which was where he deserved it. But she dared not, for there was a whip in this very tent. She'd seen it upon her entry, and thought with disgust that such a man as this would probably use it on his lovers. A lover. Is that what she was? Hardly! Unbidden her hand strayed between her thighs. The way he was controlling her, thwarting her will was making her twitch inside, inviting her to release. Would Varik whip her? He'd yet to even spank her, though he said he would.

'Do not touch yourself, Little Flame,' Varik chastised, pushing her shoulders back so she could no longer reach. Her back bowed, her neck exposed and arched, Caralissa received the promised flood. Varik's emission was warm, palpable, slightly salty. Outraged, infuriated, aroused beyond belief, she swallowed, repeating the motion over and over till he subsided.

'Go now to the furs,' he instructed, lifting her limp body till he made eye contact. 'Approach them on all fours. Kiss them with your lips but do not go onto them without permission. Do you understand, girl?'

Mouth open in rapt amazement, Caralissa nodded.

'Good,' he said, setting her down on the ground like a pet. 'Go then.'

Once again he delivered a stinging blow across her buttocks and once again she inferred it was something mild, a mere foretaste of what was to come. The journey to Varik's furs seemed to last forever, each impression of her palms and knees in the dirt being a new lesson in subjugation. Never did she imagine such a thing even for her own servants, or even for the girls in the pleasure houses where she sometimes observed, gaining entry by disguising herself as a man. Certainly the girls who served the exclusively male clientele there were slaves, being frequently made to serve their bodies along with the beverages they brought, but there'd been rules, floors upon which to walk and dance, and clothes, skimpy but real which they were allowed to wear.

How many nights she'd thrilled to the pleasure-house scenes, hiding behind her moustache, watching in rapt fascination each and every detail of the girls' ordeals as they submitted to the gropes, eventually letting themselves be led to the back rooms.

Afterwards, Caralissa's morbid appetite for vicarious female degradation sated, she'd sneak back across the moat into the castle. Her miserable elder sister, Romila, chewed her out for this on many occasions, but their father never said a word. He'd thought it amusing, even courageous on her part. It was always that way with her father, which is likely why, upon his death he'd passed over Romila, leaving Caralissa the throne.

The furs were soft upon her lips. What new sensations for her this night! The lips and shaft of a barbarian and harsh animal furs all upon her mouth in one short time span. Lowering her head she reached back to unbind her hair, allowing it to cascade over her face to the ground. She needed to think. She was unravelling, threatening to burst apart at the seams.

Her mission, she must remember her mission. What means would she use to dispose of him, then? It was a few hours at most till dawn to complete the deed and flee from the camp, returning victorious to her cheering subjects, proving herself thereby the best, the wisest of rulers. There was a sword here, and an axe. Could she lift them?

Caralissa gasped, her thoughts shattering as she felt the soft fur on her fingertips. She was touching them by mistake! As if from a hot fire she pulled them back to the ground so that she might be fully in accord with Varik's will. The action shamed her at once, for it was that of a captive girl, a mere slave.

And what if she were? said a voice deep in her head – the implications enflaming her between her clenched thighs. What if she were Varik's slave already?

She shuddered as he moved by her, his calf muscle brushing her leg. Looking up, through the tangle of her hair, she watched as he knelt in the middle of the furs upon one knee. 'Come here,' he commanded, slapping his palm upon his thigh. 'Lay yourself across me here.'

Caralissa crawled to him, painfully aware that by doing so of her own free will she was revealing herself to be not a queen, but a common slut. Varik lifted his arm so she could put herself into position. He made her slide to and fro several times, in ever finer increments till she lay exactly as he wished: her sex pressing directly onto his solid thigh muscles. Almost immediately she began to seep her fragrant juices onto him. When she tried to move to her knees he pushed her back up so that she was forced into the shape of a bridge, her feet and hands bracing her on the furs.

'Widen your legs,' he said, using his hand to induce her to spread herself. 'Good,' he praised, finding access to her wet opening, manipulating her clitoris till she whimpered. 'Now we are ready to begin.'

Caralissa clawed at the ground. The magical fingers were gone and she was alone. 'Varik, please don't stop. I'm so close.'

'I want you to count for me, Little Flame. Can you do this?'

'Yes, Varik,' she panted, having no choice but to find her pleasure in obeying him, in responding to his condescension.

Varik patted her twice, cupping her cheeks. Caralissa had never been spanked, never even been touched by her father or her nannies. Alinor, the young man who wrote so eloquently of her nipples, also composed verses on corporal punishment and on a few occasions he'd let her spank him as 'punishment' for his naughty words. But that was as far as her experience went.

It was, of course, no preparation whatsoever for the barbarian's treatment of her.

Caralissa cried out with the first blow, the tears coming quickly to her eyes. Varik's hand burned and it sent spasms up and down her body. The worst part, the really terrible thing, was that she couldn't move, Varik having pinned her across his knee to prevent any escape. It was going to continue, on and on, as long as he wished.

'You did not count, Little Flame. We must begin again.'

Varik's second blow was as evil as the first. She swore she would die, that she would never make it beyond three. 'One!' she called out hastily, nearly missing the count a second time.

Two more blows followed and then she was begging, pleading for him to stop, promising him anything, anything at all for him to let her go.

'Be careful what you wish for,' Varik said, as if thinking out loud.

Caralissa didn't have long till she understood what he'd meant. For in place of his firm spanks he now re-substituted the grinding of his fingers against her sex. Biting her lip and balling her fists, Caralissa was in no time begging again, this time for sexual release.

'No,' Varik said. 'I do not give you permission to climax.'

Sweat beaded on her forehead. He was holding her back, as if on invisible chains, preventing her from reaching the point of orgasm. 'I – I cannot bear this!' she wailed as he worked her, stripping bare her nerves and laying her open as if she were a lute to be stroked, string by string. 'Please, warrior, I beg mercy!'

'I will stop,' he informed her. 'But the alternative is spanking. One or the other. You choose.'

Caralissa groaned, knowing herself defeated, utterly outwitted. 'All right, all right,' she cried a moment later. 'Spank me again, only take your hand from me!'

She missed the count, which meant they would have to start again from one. The pain flared more quickly this time, and after the second she was forced to ask Varik to resume his caresses. She assumed he would have to ease up on account of her being so super heated, but it turned out there were more tricks up his sleeve. Using only the surface of his fingernail, he brought her back from her stupor, managing to rekindle the throbbing ache without pushing her over the edge to release.

With all her might, sweat-soaked, confused and wild-eyed, Caralissa convulsed against his hand, her motions careening her from Varik's fingertip down to his knee and back up again. On and on, and still no relief.

'Please,' she croaked, fearing she might soon lose her voice or her sanity. 'Spank me.'

Caralissa yielded to his blows, her body limp. In a ghostly voice she called the count. After three smacks he stooped his head to hear her faint request for yet another switch, to a renewed round of touching to her neglected loins. Sliding his hand over her burning cheeks he resumed his possession of her sex. This time she wailed, her very sensations of pain and pleasure having been undone, confused inexorably. 'No more,' she gasped, her head tossing to and fro, her lean body like a sinew, a wire stretched to breaking point. 'Please, my lord, no more.'

Too late, Caralissa caught herself, the word 'lord' slipping from her mouth unbidden, a confession extracted under torture. Bracing herself she awaited the storm – whether from herself or him or both, she did not know.

'It is time for you to answer some questions, my Little Flame,' he told her, his hand on her back, soothing, reassuring.

'I will not betray my people,' Caralissa countered in a raspy voice, her cheek pressed to the dirt, her damp forehead sticky with dust. 'You can't turn my body against me.'

Varik trailed a finger up the inside of her parted thighs, stopping short of the simmering volcano of her sex but still close enough to wrench from her a new round of spasms. 'Why did you come here alone?' he asked.

'I didn't – trust – anyone else,' she spit through clenched teeth. 'So I did – everything – myself.'

'That was unwise,' Varik told her, eliciting a moan as he ran the palm of his hand across her stretched calves. 'Considering that a man came to us earlier today to inform us there would be an assassin sent from the castle.'

'Then you knew!' she exclaimed. 'And yet you posted no guards?'

'Death comes when it wills,' Varik reasoned. 'We do not frighten it off with our preparations. Senelek, my brother pleaded with me, but I gave him direct orders to drink extra wine to facilitate sleep. I did the same. In addition, I relieved the regular bodyguards and removed Ahzur, my tiger, for the night. I did not even allow prayers. A man must meet his own fate, without fear.'

'Are you mad?' she asked, trying to block the sensation of his knee as it shifted in such a way as to create friction just beneath her breasts.

Varik laughed. 'I have been accused of such. Though if anything, I would say I am not insane but merely bored. There is in my life no challenge left. Perhaps that is why you are here, Little Flame. I have one more question for you then we shall try something new. If you were given the chance, would you lay for my entire army to save your kingdom?'

'The question is not fair. Nor is any other when the person being asked lies unclothed across your knee.'

He patted her glowing cheeks, inducing a mild wince. 'Well said, Little Flame. Now you may kneel upon my bed furs.'

Caralissa lifted her head, doing her best to extract herself from the man's lap. Varik was cool, calm and collected, not to mention dazzlingly gorgeous. It was probably the effect of her captivity and his powerful domination of her will, but she was strangely attracted to him in a way not even Alinor the poet had been able to invoke in her.

'I need to be relieved again,' he explained, lying upon his back, revealing a second erection every bit as vigorous as the first. 'I would like you to use your hand this time, though when it is time to finish, I will have your mouth again.'

'You are a beast,' Caralissa told him. 'An animal, with not a shred of respect or honour for a lady.'

He looked up at her where she knelt. 'It is your heated sex which speaks so harshly, on account of your heavy need,' he explained, running a hand against the lips of her nether opening, inducing a new round of shudders. 'Serve me now and well, and perhaps we shall allow you an orgasm.'

'How magnanimous,' she said bitterly, lowering her head to his crotch. 'I don't know how I'll repay you.'

Varik seized her hair, preventing further downward motion. 'Begin this time at my feet,' he ordered. 'Work your way up, using your tongue and lips and fingertips.'

Caralissa did as she was told, grateful not to have to make eye contact for the moment. If she were not careful she would wind up being impaled yet. Her progress proved to be surprisingly slow, especially as he made her begin over two times, on account of what he felt were half-hearted efforts, hardly worthy of comparison with the services of his slaves in the homeland of his people.

Which, incidentally, was precisely where she wished he would return at this very moment, he and his infernal barbarian army. Let him have the rest of the world – why did he have to trouble her little kingdom?

'Do not be discouraged,' he told her, as if somehow it bothered her that she'd no idea what she was doing. 'You are inexperienced and lacking in incentive. Tomorrow we shall undertake some training exercises and you shall see the difference.'

Caralissa clenched her thighs. No man would ever train her, despite the yearning induced by the very word. She would sooner find herself a pole and conduct her own impalement. 'Tomorrow you will be occupied,' she informed him. 'Fighting my army.'

Varik took her hand and placed it upon his throbbing shaft. 'And you too will be occupied pleasuring me with your body.'

'Why do you not take me?' she demanded, stroking him lightly, 'and get it over with?'

'I shall not force from you anything you will not give me, Little Flame. When it is time you will come to me yourself, begging for a cock between your legs, mine or the lowest ranking of my soldiers. It will matter not so great will be your need to be possessed.'

Caralissa spat at him, full in the face.

'There will be punishment for that,' he told her. 'Tomorrow. In the meantime, you will clean me with your tongue.'

Caralissa gave no argument. In order to clean his cheek fully she needed to move herself to several angles, all of which compelled her to compress her breasts against various parts of his hard flesh. His skin was smooth under her subjugated tongue. He smelled of scented leather, tinged with honey.

Varik remained expressionless as she carried out her punishment duty. Her readiness for breeching was painfully apparent, she feared, by her colouring and her odour, it would have taken an imbecile not to see she was begging to be taken, having insulted him so that he might be roused to overpower her.

'That is enough,' he told her. 'It is time to prepare

yourself for my second emission.'

She dropped her head efficiently to his lap, drawing
him in with a single caress, soft and wet. For some reason,
in the midst of all of the confusion and anguish, this one
act, servile and perverted as it was, was beginning to
make sense to her. It was almost as if it gave her an
anchor, a sense of being and purpose. Gingerly now,
reverently, she accepted him, allowing him to move her
head to suit him as he settled himself in deep, groaning
from the contact, from the sweet urgent sucking. When
he filled her at last, rewarding her with a load nearly as
thick and full as the first, she let loose with a new trickling
of tears though this time she understood not from whence
they came. For it was not exactly sadness she felt.

'Lie beside me, Little Flame,' he said when he was
satisfied.

Slowly, painfully, on pins and needles, Caralissa lowered
her fevered body. She desired neither contact nor comfort,
but he was insistent, his large hand cradling her belly.

'Put your hands above your head,' he instructed, 'palms
up.'

The position was one of helplessness, but also one of
extreme feminine beauty. She'd seen the dancers conclude
their performances this way, in the pleasure-houses.

'Do not fight me,' Varik said, as his hand began its
inevitable journey southward. 'If you surrender completely
to me you shall find your bliss.'

Caralissa arched her back, instantly transformed into a
wanton she-beast. His hand poised, Varik held her at the
brink.

'So long as you are with me, Caralissa,' he whispered,
warming her with the sound of her name on his lips. 'You
belong to me. As do your orgasms. When I choose to
pluck one from you, as I do now, it is for my joy not

27

yours. Do you understand?'

'Yes,' she agreed, though at the moment she knew nothing except the razor-edge of need, the precipice of desire over which she yearned to plummet. 'I am yours.'

Varik finished her off, neither one of them troubled over the possibility of the perfidy of her statement. In this context, in the middle of this darkened mystical night, she was his and whatever the light of day might bring she would bear his brand upon her heart forever because of it. Caralissa was sure her screams of pleasure, her pent-up passion would awaken his soldiers, perhaps even the spirits of the dead inhabiting the nearby villages.

In the end, however, no one came upon them and the moment remained private. A tableau made of two souls. The barbarian overlord, insatiable and pining for risk and the virgin queen teetering on the edge of fatal submission; the pair of them together for an uncertain number of nows, moments to be counted and allocated, their nature as yet un-revealed.

Shivering and naked Caralissa sank back into the exigencies of the hour; a thousand forgotten worries jockeying themselves for position, the chief among them being escape, revenge and mayhem, in that order.

'We will rest now,' he said imperiously as he rose to his feet to fetch a cord of leather.

'This is for your protection,' Varik explained, winding the cord about her wrist, knotting it firmly. 'If you manage to run from me, which you no doubt will do after I fall asleep, you are liable to fall afoul of my archers, or else stumble into the tiger pit. This way we shall both sleep well and awaken fresh in the morning.'

Caralissa watched in disbelief as he wound the free end round his fist, securing her as though on a leash. He offered for her to remain on the furs at his side, but she refused, preferring the honesty of the cold autumn ground to the embrace of a despicable coward and bully. Taking full advantage of her lead, stretching it to its maximum, she found a spot for herself a foot away from him.

She watched in fury as he began to snore happily, his skin toasty warm in the furs. The sword, she thought, why can't I reach the sword? Teeth chattering, miserable and cold, she tried to think of tomorrow and the freedom she would win as her troops discovered her absence and began their bold assault on the Rashal encampment.

Bold assault. Who was she kidding? The Orencian military was a shambles, a joke, thanks to Romila's meddling and that of Telos, her foppish idiotic lover whom she kept trying to foist into high places. Telos was more intent on breeching Caralissa's defences than those of any enemy, real or imagined.

A pitiful sound escaped her lips. She couldn't endure the ground. It wasn't fair, wasn't right. Intently, Caralissa watched the sex-sated barbarian, waiting for signs of deep sleep. When at last he seemed fully removed from reality, unable to witness her shameful surrender, she crawled stealthily to the furs, thrusting her tired, nerve-wracked body under the warm material. She would remain there a few moments only, she promised herself, and then she'd return to the ground, to the dignity of her self-imposed exile, away from his arrogant male beauty and his smug snores.

She was counting down the seconds, halfway to the sixty she'd allotted herself, when it hit her. Fatigue, overwhelming and irresistible. Unconsciousness was overtaking her, the closest thing to death one may know on this side of the grave and every bit as powerful. Still muttering a tiny oath to the goddess, she fell then into sleep, deep and dreamless, full of every good hope.

Hope for the morrow, hope for Orencia. Hope for a miracle. And for revenge.

Chapter Two

Caralissa awoke with a heavy weight across her chest. She dreamed it was a tree, downed in a powerful storm, but when the rasping blow of air came to her ears, tickling her to consciousness, the memories flooded back. It was Varik, on his back, his head next to hers, his oversized arm draped insolently across her breasts, the hand trailing down with disgusting familiarity to the bridge of her thighs.

Insolent pig! Somehow she'd fallen asleep on his furs and now he was holding her, like he owned her. Trembling ever so slightly Caralissa relived the orgasm, the overwhelming flood and degradation. She was sore. Her thighs, her buttocks beneath her, even her jaws ached. He'd been a beast, treating her like a domestic animal, a mere slave. In Orencia if a man were to even think such things with regard to her royal person, let alone attempt them, he would be put to death. Merely to gaze admiringly at the red-haired queen from afar was a delight many of her citizens would savour for a lifetime, a privilege not to be abused.

Varik mumbled something and moved against her. How she hated the man! By the goddess, why was this happening to her? She had prayed, taken augers and even consulted the high priest to insure the success of her journey; what more could she have done? Caralissa drew a troubled breath, giving herself a moment to absorb it all – the terrible calamity of her failed mission, Varik's surprise capture of her, his degrading 'punishments' and worst of all, the prospect of a new day dawning with her as a prisoner in the camp of a powerful enemy.

Very slowly and carefully, using her free hand, Caralissa tried to extract herself from under her sleeping tormentor. His breathing was undeservedly easy, like a baby's. Hopefully he would not rouse himself seemingly from the dead, leaping upon her a second time, terrifying her nearly to the point of ghost-hood. Squirming on her tender buttocks she began to slide away from him, inch by inch. Like an avalanche his flesh seemed to follow, re-pinning her with each motion. The arm. She needed to move the damned arm. It may as well have been a tree trunk, just as she dreamed, for all its lifeless weight.

There! She was almost free. Now to release her other hand, the one he was still lying on. But wait – why was it stuck like that?

The cord! She forgot about the cord. Flexing her unseen hand, which was obscured beneath him, she realised to her horror it was still there, unbreakable. The miserable piece of leather he'd dared to impose on her flesh. Sick with rage she replayed his words in her mind.

'This is for your protection,' he'd told her, his voice oozing paternalistic smugness. 'So we will both awaken fresh in the morning.'

Caralissa decided his death would be slow. And there would be torture, both of a conventional kind and a more intimate, sexual kind. Idly she scanned the interior of Varik's tent, looking for suitable weapons. The enclosure was square, made of thick orange-red material held aloft by poles, one at each corner, with a large opening in the roof. It was a barbarian structure, of course, unfit for civilised persons. There wasn't even any proper furniture, only these furs, and in the corner a sort of high wooden stool on which was placed a helmet, badly dented with a plume of black feathers. How charming.

Then there was the sword, the one she saw last night, huge and deadly, the scabbard inscribed with symbols, presumably from his nonsensical language. And don't forget the axe and bits of armour hung from the poles, a chest plate, knee protectors and things she couldn't even identify.

For a wardrobe he boasted several tunics that were flung over the top of a spear, which in turn was thrust into the ground at an angle. She made a sarcastic mental note to consult the man's decorator to help her at the castle. That is, if she ever got back there again. Food. She needed food. Was there something to eat, amidst the small wooden boxes, carved and decorated, or perhaps in the woollen sacks lying hither and thither across the trampled ground, the grass, largely ruined now – her grass, the grass of her fathers?

The sword. She must find a way to levitate it to her, dangling it in mid-air above them, and then release it so it fell between them, cutting the cord. And then she'd use it on him to…

Caralissa froze her thoughts. There was a low growl, very faint, to her right. And eyes; she sensed eyes. Slowly, very slowly she turned. The huge cat was sitting on its haunches, watching her. The tail was flicking, almost as if it were a household pet, one of the small furry things that were forever under foot at home. Except this feline looked to weigh hundreds of pounds. Its paws alone were the size of saucers.

The thing blinked, as if deciding on its course of action. Caralissa glared at it, mesmerised. Its fur was the colour of black pearl, mixed with irregular cloud-like patches of grey and white. The teeth were large and curved, spectacularly white. Whiskers bristled along either side of its pink nostrils. Its muscles were lean and with a single swipe of its claws, she was quite certain the creature could end her life or Varik's.

She should scream, and yet any sudden noise might set it off. Caralissa gasped. The cat was getting up on its feet, moving silently on the pads. No wonder she didn't hear it come in; it was quiet as a mouse. By the goddess, it was coming straight for them!

'Varik,' she whispered, her voice a study of compressed intensity. 'Wake up. There's a wild animal.'

He muttered something, shifting so that his hand clamped her breast.

'Wake up, you fool! We're going to be mauled!'

'Why do you disturb my sleep, woman?' he enquired, his face nuzzled at her shoulder, his eyes as yet unopened.

Caralissa exhaled, put her hand to her face. It was too late. The creature was upon them. The last thing she saw was the paw, coming straight at her, pressing down towards her bare, unprotected flesh.

'Ahzur, stop that nonsense...' Varik grumbled.

Caralissa opened her eyes. The animal was leaning across her, ignoring her as it licked Varik's face and head, slobbering him noisily with its huge sandpaper tongue. The drool fell in droplets, pebble-sized upon her head.

'Varik!' she screamed, anger replacing mortal terror. 'Get this filthy creature off me!'

The Rashal warlord sat up, his hair hanging about him in tangles. 'Can a man get no sleep in his own tent?'

Caralissa was on her feet, tugging at the tether which bound them wrist-to-wrist. If need be she would tear his arm off and hers to get to the sword or the tent flap, whichever came first.

'Ahzur,' Varik barked, seeing the purpose of her action. 'Lah-ka.'

The cat lowered its head, gingerly taking the cord

between its teeth. With a single bite, neat and clean, the tensely drawn leather was severed. Caralissa fell on her behind. Recovering almost immediately she rose again, running for the sword.

'The water jug is to the left,' he said. 'You can fill it at the stream.'

Intrigued as always by his audacity, she gave pause. 'Excuse me?'

Varik was on his back once more, the cat lying beside him, occupying her place. 'You will fetch water for my breakfast, using the jug,' he said, as though it were something patently obvious.

Caralissa's mouth hung open. 'You're not serious?'

'I am. And if I were you I would hurry. With each passing minute more soldiers awaken. They should know to leave you be, but there are one or two bad apples in every barbarian horde, as you can imagine.'

She regarded him, sprawled in his insolent nudity. Her mind turning like lightning she considered her options. She could fight him on the matter, but that would likely wind her up over his lap once more, or else slobbering over one of his incessant erections. Alternatively she might simply try to kill him, though the odds of disabling the combined weight of the man and his beast were not good. Or she could take the bucket and run. In broad daylight this would be no easy matter, but if she were to be killed – which she would be inevitably – better to have it come at the hands of some unknown swordsman or archer than from this conceited, ignorant chieftain.

'I have no clothes to wear,' she said, deciding it would be inconvenient to attempt escape in the nude.

'You may borrow one of my tunics.'

She was able to pull one down from the spear. It hung to mid-thigh and when cinched with one of the leather

35

cords that seemed to exist in endless supply, Caralissa was able to make a feasible garment for herself. It was tight at her waist and cut low at the neck, which meant it revealed a substantial percent of her charms. It might come in handy, she thought, for enacting help in getting out of the camp.

She would have liked to have her boots, but when she went to put them on she saw they were wet and gnarled, presumably from Ahzur, who may well have come in and out several times while they slept. Oh well, a barefoot escape it would have to be.

'Hurry back, Little Flame,' he called out to her as she left the tent. 'When you return I will begin your training.'

'Oh goodie,' she snapped sarcastically, knowing full well that once she was out of the man's tent she would never see his face again.

Caralissa blinked, her eyes temporarily dazzled by the morning sun. As her vision adjusted she saw she was being watched, this time by men not beasts. There were a dozen or more warriors, standing in small groups, some shirtless, others with vests of mail or chest armour. All of them wore boots and breeches and were huge like Varik, though their eyes seemed colder, unforgiving. Their conversations halted as they beheld the scantily clad beauty, the shapely redhead lithely emerging from the chieftain's tent.

Clutching her water bucket, keeping her eyes to herself, she began to walk. There were footsteps behind her and a pair of warriors trailing her to the left. She would go directly to the stream, she decided, saving her escape for later. Caralissa knew the way, having ridden horses often in this area as a child. The Rashal had greatly transformed it, felling trees, erecting barricades and raising huge tents at regular intervals along the nearby hillsides. Closer to the stream she saw rows of wooden machines, siege engines – catapults and battering rams – neatly arrayed, already facing their target – the walls of her faraway castle.

More and more warriors joined the excursion, following her as if in a parade. Others merely watched her pass as they leaned upon spears or swords. In a clearing to the left some hundred or so men partook in exercise, vigorously clashing their steel, their rounded brightly-coloured shields lying in stacks on the ground as they ran at one another, bare-chested and fearsome. There were patrols too, soldiers in helmets, holding thick chains at the end of which tromped proud, long-toothed black and grey tigers, cousins, no doubt of Ahzur.

It was clear to Caralissa as she made her survey of the Rashal camp that what Varik said was true: he had deliberately lowered precautions to allow the rumoured assassin free access. Much as she hated to burst her own pride, it was obvious that were these men even mildly vigilant last night, she would already be arrayed upon one of the sharp poles which pierced the ground at regular intervals, their tops tufted with Rashal flags, crisply flapping in the morning breeze.

So she had been betrayed; just as Varik said while simultaneously spanking and fondling her, driving her mad with desire, imposing on her the unbearable mix of pleasure and pain. Who could it have been, though? Only the royal council knew of her actions, and these were rock steady old men, the most loyal servants of her father.

And Romila, of course. She knew as well. Her dark-haired, sullen sister was displeased by her decision to end the impending war in one fell swoop, but could petty jealousy ever lead Romila to endanger her life, not to mention the security of the entire state? No, it wasn't possible. She was glad, though, that she'd removed the scheming Telos from the castle before she left. The man was a worm, a charlatan, who when not occupied in his pathetic attempts to bed young maidens, was forever finding ways to line his pocket from the royal treasury.

'You there! Halt!'

A single warrior blocked her path. His chest was mailed in black metal, worn over a tunic, also black. A red raven was painted across the front. Over his shoulders was slung a cape. His hair was tightly bound in a single braid. There was something about him, something different from the rest of the men with their casual stances and their mismatched uniforms.

'I am going to the stream,' said Caralissa, answering the unasked question that burned in the man's narrow eyes. 'I am to fetch water for Lord Varik.'

The man looked her up and down then addressed something to the entourage that now accompanied her. Several men answered at once in Rashal, their tones indicating lack of knowledge or responsibility. Caralissa held her head proudly as the man approached her, the tips of his boots touching her bare toes. 'I shall fetch Senelek,' the man decided, switching back to the language of the Valley, the language she spoke and Varik spoke. Then to the others, raising his arm, he issued an order. At once the others began to disperse.

Caralissa made a mental note to beware of the man in the future, and any others like him, with their distinctive hairstyle and uniform. She met no further trouble on the way to the stream, though when she arrived she saw there was a small group of men there already, laughing and shouting, passing among them a small horn which appeared to contain liquid. Judging by the volume of their conversation, and its boisterousness, it was something alcoholic.

Warily, she made her way to the stream.

'By the gods,' slurred one of them, a blond fellow, hair long and stringy. 'My breakfast has arrived.'

There was raucous laughter. Judging by the thicker accents and halting speech, she gathered these were common soldiers.

'To Hades with you, Galak,' roared a bearded man, his hair wild and black, a scar across his right cheek. 'This is my gift!'

'For shame,' chastised a third man, red-haired like her. 'Can't you see a lady is present? Forsooth, milady,' he bowed. 'What brings you to our fine watery establishment?'

'I am to fetch water,' she said. 'For Lord Varik.'

'For Varik?' He slapped his knee. 'Do you hear that, men? Who but Varik could win himself a trophy before the battle is even begun?'

'Long live Varik!' said a man, his voice hoarse from shouting or drinking or both.

'Aye,' grumbled a second, raising the horn. 'To Varik, a chief who knows how to take care of himself first.'

'To the perks of the chieftainship!' called another.

'Varik is waiting for me,' she told them hastily, not liking the tone of their words.

'I'll bet he is,' called the red-haired man. 'You hear that, men? I'll give you three guesses why we aren't marching yet today. And I'll wager my share of the next round of spoils we won't do any marching tomorrow, either! Not once Varik gets his water bucket filled!'

Galak shoved his way forward. 'I have something for your water bucket,' he sneered, gesturing rudely to the crotch of his tan britches.

Caralissa stiffened as the bearded man reached across Galak to touch her chin. 'Who are you, anyway?' he asked, the smell of his breath making her swoon.

'I am the queen,' she said proudly, realising too late the comic nature of her remark in the current circumstances. 'The queen of Orencia.'

Gales of laughter rose into the sky, mingling with the smoke of the dozens of campfires, rising almost as high as the highest of the white clouds.

'A queen!' the man howled. 'A queen. Shall we kiss her ring?'

'Let her kiss this,' Galak said, his attention still fixated on his genitals.

She felt a hand from behind, clenching her buttocks. 'Not till I've had a piece,' said a new man, his tongue lapping at her ear. 'It's been two months since I've spiked a wench. I'm ready to explode inside my pants.'

'It would be a very small explosion,' observed Garak.

'We'll see about that!' the man fumed, taking Caralissa in his arms. Others quickly joined in, whether to stop or encourage him she wasn't sure. She was on the verge of going down to the ground beneath the lot of them when a whizzing spear, lofted from the hillside, landed at their feet.

The men looked up, spoiling for a fight. Seeing the small company of black armoured men, however, they quickly reconsidered. Caralissa felt her pulse quicken. Among them was the dark-eyed man, the one from before.

'What is the meaning of this?' demanded their spokesman, a sturdy man, his head clean-shaven save for a long black braid rooted at the base of his skull. From the look of him, the black breastplate being trimmed in gold with a fiery yellow dragon at the centre, Caralissa took him for their leader.

The redhead, having been shoved forward by the others, became spokesman for the band of soldiers. 'Forgive us,

Lord Senelek. We were sporting with the girl. A capture of our chieftain, so it seems.'

'I am queen of this land,' she offered, deciding to play up her special status. 'Your chief captured me. And now I must bring him water.'

Senelek examined Caralissa. She felt naked under his gaze, naked and used. Uncharacteristically – and hating herself for her loss of nerve – she lowered her eyes.

'You are drunk,' Varik's brother said, turning back to the redhead.

Immediately the man's face went pale, as though just realising the severity of his offence. He fell at once to his knees. 'We heard rumours we would not march today, my lord. Behold the hour,' he pointed towards the sun. 'It is already late.'

Senelek thinned his lips. 'I need no lesson in astronomy.'

'Forgive me!' the man wailed, realising his compound error.

Senelek considered the trembling man before finally addressing the assembly. 'Be gone, the lot of you. Tomorrow when we fight you will all march in the front line.'

'Yes, Lord Senelek,' the man cried. 'We thank you, Lord Senelek.'

The revellers scattered like rats, leaving Caralissa to the sombre company of Varik's brother and his men.

'Thank you,' she said to her rescuer, though secretly she suspected she would have been better off with the drunken braggarts.

Senelek eyed her. 'I am not fooled by you,' he told her, his fingers lifting her chin. 'Not for an instant.'

Caralissa remained painfully still. Where was Varik, she wondered, when she really needed him?

'How come you to be in this camp?' Senelek demanded.

She relayed, in unsteady tones the full story of her attempted assassination, the thought of lying to the man being incomprehensible.

Senelek shook his head. 'You came by sorcery,' the man corrected. 'Not by stealth. You are a witch sent to destroy the Rashal. Varik is under your spell, it seems, but I am not. Do not think you will succeed in your plot. I shall defeat you.'

His eyes lingered a moment longer as though deciding something. 'Take her,' he ordered two of the men. 'Back to Varik with her. Let him have his toy. For now.'

Senelek's words chilled her. Their implications echoed in her mind the whole way back to Varik's tent. Who was this man, exactly? She'd heard Varik speak of her brother in such reverent tones and yet the man was seething inside with hostility, a fact plainly obvious to Caralissa.

'You took long with my water,' Varik complained as she re-entered the tent, the black warriors having left her at the entrance.

'I was detained,' she replied, a bit cross.

Varik's back was to her. He was dressed now, wearing dark trousers, boots and a red tunic, belted with a sash. His arms were crossed as he contemplated a map pinned to the rear of the tent. She recognised it as a representation of the Valley of Seven Kingdoms, of which Orencia was one, and beyond it the Forests of Night, an unexplored territory in which demons were said to dwell, along with invincible man-eating beasts. These would be Varik's next destination, logically, once he subdued her lands. That is, unless he were growing tired of building an empire. Strange, she thought, that such an idea should cross her mind. Was she capable of reading the man's thoughts?

'I encountered Senelek,' she said, trying to keep her tone neutral.

'Senelek is my greatest ally,' Varik told her, as if he could read her mind, too. 'He has fought beside me since the beginning. From the days when the Rashal were one village, unable to defend even our own hearths.'

'Why does he wear black, he and his men?'

'Senelek is the Keeper of the Way. He is high priest. He and his men enforce the moral codes. In addition he informs us of the will of the gods. He is stern, but we would not be an empire without him.'

'My sister is jealous of me, too,' Caralissa said, not knowing from whence the words came. 'She wanted to be queen instead of me.'

Varik turned, his face bearing a most peculiar expression. 'Why do you tell me this?' he mused. 'Were you sent to me by gods or by demons? Can you answer me that, Little Flame?'

'I came of my own accord.'

Varik smiled. 'We have much in common, you and I. Unlike Senelek, we seek our own ways, not those of gods.'

'And what is your way, Varik?'

She saw the light in his eyes, suddenly kindled. 'My way is conquest,' he said, his face taking on the predatory look she'd seen in Ahzur. 'I take what I desire. Remove my shirt from your body, Little Flame. I would train you now.'

'My name is Caralissa,' she defied, though her fingers were already undoing the makeshift belt at her waist. A mere handful of heart pounding seconds later, she was bared to him.

'I do not like clothes upon your body,' he told her, running his fingers through her hair. 'Were you mine, I would keep you nude at all times.'

Caralissa felt the stirrings, now familiar between her

legs. 'Then I am not yours already?' she challenged. 'But last night, I thought?'

'You think too much, Little Flame. For now, be silent.' Taking her arms he stretched them, so that she was in the form of a cross. She watched as he took the water from the jug and poured it into a small basin. To this he added an amount of golden liquid, sweetly scented. There was a sponge in the basin and he squeezed it, even as he came to her, to bathe her skin.

Varik's touch was surprisingly gentle, so much so she could scarce imagine it was these same fingers that pummelled her buttocks and tortured her loins to spasmodic ecstasy just a short few hours ago. Closing her eyes she allowed the sponge to take her. The trickling water, the small circular rubs, all of it was so delicious she wanted it to go on forever. Why could not her servants treat her so well at home? Caralissa blushed as she guessed the answer: it was because none of them were untamed warriors like Varik.

A small sound escaped her lips, one of pleasure and thanks as he brushed her nipples. Rivulets of water ran down her belly, teasing the opening of her still ripe sex. In truth she was still mightily aroused. In a way he was right; she was his Little Flame. Kindled at his touch, fanned by his presence, his arrogance, his intensity.

'You are dangerous,' Varik observed as she parted her legs in readiness for the sponge. 'Were a man not sufficiently strong he might find himself your slave.'

Caralissa glowed beneath the compliment. She'd heard such things about herself, but never from a man such as he. Proudly, almost recklessly, she thrust out her breasts. Every thought was driven from her mind: her mysteriously absent army which she'd expected this morning, the unknown traitor, the tenuous nature of her personal freedoms, none of this mattered. She lived for his words alone, for the feel of him, for his whims, his dreams his ideas.

'I shall dry you now,' he told her when the bath was complete. 'And then I shall bind you in ropes, in a manner sacred to my people. You will then kneel to me, in the way I command. Thus will you be prepared to serve my pleasure.'

Caralissa was floating above herself. As he continued with her, fulfilling the words of his own prophecy, she felt herself in the hands of a god, protected and safe. It was like with her father, when she was very young and he would play with her sometimes, tossing her in the air and catching her. However it was different with him, innocent and pure, not sexual as with Varik.

Patting her skin, almost doting on her, he brought her to a state of warm dryness. Still standing he left her momentarily as he went to one of the wooden boxes in which were contained long coils of rope, brightly coloured and of varying lengths. Choosing a coil of purple, he cinched the ends and made small loops at various places. Caralissa giggled as he worked, for with his intent concentration and stooped shoulders, he resembled more an old woman than a barbarian chieftain.

'This is Rashal Ka-an,' he said, holding the snaking, many knotted coil up before her eyes. 'The Rashal love bond.'

He began at her waist, looping the rope about as a belt. He called it a love bond. Was that what he felt for her, then? Cursing her own girlish naiveté, she braced herself as Varik pulled the long end up under her bottom, slipping it tightly between her thighs. At once she began to spill her juices upon the biting material. The pressure in her front and rear, aimed simultaneously against both passages

45

was an odd, almost overpowering sensation. She was constricted in one sense, closed off to invasion, and yet she was at the same time quite fully possessed.

'Do not forget, Little Flame, your punishment,' he whispered, nibbling her ear, the combination of words and touch weakening her knees, cutting at her belly like a hot knife. The punishment. She nearly forgot. He'd said she would be punished for having spit upon him. For a man this would mean death. But for her, a girl, it would be something small and intimate, something designed to humiliate. Something she would no doubt come to crave as much as she hated it.

Varik went to work on her torso. Brooking no obstacles he put her hands atop her head, compelling her to twist her fingers in the damp tendrils of her hair. The rope he wrapped skilfully round her ribs then over and under her breasts, forming an outline. It was tight enough that she felt the constriction and though he neither laid a hand on her nipples nor touched them with the rope, she found herself responding, the nubs being full and ready, just as Varik said they should be on a female.

There was no mistaking the femininity of the ties, the intensely sensual, sexually explicit implications. Rashal Ka'an was designed to blatantly display a woman's charms, tempting a man to plunder them. She remembered his promise, that he would not enter her unless and until she invited his presence. No, not invited. Begged for it – those were his exact words. Was that to be her punishment, then, to be teased to submission? Caralissa stiffened, trying to keep her guard up. She would not yield to this man, could not yield to him. She would not surrender her liberty.

'Place your hands behind your back,' Varik commanded, his presence a constantly shifting distraction, a mountain of potency keeping her constantly off balance.

Caralissa removed her hands from her hair, allowing it to fall about her shoulders and breasts. She was particularly vain about her hair, having been encouraged from an early age to think of it as a divine sign of the red-haired sun goddess, evidence that her life was marked for special beauty, special greatness. Certain popular statues of this goddess, banned in the capital for their overtly sexual connotations, depict her with red pubic hair as well, and so she sometimes thought her untested sex divine too.

Varik took her crossed hands and lifted them so that the flat of each palm was touching the opposite forearm. The resulting tie raised her breasts even higher as she was compelled now to keep her back ramrod straight. Looking down at Varik's work finished, Caralissa marvelled at the overall effect. Her skin was crisscrossed with purple lines, the pale flesh lovingly displayed and quartered. Every part of her seemed to glow, seemed to call out for a man's caress, a man's kiss or – if he were so inclined – a man's discipline.

'Come, Little Flame,' he beckoned, leading her by the arm, steadying her as she tried to walk upon much weakened legs. 'Come and kneel again upon my furs.'

It was an honour, of course, for a girl to be allowed upon them, though at the moment they were chiefly occupied by Ahzur, who was snoring happily, dreaming no doubt of some animal to hunt.

'Ahzur,' Varik said. 'Ja-ta.'

Caralissa assumed this meant something like 'shoo', but the big cat seemed unimpressed. Yawning heavily it sat upright, but did not budge from its spot.

'Yes,' Varik said as though the animal were asking a question, 'you may sniff.'

The cat put its nose to Caralissa's foot, causing her to recoil. Ahzur looked at her and growled.

'Do not do that,' Varik said. 'He is trying to learn your scent.'

'Could I not send him a sample of my perfume?' she asked.

The cat rubbed its nose over her foot then began to lick her ankle. When it moved up her leg she tried again to pull away, but a stern look from Varik was enough to discourage her. The cat's nose was wet and warm and the whiskers tickled. Without her arms she felt doubly vulnerable. Leaning into Varik, putting her life in his hands, she prayed for the ordeal to end.

'Oh my,' she gasped, when it reached the nexus of her legs. 'Won't it…?'

The words eluded her, but Varik assured her the cat was only curious and that in a moment it would go away and resume its nap. Sure enough it did, though not after taking very thorough olfactory samples indeed. As a parting gesture Ahzur put his paws upon her shoulders, licking her face and even tasting her hair as though she were some savoury morsel or a small version of his own kind.

Caralissa was visibly rattled as Varik helped her to kneel.

'Do not move,' he instructed, issuing the all too familiar command.

'Where am I to go?' she asked, shrugging her trussed shoulders.

She heard Varik leaving and for a moment she imagined she might run away. At the very least, she reasoned, she ought to move from this demeaning position. Could she undo the ropes? It was a very disturbing thing, being left like this, dominated by a man when he wasn't even there. What did he care how she stayed when he was gone? What right did he have to determine if she sat or knelt or anything?

Caralissa rose to her feet, unsteadily. At once Ahzur raised his head and bared his teeth. He continued to do so until she went back to her knees. Wonderful, she thought bitterly, now I am being bossed around by animals as well.

A short while later Varik returned with food. 'Are you hungry?' he asked, with typical male denseness.

'No,' she snapped. 'I dined on a roast and some suckling pig while you were gone. I fixed it myself.'

'No doubt carving the flesh with your sharp tongue,' he countered.

He let her stew awhile longer while he prepared several bowls, using the awkward wooden stool in the corner. One at a time he laid them at her feet. Finally he stood before her, holding in one hand a bunch of pink grapes and in the other a thin strip of wood, green, the thickness of a twig.

'A Rashal warrior brings to his slave girl many things,' he explained sombrely, as though addressing a temple full of worshippers. 'In general, these things may all be subsumed under two categories: pleasure and pain.'

To demonstrate the former he held up the tiny pink fruits. For the latter he showed the strip of wood, which she now recognised to be an instrument of torture. Instinctively she drew her knees tightly together.

'Open your mouth, Little Flame.'

She regarded him, tight-lipped. So long as he held that thing, he would get no cooperation from her.

Varik tapped the switch against his thigh. As usual he enjoyed the distinct advantage of clothing. 'Did you know a Rashal slave can be made to orgasm,' he lectured, 'upon command?'

'No,' she said. 'I guess Rashal slaves have no minds of

49

their own, then do they?'

Varik flicked the tip of the switch across Caralissa's captive nipple, just hard enough to get her attention. This achieved he flicked her again, more sternly.

'That is the level of pain you will receive,' he explained to his wide-eyed prisoner. 'Each time you answer me with disrespect. I will now repeat the question.'

'No,' she answered when he was done. 'I did not know that.'

'Your legs must not be closed like this,' he said, switching subjects. 'When you kneel and a man approaches with a whip, you will part your legs. Consider it an unspoken signal.'

Caralissa swallowed. He would punish her if she disobeyed, but once her sex was exposed there'd be no limit to what he might do. Then again, what limit was there now? In the end, she opened herself.

'You were told previously to open your mouth as well,' he said harshly, striking her upon the thigh, the switch whistling as it sliced the air.

'Ow!' she cried out, looking at him in shock and pain. His face expressionless, Varik lifted his arm once again, taking aim.

Like a tiny bird Caralissa gaped, arching her neck. It was a knee-jerk reaction, one that shamed her for its cringing servility. He fed her the grape, even as the tears began to well in her eyes.

'Look at your thigh, Little Flame,' he commanded, after she managed to swallow the sweet little grape down her trembling throat. She did so, seeing the welt, some two inches long, red and angry, which now marred her perfect skin. Indignation rose from deep in her belly, burning and souring the juice of the single grape that occupied her empty stomach. It was unthinkable! Caralissa of the house of Lysor, daughter of Lysanis, sovereign of Orencia, guardian of the people, was being tortured like a common slave.

'That was the result of disobedience, Little Flame. Note the different punishment it receives than does your disrespect,' he explained. 'Note, too, that neither of these constitute your punishment for last night's more serious offence.'

Defiantly she glared up at him, straining at the ropes. 'Are these your love bonds, Varik? Must you hit your women for them to love you?'

Varik leaned forward with the switch, taking careful aim as he flicked her other nipple, treating it just as the first. There was in his action no animosity, no trace of emotion. She'd been disrespectful again and he was merely following through on his words, accustoming her to his techniques. In short, he was training her, just as he said he would, and just as she assured herself could never happen.

'No more games,' Caralissa declared, summoning her strength to rise to her feet. 'You may kill me now or else release me.'

She'd risen halfway when Ahzur began once more to growl.

Stamping her foot petulantly, boiling with rage, Caralissa went back to her knees. 'I hate you,' she told Varik. 'I will always hate you.'

The switch whistled across her exposed breasts, catching both nipples.

'I am sorry!' she cried. 'I am sorry!'

'I did not strike you for hating me,' he explained, as though the distinction made one bit of difference for her throbbing breasts, 'but rather because you lied. I know you do not in fact hate me.'

She looked at him through tear soaked eyes, a wicked smile rising to the surface. 'So I may tell the truth, then?' she challenged. 'With impunity?'

He wrinkled his brow. 'I hadn't considered it that way, but I suppose you can, yes.'

'Good,' she spat. 'Then I am free to tell you that?'

'Open your mouth,' he interrupted, cutting off her intended string of vituperative directed against his many shortcomings.

Caralissa obeyed, but not without showing him with her eyes all the things she intended to say with her tongue. The second grape was sweeter than the first, and as it joined the other in her barren tummy she was painfully reminded of the extent of her hunger. The barbarian had fed her nothing in nearly twelve hours, despite his having put her through gruelling paces and exploiting her body in the most outrageous ways.

'Open,' he repeated, and she did so in a much more pliant way this time. Five grapes in all he allowed her. She made no moves to speak in between. Eyes wide like a hawk's she watched as he set down the remaining grapes and took up one of the nearly forgotten bowls. She saw that it contained meat, finely cubed and browned, and she watched him pop a piece into his own mouth.

Whatever happened, she told herself, she would not stoop to begging.

'A bit salty,' he shrugged, sitting himself beside her on the furs, his legs crossed. 'But not bad. Ahzur, fetch!'

Caralissa gasped in protest as he took a handful of the meat and tossed it to the sleeping cat. Raising its head, yawning widely, it looked down at the tiny offering and wrinkled its nose.

'He is spoiled,' Varik muttered, shaking his head as he took another piece for himself.

'Varik!' she cried, unable to still the riot in her belly. 'For the goddess' sake, give me something to eat!'

Varik considered her. 'You may help yourself,' he decided, pouring out a sprinkling of pieces on the fur in front of her.

Caralissa looked down at the meat, impossibly out of reach. 'How am I to eat this?' she demanded.

Varik swatted a nipple, causing her to yelp.

'What I meant,' she began again, wincing as she chose her words with distinct care. *'Your lordship*, is that I cannot eat without my hands.'

Varik stayed the whip, apparently having overlooked the sarcastic edge to her use of his title. 'Ahzur eats without hands,' he pointed out, inclining his head towards the slobbering animal.

'Fine,' she hissed, 'suit yourself.'

Before he could lash out at her tender nipples Caralissa dove forward, collapsing on her own shoulder. Manoeuvring her mouth, facedown, still on her knees, she grabbed at the meat, greedily inhaling it.

'Clever girl,' Varik acknowledged, sliding the bowl within reach.

Caralissa inserted her face, all pretence of dignity lost to the desperation of hunger. So much so that she didn't even notice him changing positions, placing himself behind her.

'Do not move,' he said, repeating once more the words she was coming to dread.

Her body jolted as the object found her opening, the smaller one, slipping in past the rope. It was the switch, she was sure of it. Varik was using it on her, in her, finding a way to circumvent her defiance. Eyes closed, panting, her jaws still chewing, Caralissa submitted to the invasion, to her anal possession by a piece of wood, a green sapling.

Never did she dream a woman could be taken in such a way. It was terrible, revolting, and yet it heated her loins, made her feel even more under Varik's power as his property, his toy. Shamed, humiliated, Caralissa raised her buttocks to the odd but not unpleasant sensation, silently begging for more.

'Try the vegetables,' he suggested, pouring the contents of the second bowl into the first as he removed the switch from inside her anal opening.

She moaned into the rounded container, feeling the sudden, painful vacuum. Subtly, passionately, her body weak and fever-wracked, she went from biting to licking and nibbling, savouring the flavour of the tiny pieces of meat and vegetable. Suddenly it was something else she craved, a different flavour altogether.

'Let me please you,' she begged, lifting her head to look into his eyes, her hunger forgotten. 'Let me please you like I did last night.'

Varik opened the fastening of his trousers. Caralissa took him deep at the first contact, deeper than she dared go before. It was as if with each session between them, the harder he pushed her, the more he shamed and infuriated her, the more he was bringing forth from inside her true self. Could it be she in turn was testing him somehow, seeing if he was worthy to control her, seeing if he would protect and keep her safe, even as she submitted to his bonds and his discipline?

'More slowly,' he said, tapping her back with the switch.

Caralissa released him and began again. She was working her way to the perfect rhythm when she heard Varik speak, not to her or to Ahzur, but to another. She felt her blood chill as she realised it was Senelek. She tried to lift her head, to hide herself, but he put his hand on the back of her neck, not hurtfully but firmly, in order to make it clear she was to continue serving him.

'Well,' she heard Senelek say. 'I understand now why we do not march today to subdue Orencia.'

Varik ran the switch up Caralissa's back, across her bound arms. 'Orencia seems to me well subdued already,' he observed.

Caralissa stiffened. With the Rashal warlord's shaft in her mouth and his bonds biting deeply into her flesh, there was little to mitigate his argument.

'The men grow restless,' Senelek responded, his voice devoid of humour. 'They wish to know why we linger in this place.'

Varik ran his hand over Caralissa's glossy hair as her head continued to bob up and down. 'We linger because it is my will.'

Senelek was silent for a moment. 'Yes, my brother, that goes without saying. But surely they are owed something more?'

'Tell them I am negotiating for a ransom. A fitting cost for the return of her majesty the queen.'

'Indeed.' He cleared his throat. 'In her present state, I should say that value to be a few copper coins at most.'

Caralissa increased the intensity of her suctioning, it being the only way to vent her outrage. Senelek was effectively calling her a whore, a copper coin girl of the sort to be found in the pleasure-houses.

'I think her royal personhood takes umbrage,' Varik observed, no doubt sensing the sudden friction on his manhood.

'We have never taken hostages,' Senelek said. 'It is not the Rashal way. Nor is keeping enemy sluts for one's self when one's warrior brothers go hungry.'

'The girl is worth fifty thousand, maybe a hundred thousand crowns. The Orencians will beg, borrow and steal for her more than we could loot in a year from these petty little kingdoms.' Varik inhaled, his body stiffening. Caralissa moaned. He was going to discharge, right in front of Senelek.

'The empire is run on steel,' Senelek declared. 'Not on gold.'

Varik grasped Caralissa's hair, pushing forth his pelvis to find the sweet spot at the roof of her mouth. 'Perhaps,' he acknowledged, filling her with a fresh load of his sperm, the largest yet. 'But steel may be more easily acquired with gold than without.'

A moment later he lifted her from his lap, putting her back onto her knees beside him.

'Good girl,' he said, rubbing her head for having swallowed properly.

'You offer a clever argument, as always, brother,' Senelek replied, his eyes on Caralissa, shaming her more deeply than could any act of Varik's upon her flesh. 'And yet I fear it is not with your brain that you are reasoning.'

She tried to evade Senelek's stare, but Varik, seeing this, cautioned her to keep looking straight ahead. At the same time he tapped her thigh with the whip – her marked thigh. Having grasped the meaning, very reluctantly then, she opened her legs in full view of the dark-eyed priest.

'Would you like to try her?' Varik asked, seeing his brother's obvious interest.

Caralissa gave a desperate cry, piteous and filtering from the back of her throat. It did not dawn on her till this very moment just how absolute was Varik's power over her. He had not yet taken her himself, and yet if he wished he could give her to his brother, or to the entire army for that matter.

'Please, Varik,' she cried, throwing all caution to the wind, thrusting her face to his foot. 'Take me yourself. I beg you to have me, only do not?'

The blow to her back was unlike anything felt so far. It had come from the switch, a clean stroke, neatly delivered to one of the open sections of flesh between the intricate crisscross of rope. The pain was searing and did not let up even when the instrument was removed.

'Sit up,' Varik commanded, his voice as sharp as the steel of his sword. Caralissa hastened to obey so that she once more looked Senelek in the eye.

'You have insulted my family and my honour,' Varik declared. 'You will go to my brother at once and beg his forgiveness.'

Caralissa looked at Varik, her eyes pleading.

The warlord's jaw tensed slightly. 'Go,' he said in a voice that she was quite certain none would dare refuse, either man or beast. Pitifully, Caralissa struggled to rise.

'No,' Varik countered, pulling her back down by her bound arm. 'You will go to him on your knees. He is high priest here, you will address him on your belly.'

The ground brazed Caralissa's knees. The way was long in her current condition. Putting her head to the dirt finally, the black earth clinging to her lips, she begged forgiveness at the high priest's feet.

Senelek ignored her. 'I have no interest in these games, Varik. Nor in your latest plaything. I am sure, however, that she would amuse the men. I shall arrange a raffle.'

'No,' said Varik, in a voice whose intensity surprised the prostrate Caralissa. 'If it be women they desire, than we shall find some. Order a raiding party to scour the nearby villages for wenches.'

Senelek regarded him. 'Indeed.'

'This one is worth too much to us,' Varik offered, rising to his feet as if to cover his show of emotion. 'I do not wish to waste a hundred thousand pieces of gold.'

'As you wish,' Senelek bowed, his voice rich with irony, 'my brother.'

Caralissa waited till the man was gone to fall at Varik's feet. 'Thank you,' she offered breathless. 'For sparing me.'

Varik growled from the back of his throat, sounding like Ahzur. Seizing both her arms he yanked her to her feet, holding her before him on tiptoe, like a rag doll. 'Do you dare to insult me again, wench?' he fumed. 'Do you think I care one whit for your feelings? Think yourself more to me than a momentary diversion from my battles?'

Caralissa shook her head. 'I – I meant no offence.'

Varik frowned, his eyes a raging sea. 'I grow tired of these games,' he declared, unwittingly echoing Senelek's words. 'We shall end them. Now.'

Lowering her to the ground, on her back in the dirt, Varik fell upon her. Using the dagger at his waist he cut the rope that held her crotch then spread her legs painfully apart. He took her in a single stroke, not bothering to free her hands. The barrier of her virginity was torn as a sheet as he pressed himself as deep as a man could go.

Caralissa clutched him with her thighs, issuing sounds of shock and wonder and ultimately pleasure. He was taking her, at last, at long last.

'Oh, my lord,' she whispered in ecstasy. 'My barbarian lord, I beg to come for you.'

'No,' he said fiercely, gripping her chin between his fingers. 'You will not climax beneath me. That is your punishment. Is that clear?'

Her acknowledgement was lost in a long wail as she set herself down the torturous road of obedience. Round her the world faded as everything focused on her subservience, her grip in his iron will. Until at last, trembling, shaken, her will broken, her body bound beneath him, she accepted the gift of his lust, the sign of his dominance and her submission. The cycle, ancient as the goddess, ancient as the moon, was now complete. Silently then they lay together, he sated, she yet burning till at last they were able to speak.

'This changes nothing,' Varik said, his loins already pumping towards a renewed erection. 'When I am finished with you I shall take you home and collect your ransom.'

'Yes,' she acknowledged, 'my lord.'

Though still a helpless prisoner, she welcomed him yet again, for he alone among men dared to do with her as he pleased, dared to ignite her secret submissive passions. She sought to meet him with every thrust, telegraphing his conquest of her with moans and yelps and with the soft, bound flesh of her, desperately pressing, seeking contact betwixt the ropes that harnessed her breasts and torso.

On and on he pressed, till he was satisfied, and satisfied again, caring not one whit for her pleasure. When he was finished, Varik sliced away the ropes to announce that he would lay hands on her never again. Once freed she continued to beg him, on her knees. Fists clenched, sweat beaded at his forehead, veins protruding from his forehead, Varik lifted his head to the unseen sky and cried a man's cry, the unrestrained roar of the wolf or perhaps some unknown beast, noble and surefooted, sleekly furred of the sort that roams the plains of purer lands as yet undreamt. Naked and splendid, hair wild about his shoulders, he screamed his troubles to his gods, or hers, or perhaps to no gods at all.

Chapter Three

Varik thrust the gag into her mouth, having swathed it first between her outstretched legs to catch the prodigious juices, hers and his. His eyes were cold and distant. He did not even bother to fetch clean material, employing instead the sweaty handkerchief of a nearby soldier. The action was meant to spurn her, to douse their flaring passions, but its effect was quite the opposite.

As he gave the order to deploy the massive machine to which she was bound, Caralissa strained at the thongs, offering herself with muffled whimpers. How could he deny what was between them, how could he deny that she was his now, as fully and absolutely as if she were his slave?

And yet deny it he did, ignoring the whimpers, the pleading eyes. It was, of course, a splendid Rashal joke, rolling the queen of Orencia home, naked and spread-eagled on the front of a battering ram. Its symbolism would be unmistakable, both to his troops and hers.

The afternoon sun was golden upon her skin, which still burned from Varik's touch. She laid her head back, so that her hair whirled in the breeze. Closing her eyes she prayed to the goddess, seeking things of the heart too deep for words. It mattered not, the lust-filled eyes of his warriors, the thousand takings she endured in their minds' eyes as the ram rolled slowly past their waiting ranks. It was irrelevant now, too, what might happen in the future, of no import whether she returned to her old life or died instead in the midst of battle.

All that lived in her mind were the memories of Varik's possession of her. How wild he had looked, the heat in his eyes beyond reason as he took her.

They brought the ram to the edge of the Rashal camp. Varik and Senelek, mounted on their stallions waited beside the machine, flanked by a picked number of men, cavalry and foot soldiers. Riders were sent ahead to the castle, some forty minutes' hard ride to the east, with orders to summon the senior Orencian leadership for an immediate meeting with regard to the queen. It would be Romila who would come, no doubt with members of the royal council. It was a smaller council these days, a number of them having been sent packing by Caralissa along with the halfwit Telos.

It infuriated her still to think how she'd found four of them in the council chamber, holding down a hapless serving girl over the oak table while Telos rammed in and out of her squirming body. They were supposed to have been in session, looking for solutions to the impending Rashal invasion.

It was this incident that set in mind her own determination to deal with the Rashal in her own way: alone, in the way of her father.

Then again, there was no telling what the headstrong Lysanis might have done. Truth be told, he was said to favour serving wenches himself and even, upon occasion, to have visited the pleasure-houses much as she was wont to do herself. Needless to say, however, it was likely King Lysanis did more on these outings than observe.

'What is taking so long?' she heard Varik ask, with uncharacteristic impatience. 'They should be back by now.'

Senelek allowed a moment's silence, which she knew now was his way of exposing weakness. 'Perhaps they

61

are having trouble catching the Orencians,' he observed at last. 'The sight of even a handful of Rashal warriors has likely sent them fleeing clear to the Forest of Night.'

Caralissa clenched her captive fists. It was one thing for her to criticise her own people, but it was quite another coming from the mouth of an enemy. Then again, she thought with shame, Varik was her enemy and she was doing something with him far worse than running away. Colour came to her face as she entertained the possibility that her recent behaviour might smack more of treason than of passion in the minds of her subjects.

There was a cheer from the right, and as Caralissa looked she saw it was some of the soldiers, raising their spears and swords in joy at the sight of an approaching column of mounted riders. She thought at first it was the castle delegation, but as she looked more closely, she saw it was another Rashal scouting party. The horsemen were riding slow and lazy, as beside them, on a long chain, hands bound before them, each one attached to the waist of the one ahead, was a line of women. Though the warriors were only trotting their horses, the captives were forced to run to keep up.

They were all of them young and beautiful in their Orencian peasant dresses. Some were fair-skinned blondes, others raven-haired or chestnut-haired. As they came closer the fear in their eyes became palpable.

'You would stand a better chance to get your hundred thousand gold coins for one of them than for the queen,' observed Senelek, as the party passed quite close on its way back to the camp. 'Ask any merchant. Used merchandise inevitably requires discounting.'

'Stick to religion, Senelek,' Varik replied curtly, digging his booted foot into the side of his horse. 'Economics is not your forte.'

Varik galloped past her, a look of dark intensity on his face as he headed back towards the camp ahead of the column.

'Did you hear that, majesty?' Senelek called to her once his brother was out of earshot. 'My abilities have been called into question. But you and I know better, don't we? Varik may understand steel, but he knows nothing of the difference between copper and gold.'

He was referring again to his earlier remark about her being a whore, with only the value of the cheapest copper coins, the kind that can be thrown upon an oak table in exchange for the having of a hapless pleasure-house slave whose life consists of the endless serving of ale in the common drinking area betwixt trips to the pleasure rooms, the mats thick with the scent of stale sex and fermented hops. She'd imagined such rooms, and the things that happened within them many times; even as she watched the doors slam shut, excluding her eyes. And yet on all those occasions, she never dreamed she herself might one day be evaluated in anyone's mind as chattel, her value being that of her flanks, her worth tied integrally to her ability to writhe under a whip.

As for Senelek's insolence, were she given license to speak she would certainly have told this sorry excuse for a holy man that he might pray all he wanted, but he would never have her heart or her soul, much as he might lust after her. For these belonged to Varik and Varik alone.

Though Senelek said nothing more, she was infinitely relieved a few minutes later when she heard over her shoulder the resounding hoof beats of the chieftain's returning horse.

'What was that all about?' Senelek asked, after his brother resumed his place beside him.

'I was instructing the camp watch commander to treat

the women as our guests, to provide them with food and drink,' Varik replied.

Senelek brushed a bit of dust from his arm. 'Such generosity,' he noted dryly. 'Coming from a chieftain; I do hope the Orencians arrive soon, as I fear we will need their capital if we are to finance any more of these new invasions of yours.'

Varik ignored the insult. 'You there!' he shouted to an officer at the head of the cavalry line. 'Send fresh riders! Find those messengers and get them back here with the Orencians!'

'I think that will not be necessary,' Senelek interjected, inclining his head to the horizon.

All eyes focused on the tiny dots, rapidly enlarging. There were eight or nine in all, some in Rashal armour, others in the brilliant colours of the Orencian court. As they approached Caralissa recognised Romila, in a hooded cape of red. Beside her was a man in a uniform of light blue, richly decorated in gold. She thought for a moment her eyes were playing tricks on her, and then it dawned like a blow to the abdomen.

The man was Telos! He was back, and worse still, he was wearing the uniform of a general! Desperate for an explanation, her eyes scanned the remaining three of her people for familiar faces. They wore the cloaks of green reserved for the royal council, but she knew none of them. Not one. As the party approached the Rashal escorts fell to the rear, allowing the Orencians to approach their chieftain directly. It was Telos who galloped to the lead, taking the vanguard place.

'Greetings, Your Lordship,' the man bowed with a ridiculous flourish. 'The nation of Orencia welcomes its liberator, the feller of tyranny, the new sun upon our cloudy and oppressed land, the great and noble chieftain of the

Rashal!'

Caralissa stiffened in her bonds. What nonsense was this buffoon spouting and why was he speaking for the state?

Varik frowned. 'Your words are unclear to me.'

Telos wrinkled his nose, causing vibrations in his short black moustache. Across his forehead a pile of black hair poured forth from under his gleaming, tufted helmet. 'Why, the tyrant Caralissa,' he laughed. 'But you are jesting, obviously. The Rashal, we know, are renowned for their sense of… the absurd.' Telos had paused briefly before concluding his thought, his eyes having fallen blatantly and lustfully upon the body of the bound queen. Behind her gag, Caralissa screamed at him in rage.

'We are most grateful,' Telos continued, seeing that Varik had nothing as yet to say. 'As are the people of Orencia, our humble peasants, whom the cruel queen has bruised so heavily beneath her iron fist.'

Caralissa shook her head frantically. It was a lie. All of it. It was Romila and Telos who wanted to increase the taxes and impose levees on the peasants, not her. The people loved her, as they'd loved her father.

'The queen seems to take issue,' Senelek said, noting the squirming girl. 'Personally I think her a bit puny to wield an iron fist.'

In a rare show of commonsense, Telos said nothing.

'Either way,' Senelek continued, interposing himself for his strangely silent brother, 'Lord Varik has no interest in the internal politics of your regime. He merely seeks to bestow upon you terms for the release of your queen. And they are, I might add, most generous terms, unprecedented in the history of our people. My advice to you, then, is to identify yourselves to his lordship and then wait humbly upon his pleasure.'

65

'Forgive our boorishness,' Telos effused, with another bow of the sort more appropriate for the comic stage than the battlefield. 'I am Chief Regent Telos, Commander of the Home Militia and Royal Consort to her highness, the Princess Romila, soon to be Queen Romila.'

Caralissa looked at her sister. There was upon her face no emotion, no sign of recognition.

'We await your terms, Lord Varik,' Romila said, employing the bravery of cold reason. 'Our lives are in your hands. We have nothing to lose.'

'Lord Varik requires the sum of one hundred thousand gold pieces,' Senelek declared. 'To be delivered by sunset tomorrow. Upon receipt of it your queen shall be returned to you.'

Telos smiled in a failed attempt at irony. 'That is a good deal of money, gentle sirs.'

'Enough, Telos!' This came from Romila. 'We shall bring the money,' she said to Senelek. 'Precisely as you say.'

Senelek curled the right side of his lip, revealing to Telos and the rest the true nature of irony. 'We have no need of your words, princess. Everything you own is already ours.'

'This meeting is at an end,' Varik declared, breaking his silence.

'Go home,' said Senelek to the Orencians. 'Go home and give prayers of thanks to your gods. Apparently they have been watching over you of late.'

Romila bowed her head, rapidly, mechanically. Before she turned, as she seized upon the reins, her eyes met her sister's for the briefest second. Caralissa felt a chill down her spine as she saw in them the truth. Romila hated her.

'Good day to you, esteemed ones!' waved Telos over his shoulder as they galloped off; a gesture Caralissa was convinced was done solely to allow the man to burn into his brain one final image of her ripe and helpless body.

'So,' said Varik, some time later, his mouth full of fruit as he addressed the kneeling and obeisant Caralissa, her head to the dirt at his feet. 'It seems you are a tyrant just as I am.'

'When I return home,' the naked queen informed him, maintaining her position of subservience, 'I will have my sister and her blue-suited pet monkey executed, along with every one of their allies.'

Varik reclined upon the cushions, taking another bite of the apple, complements of a nearby Orencian orchard. They were in the Tent of Pleasures, the place in the camp where Varik and his chief officers gathered for celebrations. There were guests today, in the form of a dozen captured maidens. Their laughter could be heard, bright and sweet as the soldiers fell upon themselves to impress their particular favourites. A few of the girls seemed already more than impressed, having descended to various states of undress in the arms of would-be lovers.

Varik extended his goblet, signalling Caralissa to refill it from the pitcher by her side. His stomach was filled with wine and it was beginning to tangle his thoughts. Or perhaps it was the girl, with her unique power to drive him into a blinding rage at one moment and then at another to pluck from him the most peculiar protective and nurturing instincts. He'd hoped putting her upon the battering ram would end his growing addiction for her body by reducing her in his eyes to a mere object, a pawn with political purposes only. Were he a pragmatic man he would have her chained in a dark tent, out of sight till the Orencians saw fit to bring him his gold. Or else he ought turn her over to his men, to remove her entirely from his thoughts. Instead, he had lain with her again and brought her to a feast. His Little Flame. The fire that burned too hot even for a warlord.

'You have not answered the question,' Varik observed, renewing the verbal banter for which he was rapidly developing an insatiable appetite. 'Are you or are you not a tyrant?'

Caralissa curled her lips, a sparkle in her eye. 'My Lord Varik has possessed me to the depths of his soul. Can he not tell this for himself?'

'All women are tyrants,' he replied, gulping the sparkling beverage. 'Until they are mastered.'

'I serve the goddess,' she said proudly. 'And in her name, justice.'

'Indeed. This can be verified, you know.'

'How?'

'By means of a character witness.'

Varik signalled to a nearby guard, one who'd drawn the lonely job of watching over the feasters. 'You there, bring me one of the Orencian wenches. Any will do, they all seem equally overjoyed to be witnessing their queen's degradation.'

He fetched a buxom blonde, her bosom sharply accented in a low-cut dress of yellow with white trim. Her cheeks were rosy and her lips engorged, presumably from kissing.

'Yes, milord?' she chimed pleasantly, her pitch and volume indicative of having consumed a fair amount of the sparkling wine herself. Either that or the girl was in shock from having been kidnapped by ruthless barbarians only to be invited to a sumptuous feast. Chalk it up to the legendary Rashal sense of humour, he told himself.

Varik watched her attempt at a curtsy, a nicety rather lost on one such as him, raised in a remote warrior village. Senelek, whose early years were spent among civilised men as a hostage, would better appreciate the action. It was an experience he spoke little of to this day.

'What is your name, girl?'

'I am Eliana,' she replied. 'If it pleases, milord.'

'It takes more to satisfy me from a woman than her name, but if you would like to try, I might not object.' He glanced to Caralissa, hoping for signs of jealousy in the wench. 'But tell me, Eliana, what is your opinion of your queen?'

Eliana beheld the kneeling girl, roughly her own age. Apart from prior station in life and hair colour they were much the same. Varik watched as Eliana's facial expression changed, from glee to mounting sadness. Tears formed in her eyes as if it overwhelmed her to look too closely upon her monarch.

'Be strong,' Caralissa whispered to the girl. 'Remember what I told you. Do not disgrace me!'

'Oh,' she whispered, putting a finger to her full red lips. 'Your majesty, forgive me, but I cannot let you suffer alone.'

Remarkably, Eliana now commenced to remove her clothing, as if to give it to Caralissa. At Varik's signal the guard grasped her arm to stay her action.

'What mean you by this?' Varik demanded of her.

The girl's lower lip began to tremble. Looking to Caralissa and then to Varik she began to weep. 'Alas, I have betrayed my queen! I could not help myself! I felt sorry for her.'

Varik shook his head, baffled as always by the ways of civilised people. 'I understand none of this.'

Eliana fell to her knees, crawling to Caralissa, to kiss her feet.

The queen lifted her, offering embrace. 'It is all right, child. I forgive you.' Turning to Varik, she offered him explanation. 'By means of one of these girls, whom I was able to speak to earlier, I passed to them orders to reveal no emotions toward me tonight, to offer no pity.'

'Ah.' Varik nodded in satisfaction, taking another sip, allowing the wine to wind its way through his mind. 'Then you do not hate your queen after all, Eliana?'

Eliana laughed through her tears. 'Hate her? But sir, we love her. She is kind and fair like her father before her.'

'But also vain and petty,' Varik observed. 'And overconfident, wouldn't you say?'

Eliana's face grew pale. 'No sir, I would not say that.'

'I shall prove it to you. And in a way which will simultaneously demonstrate that unlike your fair ruler, I am neither kind nor fair.' Varik clapped his hands. 'The Dance of Cords!' he commanded.

The dance was a simple one, ancient and beloved among the Rashal. Most appropriately performed round the campfire, in the dark of night, the flames kissing the sky as warriors, hundreds in number reclined upon cold earth, passing flagons and slapping one another's backs. There was only one dancer, a female, naked and invariably a prisoner, taken in battle. Several men were required to inspire the dance and to keep the woman attentive and sufficiently sensual in her responses. No pre-set moves were recorded, no requirements as to length or details of performance. The magic was in the cords, the long strands of leather or rope wielded by the Cord Men. The dance was best served up as a surprise, the girl learning upon impact the stakes of her dancing.

The cords left faint marks, thin and red and a good cord man would test his device upon himself and his fellows prior to the start. It was a stinging more than a wounding, and the girl's pride was the victim first and foremost. Purists would argue that the dance be choreographed and the girl guided by means of the

70

corrective lashes to improve her sensuality. For most men, however, the chief pleasure lay in seeing the girl perform under duress and watching her yield sexually to the very concept of public correction and forced display.

Varik was rather more in the second camp, being less concerned with seeing a perfectly executed performance than with witnessing a girl's struggle with and ultimate surrender to her own passions. It was especially delicious when the girl was so new to this, when she retained in large part her pride and self-image as a free creature. Caralissa was of this type, as were her captured countrywomen. While he had no intention of subjecting these maidens to the Dance, he would coax from them their own vicarious surrender through their observation of it.

'Fetch the cords,' Varik said, 'and chains as well.'

There was laughter as a large number of the men set about a good-natured competition for the right to wield the cords.

'Here, Lord,' shouted a man, holding up the leather strands. They were binding cords, useful in securing wagonloads or, alternatively, pretty girls. Out of the corner of his eye he regarded Caralissa, who was watching, warily, suspiciously, deliciously. Her eyes were glassy as she beheld the cords that would all too soon nip at her heels, singe her buttocks and braze her calves and thighs, not to mention her breasts and buttocks. There were Rashal men who wished heavier markings, employing whips for the Dance. Senelek was one of these, Varik was not. For him it was a far greater thing to tame a woman with minimal use of force, this being a fulcrum, a mere catalyst to invoking the far greater weapon which is a woman's own passion.

Handled properly, the Dance would make for a night of

71

ecstasy for all. Which would go a long way to quelling the grumbling, thereby keeping the officers satisfied till the morrow, when the Orencian gold would arrive. There would be, he decided, a fair share for everyone. Even Senelek.

It was his brother's hostility that troubled him most. At one time he could have read the man's every thought, and yet now he seemed a stranger. What had changed him so much? Or was it Varik who was changing, growing softer somehow, less able to endure the rigors of military campaigning, the travails of empire building. Where would it end? Would they stop at the Forest of Night, or would Senelek's infernal augers, his endless and arcane consultations with their gods – his gods – call them to raise arms even against the supposed demons that inhabited that lonely and miserable place? Personally, he had no use for demons. Nor had he any use for wives or even slaves to whom one might become overly attached.

Caralissa was conveyed to the dancing place, a circle in the dirt, drawn by the blade of a warrior. The circle was crucial, being both a religious and a sensual symbol. They put her in the irons then, locking the metal bands on her wrists, connecting them with a mere six inches of chain. On her ankles were locked another set of irons, these having a larger lead between them. Some would consider it in poor taste to dance the girl in shackles, but again it was not technical proficiency he desired, but erotic stimulation. If his calculations were right, Caralissa's yielding beneath the cords would be intensified a hundredfold by means of steel. If so, then the maidens would be given little choice but to give in to lusts of their own.

'I do not understand what I am to do,' Caralissa said, her tone entirely too haughty for a slave.

72

'You are to dance, Little Flame,' he told her, delighting as always in encouraging her resistance only to sweep it aside for his own pleasure. 'Do not tell me you have become shy?'

She looked at the three men holding the cords, and then at the expectant maidens, all of whom were lined up now at Varik's feet. 'You would have me do this in front of my own people?'

He shrugged, eyeing Eliana, who squirmed uncomfortably on her knees. 'If you would like we can supply one of them as your substitute.'

'No, warrior,' said Caralissa with surprising vigour. 'You will abuse me alone.'

'As you wish.' He clapped his hands, signalling for the piper and the reed flayer, the reed flay being a flat disc of woven air-filled stems which one strikes with a kind of thick brush. 'Let the Dance begin.'

The tune was a variation of a Rashal nursery rhyme, though played with rather more gusto. The piper and flayer together were a pleasant combination, though one could enact the Dance with any instruments, or for that matter, with none at all. Predictably, Caralissa did not know how to begin. As much as thirty seconds may be granted the girl to gather herself under these circumstances or, alternatively, she may be lashed at once.

Varik felt his manhood swell as she looked at him in confusion, her chained hands hanging down, her arms framing her ample breasts as she cupped her wondrous sex. They were nearly a verse into the song and all three of the cord men were poised, awaiting Varik's command. He was the host, the dance maker. The right to punish and to take pleasure was his and his alone. In most circles it was considered a matter of courtesy to allow the cord men use of the girl, and she is oft times instructed to

73

dance with her eyes at belt level, which means that she is to gauge her performance by her ability to visually arouse those men to whom her body is to be given.

Caralissa's own fate was yet to be decided. Within him warred two impulses, each quite powerful and striving for mastery. On the one hand there was the call of duty, his obligation to divide the spoils. To remain aloof from his own desires in the role of chieftain, the one who shares the fruits of victory. And yet there was the other voice, dark and compelling, dangerous and unpredictable which told him to hold on to this particular woman. At any cost.

Varik scowled. This dark voice was, of course, treason, a flirtation with the spurning of the code of the Rashal. For a warrior, let alone a chieftain, to keep a captive woman as his own, to set up house like a civilised fool denying his friends and allies their rightful use of an enemy wench was the greatest of sins. Were one of Varik's own men to even speak of such a thing, he would have the man flogged and the woman passed through the ranks until every last warrior had tasted her charms.

The Racial chieftain drained his goblet and threw it to the ground. By the gods, he would not succumb to the wiles of any female, even those of a charmingly seductive queen with hair of fire and lips of wine.

'You may strike her at will!' Varik called to the cord men. 'And to the man who makes her writhe the best, goes her body for the first hour of the night!'

Caralissa saw stars as the first cord struck her on the left calf. Yelping in shock she leaped from the spot only to land herself another blow, to the right thigh. And so began a hissing, stinging rain of cords, infernally delivered, impossible to avoid. Varik was a beast, an animal for expecting her to fend off these nipping demons with her hands and ankles chained! He was no gentleman, no man at all to put a girl to such misery.

And yet, in her undulations, in her tiny world of closed torment, she found a rhythm, a pattern to be followed. It was so shameful, and yet it was beautiful at the same time. To be a female, only a female, and to be under the power of strong men, men able to control her, to rouse her with the cords. She must perform for them, in her chains; she must be pretty, she must be pleasing to the men with the cords. Her naked body was theirs; they would have her, do with her what they wished. It was Varik's will. And so she danced, finding the ways to move, to show them she was a woman, that they were men and that her place was at their feet, subject to their whims, their steel, their discipline. Her sweet breasts, made to be gripped by strong hands, her sex made to liquefy at the touch of a strong man.

There were sounds of awe coming from the maidens, shocked gasps. At the same time from the warriors there came the sound of palms slapping together in the way of Rashal cheering.

'Seize the wenches!' someone cried.

One by one the maidens fell, willingly brought to the floor, their clothes opened, torn, thrust aside in service of iron hard shafts. It was like a fever filling the whole of the tent, and it was cantered in Caralissa, in her swaying thighs, her honeyed undulations.

What was it that drove her? Was it the incentive of the biting gnat-like cords, the nipping tendrils, or was it something else that invoked her passion? Could it be the knowledge that these men were going to possess her? Between her legs she was like a waterfall roaring, and that wetness she knew would serve the best of the cord men, and then the second and then the third, in that order and after that, maybe all the men in the room would have

75

her.

Use her like a slut. A pleasure-house girl.

Rage came, and indignation then self-pity. Though it seemed now that every emotion she could conjure was feeding into the Dance. Especially her hatred for Varik. Who was this man to award her favours to these warriors? Who was he to bind her and punish her and keep her naked? She was a queen, and among these witnesses to her shame were her own people, people whom she ruled, and who must respect her. A curse on Telos and her sister Romila, too, for their impudence, their utter lack of support and respect. They could have freed her today if they'd tried!

This mere peasant Eliana had done more to defend her ruler than her own kin! She made a mental note to reward the girl, perhaps with a title or even the services of a particular male slave, one with a ridiculous little moustache and unkempt hair, a new slave whom she would inaugurate herself.

'More!' she heard Varik roar. 'I demand more!'

Caralissa's eyes slid shut. It was voices alone that carried now to her senses. There'd been moans from the females, and Caralissa was sure they were succumbing in their heat, opening their legs and mouths, giving in to warriors of their own choosing. She prayed that Eliana would find a strong one, a kind one, the sort of man Varik himself might be if not for his arrogance, his stubbornness. She moaned as she heard the crack of a palm upon bare skin. Someone was being spanked.

'You heard Lord Varik,' called one of her tormentors. 'Give us more. Touch yourself. Move for us or we shall go for your little friends instead of you!'

Caralissa had never done such a thing, not even in the privacy of her own quarters. She told herself she would do it now only for the maidens, to spare them what she now felt. But there was more, something deeper, a call from her own soul perhaps, which drove her ever onward to greater and greater acts of self-abasement. Was Varik watching? Could she bear to look herself? The feel of her fingers, like silk on her breasts, made her nipples throb. Echoes of their stirring reverberated to her fleecy triangle.

Like slaves to a master, her fingers slid over her stomach in search of her honeyed heat. Fingers attached to hands in turn attached to arms, and none of it at this moment her own as she worked towards her goal. Let them be Varik's fingers she thought, or any man's for that matter. For what was she now, if not a girl who belonged to men? It was a temporary haze to be sure, the result of captivity, of corporal punishment and teasing and humiliation, and yet it was all too real at the same time, as real as the steel which held her, as real as the cords, as real as the jeers and mocking music, as real as Varik's voice demanding more, still more.

Caralissa drew a ragged breath, her fingers sliding into place. She cried out as she reached the soft nether lips. She no longer felt the cords as her own self-manipulation took centre stage. Mercilessly, giving no quarter, she flicked her own clitoris, piercing her pride with swirling circles across her oozing lips. Elsewhere girls were climaxing; she could feel their saturated heat pouring into the air from tiny vessels, mouths exhaling as men, true men, took them blatantly, definitively.

She tried to picture them, virgins no more, legs splayed, buttocks on the ground, mouths forced open, warriors pounding at them as their commander sat gloating. What a proud victory for Lord Varik! The chieftain who wins wars without crossing blades, the king who plants his flags between the thighs of helpless women. How many others, and from what countries were his other conquests?

No, she thought, this matters not. Revenge, this was the dish she should be savouring. Revenge on Telos, on Romila, on their rump council and for that matter, upon each and every man in this room, and all of those outside, even the unlucky foot soldiers, the men of no rank being denied the pleasure of Orencian girl flesh.

Round and round Caralissa spun, whether moving in space or only in the landscape of her own desires, she knew not, nor did she care. It was her own orgasm she claimed, even as those about her sought to claim it for themselves.

'She finishes herself off like a whore!' someone cried, while another wagered he could make her dance upon his spear.

'No, worse than a whore!' she heard, and then there were fingers clenching at her, pulling her away from herself.

'Looks like I'm the lucky winner,' one of the cord men spat into her ear with fermented breath, though truthfully she never heard the contest's end, never really acknowledged its beginning. Hands were dragging her from the floor, taking her to a corner, dark and pillow-strewn.

'Could you feel my cord the best?' he crooned, the odour of his air sickening her. 'It was the biggest.'

More laughter. There must be an audience. Or was it the others who were to come after him? Were they already waiting in line? She felt the ground rising to meet her, or rather she felt herself being forced down. No matter, it was all the same. Perhaps she would die here, in this very spot, and then her sister would have to live with the guilt, and Telos, too. Was there any doubt now, she thought bitterly, as to who the betrayer was? How far had she gotten from the castle, she wondered, before the informant was sent ahead to Varik? Did Romila's lips even have time to grow cold from the kiss they shared, the one she gave Caralissa to wish her good luck?

'Have you ever seen a shaft so big?'

Caralissa pictured the man shouting stupidly, waving his manhood like a flag. If such a word as manhood could be applied to a creature who stings naked girls with nasty little strings making them do terrible things to themselves, requiring them to drip their own juices down welt-ridden thighs to the sound of cacophonous music, the echo of orgasmic maidens filling the air.

'No!' she heard a man roar into the void. 'It is enough! No more, I say!'

Caralissa opened her eyes, to see if it was a shattered dream or some taste of afterlife, but instead she saw the shadow of Varik, wrenching the foul-smelling man away, his penetration having failed, been disallowed before it ever occurred.

'But, my lord,' the man wailed. 'I never even got to touch her.'

'Find a maiden,' she heard Varik growl. 'Leave this wench to me.'

Caralissa lay beneath the furs, her breath soft in the darkened air. Making herself as small as possible, she tried not to listen even as the men's voices increased their hushed intensity. Just outside Varik's tent, where he'd carried her after rescuing her from the aftermath of the Dance, he was speaking now with his brother. It had been several hours now, and in that time Varik made love to her twice more. At least it felt like love, his hands firm and gentle, his taking of her marked with possessive concern and relentless attention to detail. She was glowing still as she huddled herself, making herself small, invisible. Yes, it felt like love.

There must be something to it, she thought, something more than barbarian custom alone or mere barbarian lust. Hadn't he even given her an ointment, a healing cream brought long ago from the Forest of Night to ease her smarting legs and buttocks? Almost at once she'd felt the cord marks ease and shrink. A small thing, perhaps, but for a woman in her position, desperate for any sign of her future, for a vision of her true allies in a world of danger, it was a lifeline.

Varik was growing angry with his brother, this much she could discern. Senelek, by contrast, was maintaining his usual clipped style, his biting sarcasm. Straining her exposed ears, she sifted the air for their words.

'Let them come to me themselves,' Varik declared. 'If they dare. Or is it that the complaints are yours alone?'

'Truth has many voices, brother. It uses what messengers it will. Though more often than not it is more a curse than honour to be chosen as its mouthpiece.'

Varik exhaled noisily. 'Why must you always speak like one of them, in riddles with such high sounding phrases? Is it not enough we must forever be conquering them and living in their lands?'

'The city dwellers, you mean – the civilised ones? Perhaps you've forgotten my childhood, then, how I served as hostage among their kind in order to save our village?'

'How could I ever forget, Senelek, when you remind me each and every day?'

'A Rashal never tires of hearing of his obligations and his debts.'

'A Rashal allows a man to pay those debts,' Varik countered, 'at a fair rate of interest.'

'I will not debate you, Varik. There is no defeating you

on any front, which is why you are chieftain instead of me. My humble lot in life is to serve you, and this compels me to issue you this warning: Lie with this Orencian slut much longer and you shall incite rebellion.'

'And I warn you, Senelek: raise the point again to my face and you shall court treason.'

The space of several breaths passed before Senelek replied. 'It is not your face you should concern yourself with, my brother,' he said, his voice devoid of emotion. 'But rather your back.'

A moment later Varik returned to her, having closed the tent with an angry flourish.

She clung to him in the blackness, seeking to ease his worries with her warm and willing body. 'Tell me what I can do for you,' she whispered, stroking his cheek with the tips of her fingers, 'and I will do it. It would be my pleasure to best that brother of yours.'

Varik took her wrist and slid it behind her back, applying sufficient pressure to make her wince. 'Have you been eavesdropping, Little Flame?'

'No – I mean yes, but only a little.'

He slid his free hand down between her legs, to her waiting moistness. 'This makes three offences, then,' he declared, stroking her slit, commingling the sensation with that of the tension on her wrist. 'The first being your continued insolent disrespect for the high priest, the second being your dishonesty with regard to the incident, the third being your invasion of our privacy. How am I to handle this – Orencian slut?'

Caralissa writhed against him. How unfair it was to be a woman; to be so easily put into one's place and to be aroused in the process. 'I – I should be punished,' she confessed breathlessly.

Varik released her. 'Show me how,' he commanded,

sitting upright.

With a whimper, her spurned sex stinging with need, Caralissa crawled across Varik's lap. Crying out in frustration, her nether parts rubbing against his thighs, she put herself in a position to be spanked. It was a trifling punishment, a girl's punishment.

'Now tell me,' he demanded, making her wait, her sex wet over his skin, her buttocks twitching enticingly. 'Tell me what I am to do to you.'

'I've been naughty,' Caralissa trembled, her voice barely audible. 'I need to be spanked. I beg for you to spank me.'

His palm sat heavily on her buttocks. 'And what about your pleasure? Should I allow you to climax tonight?'

Caralissa clenched her small fists, knowing he intended this night to bring her to new depths of shame. 'Not at first,' she wheedled. 'But after I am punished enough, when I am very sorry, and if I beg and if I am pleasing, with my mouth and my sex, maybe yes, you should let me.'

Varik struck her with the palm of his hand, drawing a low gasp. 'No, Caralissa, not at all. There will be no climax for you tonight. I shall keep you at a fever pitch; I shall use and tease and torture you till I am bored and then I will sleep. In the morning, when I awaken, I will send you and you will fetch water for me and make me breakfast, which you will serve on your knees. You will do all these things to remind you to behave more pleasingly in the future. Is this acceptable to you?'

'Aaah,' she cried as he snaked a finger in and out of her. 'Yes, yes, I'll do as you say.'

'And another thing,' he added, his hand having impacted upon her pert behind a second time. 'If I do decide to keep you, it shall be because I desire it; your will is of no import.'

'I hate what you do to me,' Caralissa moaned as he touched her yet again. 'I hate it! Do you hear me?'

'Your body says otherwise,' Varik countered, taking his sticky finger and putting it to her mouth.

Caralissa rubbed her breasts helplessly against the furs as she tasted her own juices, her tongue and lips obediently paying homage to Varik's finger. It was going to be a long night, she decided as he spanked her yet again. A very long night indeed.

Chapter Four

As the first rays of dawn rose over the camp, Caralissa was a shattered mass of need. Her pride surrendered, reduced to grovelling and begging for even the most incidental of touches, she lay at Varik's feet, his great toe inserted reverently in her mouth as she sought to earn for herself the right to lie once more across his lap, to rub herself lewdly against his knee, to have his hand swatting her mercilessly. Anything, anything at all to fill the terrible emptiness, the burning need to be used.

'I grow weary,' Varik said, rolling over to his side, his manhood having drained itself a total of three times in Caralissa's mouth. 'Do not disturb me further.'

Caralissa moaned in self-pity. He was going to leave her this way, in a state of utter desperation, unsatisfied. Which is exactly where the night began. It was more of his infernal training, his conditioning of her responses through gradual transference, inducing her to respond evermore passionately and desperately to a series of increasingly mild and innocuous sensations.

Longingly, she looked at him. It was out and out penetration she aspired to, the plunging of his ever-throbbing manhood into her overeager womanhood. She knew this was folly though, a pretentious dream, something infinitely more pleasurable than she, a slave, deserved. She had no right to intercourse with him. It was not her place to choose when he might have her, but his alone, and tonight it was only her mouth he had sought, not her hungry nether opening.

'Please,' she begged in his ear, trying to entice him with her lips and tongue, suggesting to him the possibilities of her own ravishing, 'have mercy on me. My body burns. If you will not have me, will you not give me to one of your men? I will accept whomever you choose; I will crawl, I will make no complaint. Let me be whipped, even. I don't care.'

Taking a deep breath, Varik began to snore.

Caralissa moved to her haunches. Arrogant dog! He was so utterly certain of her captivity that he'd gone to sleep, having made no effort to bind or restrict her in any way. Desperately she looked down at her swollen nipples, her sex seeping with the juices of her submission.

Did she dare to touch herself?

Hands trembling she reached for her nipples. No! She couldn't do it. Not without permission. She could wake him, but he would be more likely to punish her than grant her request.

Lost to her own passions she made one last attempt to bargain for his attention with her body, seeking to arouse him in his sleep with her lips, her soft hair, her eager breasts. Perhaps in his dreams he might unwittingly reach for her. Sliding her belly across him she gained access to his sleeping member. Hungrily she took him once more in her mouth. An ordinary man would never stiffen again so soon, but Varik was anything but ordinary. He tasted sweet and powerful. Full of hope she lowered her lips down the length of the shaft, taking him deep.

If only he would awaken and touch her one more time – his finger grazing her earlobe, the back of his thumb brushing across an agonised nipple, making her whimper and beg like a pet. All this he'd done to her already this night, this and much more. And the most awe-inspiring thing was that he accomplished his cruel domination without even putting her body beneath his driving manhood. It was this she needed above all else, even more than the air she breathed, though she knew this act of conquest would likely do her in altogether.

Tears in her eyes, moaning to herself, she felt the spasms in her forbidden sex, glistening and needful. As the warrior's snores increased she yearned to touch herself, to bring even the imperfect relief of masturbation. And yet those lips and that slick opening were no longer hers. It was Varik who owned her body, owned her pleasure, even her very right to feel.

'Leave me be,' he warned at last, pulling her off by means of her sweat-soaked hair. Her head throbbing, forced back to the dirt at his feet, she tried desperately to think of something other than sex. It was then that she recalled her forgotten hunger, the pangs of which returned with a vengeance.

Crawling back to Varik's ear, being careful not to allow too great a friction between her thighs lest she steal an orgasm for herself, she tried her luck at breakfast.

'I am hungry,' she whispered, barely catching herself before she called him 'master'. 'Please, Varik, I am hungry.'

'Fetch water, girl,' he grumbled, swatting her nuzzling lips from his earlobe as though she were some annoying insect. 'You will eat later.'

On shaky legs Caralissa rose, doing her best to walk to the inverted spear, over which Varik's shirts were hung.

'No covering for you today,' she heard him say over her shoulder.

Her heart stilled in her chest for the briefest of seconds. Wheeling about on her bare heels, arching her back she confronted him, her hazy slavish feelings vanishing like mist. 'What did you say?'

Varik rolled onto his stomach, showing her nothing but his shoulder blades and sloping back above the coverings. 'You will go to the stream as you are,' he said, his voice largely muffled by the furs. 'I would have my warriors behold the beauty of my prize.'

Caralissa's knees were close to buckling. Shame washed over her, and with it a rush of heat and desire. She swallowed hard, her dry throat aching. He considered her beautiful. He considered her a prize.

'There are thousands of men out there,' she reminded him, trying to keep her voice steady. 'Do you think it wise to send me out like this?'

'It would be death to touch the chieftain's property without his permission,' Varik noted, his face still buried.

She inclined her chin proudly, defiantly. 'I am no man's property, fetch your own water,' she declared, picking up the jug from the doorway and tossing it across the dirt to a place some inches from his half exposed body.

Varik did not budge. For agonising seconds she waited, her body trembling from unquenched desire mingled with mounting trepidation. As usual he was allowing her to resist, but how and when he responded, putting her back in her place, was up to him.

'If it is covering you wish,' he said, opening one eye lazily to behold the jug, 'then I can offer you some. A lovely shade of red, in fact, the sort appropriate for disobedient girls.'

Caralissa's cheeks flushed the very colour Varik was invoking. The reference to punishment, to marking her with his hand, or perhaps even the switch – that horrible little device which made her wet and weak just to think of it – was all too clear. How dare he? The man was a despicable beast, a blasphemer to the goddess. Fine, she would do what he wanted, but heaven would make him pay.

'No decent human being would ever speak so to a queen,' she said, even as she stormed over and scooped up the jug. 'Do you think me a common slut that you can bully – disrespecting my womanhood, threatening to beat me? Do you think the goddess won't punish you for such things?'

Varik seized her ankle, preventing her intended exit, which she meant to be both haughty and blustering.

'Ow!' she exclaimed, not hurt so much as shocked by his sudden grip, strong as steel.

'Do not offer curses,' he said, his emotions clouded, unreadable. 'Or I shall have you branded by the iron, that the gods will never again hear your prayers.'

Caralissa felt the blood drain from her face. It was a well-known fact that the gods and goddesses ignored as a practice the entreaties of branded slaves. 'I understand,' she stammered. 'Please forgive me.'

He released her. 'Bring my water, girl. And quickly.'

'Yes, my lord,' she heard herself say, scampering away as though she were his slave.

It was another of his tricks, of course, manipulating her emotions, redrawing the lines between them, lowering her standards so that she'd gone from legitimately protesting her right to clothing and fair treatment to running obediently to do his will, as though it were a privilege to do menial tasks for the man as his naked errand girl.

The fresh sun was warm upon her tender, aroused body. She was painfully aware of the swell and jiggle of her breasts, and of the sway of her hips. She'd not gone about naked since she was a child, and that was under the safe eyes of her nannies. Caralissa was far from a child now. She was a woman, bothered and in heat, a prisoner in a camp filled with sexually starved warriors.

Her heart pounded as the eyes began to follow her. Though no one pursued her, she could tell by the sudden silence, the predatory glances that they desired her, all of them.

She clutched the water jug. She was Varik's property. As demeaning as this fact was, she held to the label as strongly as to his water jug. It was that ownership which was saving her now, an invisible truth which alone prevented her from what she was sure would have otherwise been mass rape at these men's hands. Trying hard not to arouse them unnecessarily with her exposed flesh, she made her way quickly and efficiently to the stream.

It was eerie, the complete change from their manner of the day before. All along the path warriors stepped back, their muscled bodies a powerful lesson in discipline, controlled power. She did her best to avoid eye contact. At her current level of need she did not trust herself to keep from falling at their feet and begging them to do what they so obviously wanted to in the first place. Was it the sight of her, flush from a night of unquenched arousal that made her so irresistible? Could they smell her need, like a bitch in heat, silently begging the attention of every available male? Or was it what Senelek hinted at – that Varik's ongoing possession of her was becoming a source of rage and jealousy in the men? She could never resist them, she knew that. Any one of them could overpower her, attaining her easy sexual surrender. It shamed her deeply and yet it aroused her too, to know that she could be made to give herself to any one of them with a mere glance or a snap of fingers.

Would that make Varik jealous? Her mind moved yet again, towards the madness of thinking herself in love with the cruel chieftain. No, she could not think such thoughts. Varik was a sworn enemy, one whom she must now personally repay with torture and death, lest her own reputation as a sovereign, her own place as a queen be lost forever. After she was ransomed, that was when she would plot her revenge. As soon as she was free and the warlord's back was turned, she would concoct a plan for his demise.

If he let her go, that is. A secret thrill passed through her at the thought that he might not. What if he cared for her too much to free her? Could it be he loved her, even? Yes, he'd been harsh with her, denied her pleasures, subjected her to his hand and to the whistling, stinging switch, but did that not merely reinforce the strength of his desires, his need to control and conquer her completely? He'd warned off Senelek, been prepared to violate the trust of his own men, violate even the very customs of the tribe. What more proof could anyone need that he felt things for her? And the way he disallowed her use by the cord men, too, that was also proof, was it not?

'Greetings,' came a voice, sinister and crisp. 'Majesty.'

A hand clasped her arm. Caralissa looked up from her reverie and gasped. It was the black armoured soldier from the day before, the one who'd blocked her path and whom she later identified as one of Senelek's so-called warrior priests.

'I must fetch water,' she told him. 'For Lord Varik.'

The soldier gave her a slanted smile. 'Lord Senelek has your water,' he said, reaching out to cup her breast.

The sudden contact, as unexpected as it was openly sexual, caused Caralissa to leap backwards, her heart thumping like a threatened doe. 'I – I must go,' she stammered, attempting to bypass him.

The soldier collared her, his hand gripping at the back of her neck as he drew her into his embrace. His kiss was wet and offensive, and yet, in her boiling need she found herself moaning, opening, yielding.

'You will see Lord Senelek,' the man confirmed, worming his tongue from between her lips. 'Now.'

The command was punctuated with a stinging blow to her exposed buttocks. It jolted her all the more for its coming from a hand other than that of Varik – her punisher, her one and only lover, her lord. 'You won't get away with this,' she told him, even as she hastened to keep ahead of him so as to avoid any more blows. 'Varik will find you out.'

'Just keep moving, wench,' he advised, his breath hot in her ear, his hand insolently caressing her bottom cheeks. 'And save your tongue for my prick.'

A chill of fevered weakness passed through Caralissa's body as she contemplated the man's threats. She was going to be made to serve him, intimately and with her mouth as she had Varik. And even now she was walking towards that fate, her own degradation awaiting her in Senelek's tent. Would there be others, she wondered? And what about the high priest himself – would he have her too?

'Inside,' he snarled, shoving her through the opening of the black tent striped in red. 'Time to teach you some respect.'

The man sealed the tent opening behind him. It was dark inside, save for a single glowing light, green and flickering, contained in a glass lantern hung from the centre pole. The ground was soft. A rug of some kind lay over the bare ground. She looked about her. The tent walls were thick and overhung with layers of tapestry. Shining chains of gold and hanging metal bowls were arrayed from the corner poles. It was a damp, misty gloom that pervaded the room, an aura made even more sinister by the smell of burnt incense.

Caralissa sought to adjust her eyes, sought to make sense of the strange shadows that hung across her field of vision preventing her from seeing anything clearly. There seemed no signs of life about her and yet she felt eyes in the blackness, peering at her, probing and poking.

'Kneel, Orencian slut,' the soldier barked, snatching the jug from her and pushing her down by her shoulder till she was on her knees, the rug ticklish against her skin. 'Kneel and pay homage.'

The robed figure emerged from the shadows as though he were one himself. Caralissa was on the verge of looking up to identify the face when she felt a sudden force on her back, compelling her to lower her head till her lips were touching the red slippers, narrow and curved at the toe. Grasping the hint, Caralissa puckered her lips and kissed them, one after the other, rapidly, gingerly.

'See how naturally the slut abases herself, Gatal,' she heard Senelek say to her escort.

'All the world shall kneel to you, Lord Senelek,' Gatal replied, his voice thick with religious fervour.

'Varik will have your head for this, Lord Senelek,' Caralissa retorted, straightening herself to look up at him defiantly as she spat out his title with as much contempt as she could manage. 'You know he will.'

He was looking deeply into her eyes, but she did not flinch. Kill me, her gaze told him silently. I have nothing more to lose.

She heard the sound of scraping metal coming from beside her. It was a scabbard out of which was being drawn a sword. There was another man now, standing beside the unspeaking Senelek. A second later she felt sharp metal as the lethal blade was placed across the back of her neck.

'No, pretty little whore,' came the new man's voice,

slightly nasal as he pressed the sword a tiny bit harder. 'It is Lord Senelek who will have yours.'

'Put that away, Birat,' chided Senelek, sounding for a brief moment as if he sympathised with the prisoner. 'It is not our place to kill her. The law is very clear on the treatment of whores. They must be dealt with according to their sex and status.'

'I am not a whore,' she defied, not caring if they chose to strike her dead. 'I am a queen.'

'How dare you?' growled yet another man, emerging from behind to threaten her with the back of his hand.

'No, Voorash, do not strike her. Let us use reason instead.'

'Yes, Lord,' the new man deferred, lowering his arm at once.

'Reason?' Caralissa scoffed. 'What would you know of such things, barbarian?'

There were growls of indignation from every side.

Senelek calmed them with a single word in Rashal, delivered with clipped intensity. His minions reminded her of snarling dogs, obedient to the one man who was more vicious than they.

'I am a barbarian, yes,' Senelek agreed, his voice showing exaggerated calm. 'It is a fact I am quite proud of. Among the civilised peoples – the so-called civilised, I should say – I saw such horrors and atrocities, all hidden and couched in finery, of course, as to make me vow never to even remotely resemble them in any way. Do you see this mark, majesty?'

Senelek bent to show her his forearm. She attempted to twist her head, to avert her gaze from the mark, deep and red, a groove in the skin, intricate, made of lines, crossed with other lines. It was deep and ugly.

'Why do you look away, noble queen?' Senelek asked,

grasping her chin to compel her attention. 'Does it disturb you to see upon me the mark of civilisation?'

'Orencia practices no such mutilations,' she said. 'Nor is there any form of branding in all of the Seven Kingdoms of the valley, not even upon slaves.'

'How pleased your slaves must be,' Senelek snorted. 'To know they are spared any unpleasantness.' He released her, thrusting back her chin contemptuously.

'I am not responsible for what happened to you,' she persisted. 'Nor are my people.'

'Then I shall make them responsible!' Senelek thundered, shaking his fist. 'I shall make them pay. And I can, you know. Varik controls the army, but I have at my disposal holy warriors. Fewer in number, but highly effective.' He paused, watching her, gauging the effect of his words, the anticipation of what he said next.

Bending even further forward, he spoke nearly in a whisper. 'I need only give the order, my queen, and Orencia will cease to exist.'

Caralissa fought to keep her face devoid of expression. To be conquered by the Rashal was one thing. There would be fires, hostages taken tribute to pay. But to face the kind of attack Senelek was hinting at was unthinkable. 'What do you want?' she asked, seeking to hide her terror.

He folded his arms inside the thick robe. 'To begin with,' he said with deep satisfaction, 'I wish you to put your hand between your thighs, my little foreign slut. Then I want you to stroke yourself deeply and show me upon your fingers whether you are wet or dry.'

Caralissa heard the words as if from the end of a tunnel. Just as distant seemed her own response, as she put her fingers to her sopping sex, drawing off a thin film of the musky substance. The feel of her own vaginal opening nearly made her swoon. It wasn't fair, not fair at all to employ such power over her, to invoke in her such feelings, such needs. What was it about being commanded by strong men, about being made to surrender her will that so excited her?

'Hold up your hand, now,' Senelek said. 'Show us the results.'

Caralissa bowed her head, lowering it below her upraised arm as she presented for his inspection the glistening tips of her fingers.

'It is as I thought,' he hissed. 'You are a slut. Even when faced with the extermination of your own people you juice like a whore, a she-slave.'

'Do what you will to me,' she declared. 'But spare my people.'

'Touch yourself again,' Senelek demanded. 'More deeply this time.'

Caralissa looked at him in horror then lowered her eyes. He did not intend to relent; he would never relent. She saw that now. Spreading her legs more widely she gave him what he wanted. A demonstration of her true nature as a slut. Biting her lip, her fingers hot over her clitoris, she resisted the impulse to beg them to take her.

'Yes,' he confirmed a moment later as the spasms began to hit her, 'that is how you must be in my presence. Show me what you truly are. Yes, make yourself flow hotly. There – that is enough. Now put your fingers to your lips; use your tongue, taste your own evil fluid.'

Caralissa trembled, her climax cut off prematurely. She did not know if she could remain upright, if she could manage to move her own arm, to complete the terrible deed. Eyes glued to her fingers, tears brimming, she watched their approach, inexorably moving towards her waiting mouth.

He could not make her do this. It was too shameful!

'Now!' hissed Senelek, his cruel command enforced by the resurgent blade of Birat, now pressed pointedly at her left nipple. 'Lick yourself now!'

Caralissa nearly fainted. Moaning, arching her back, she sucked her fingers till they were clean. Desperately, in the back of her mind, she tried to rationalise the act, even as she performed for them as a captive slut. Repugnant as Senelek was, after all, he was Varik's brother and deserved her obedience on account of her feelings for him. Besides which, he was male and she was female; how could she do aught but obey one of them after having been dealt with so thoroughly on their behalf by Varik? It was a result of her captivity that was all. And her people – how could she risk their deaths by disobeying?

'Enough,' said Senelek to Birat, who withdrew the sword. 'You may take your hand from your mouth,' the high priest declared, stepping forward so that his midsection was an inch from her face. 'You will now put it back between your legs,' he added, his voice thick with the satisfaction of complete victory of his will over hers. 'You will continue in this manner as we converse.'

Caralissa returned her fingers to her burning womb. Would Senelek allow her to come? And if he did – given the current circumstances – would it be a blessing or a curse? And what of Varik – would he forgive his brother such liberties, or would he fly into a rage when he found out? She laughed to herself, thinking of the beast. More likely he'd encourage his brother, Caralissa thought, rubbing herself harder, the warlord's presumed insolence arousing her to fever pitch.

'Aah,' she cried, the sound a long hiss as the convulsions began, the preliminary waves.

'Silence, slut,' Senelek commanded, showing his utter indifference to whether she pleasured herself to climax or not. 'And open your ears to listen to my offer. It is an offer I do not think you will dare refuse once you have heard it.'

'The Rashal are noted for their generosity,' she observed, the words coming in short stabs of breath as she tried to recover herself.

'The Rashal are destined to rule the world,' corrected Senelek, snapping his fingers so that the lantern might be adjusted. Caralissa grimaced, the greenish light having been redirected to her body. Her flushed skin shone with an eerie glow.

'Varik does not seem to share that ambition,' she countered boldly, attempting to keep her breathing steady. It was not her intention to climax, to shame herself in such a manner in front of these men, and yet how would she be able to resist, as long as Senelek compelled her to touch herself?

Senelek stepped from his pointed slippers. His toes bore rings and his skin smelt sickly sweet. 'The will of an individual means nothing among the Rashal,' he said. 'Not even that of a chieftain.'

Caralissa bit her lip, needing the pain to keep her focused. It was madness, having to stimulate herself all the while fighting the inevitable release, the craved for conclusion she'd been needing for so long. 'And yet you seem to place so much stock in your own will,' she suggested, approaching his blatant megalomania in as subtle a manner as possible.

Senelek shook his head. 'Not my will,' he declared, opening his robe and shedding it from his broad shoulders. 'The will of the gods.'

She beheld his naked body. It was oiled and muscled, but strangely pale in comparison to his brother's.

'Praise be the gods of the Rashal,' repeated the men in

unison.

Caralissa regarded Senelek's limp shaft, which was close enough to touch. Or kiss. 'I know what you worship,' she said pointedly. 'I know what you serve.'

'Insolent slut,' he hissed, stroking himself, his eyes slowly closing. 'You know nothing. But you will be taught.'

There was silence as they all waited for the high priest to bring himself to erection. This achieved, he reopened his eyes, refreshed, as if having just completed a long nap. 'Let us begin the conversation anew,' he said, taking a deep breath, 'shall we?'

'I'm a captive audience,' she shrugged, conveying as much irony as possible.

Senelek began to pace in front of Caralissa, from left to right and back again. 'We have a problem, you and I, a common problem, one which begs a single solution.'

'Oh?' She tried not to laugh at the sight of his erect member, preceding him as though he were a man being walked by a worm. 'And what problem is that?'

'Why, Varik's deep attachment for you, of course,' he laughed. 'Isn't that obvious? So long as my brother craves you, in this most unhealthy, unholy manner, he will never return you to your home – which I assure you, highness, is the outcome we both desire.'

Caralissa braced herself. It was too late; she was going over the top. 'What do you care if I make it home alive?' she asked, the first waves of her orgasm closing over her.

Home. What was home any more? It felt now as if she'd been born in this place, in this camp, on the furs of the warlord Varik, and here again, here and now upon the rugs of a wicked, lust-filled priest. Home was the iron will of Varik, his implacable need pressed upon her, his hand, smoothly striking, making her wince and beg. Home was the empty craving in her heart which needed filling by Varik's arrogance, his wild-eyed lust. How her being a queen fit into this, how the needs of Orencia and her people configured in this new scheme, she did not know. It was a shameful truth, one that dishonoured her in her father's immortal eyes, and yet she was a female, a girl with needs and she could no longer deny this.

Senelek honed in. Directly in front of her again he absorbed her anxious trembling, the self-yielding. Unable to hold back or hide it, she gave it to him, her passion's flower, callously beheld by his indifferent eyes. Weeping, she convulsed again and again till the throes of her orgasm passed.

'The reason I care,' Senelek said after she subsided and was able to focus on his cruel, contemptuous face once more, 'is because you and I both know that so long as Varik burns for your unworthy body, he is of no use to the Rashal. We must, therefore, work together to break his attachment.'

How badly she wanted to lay down, to close her eyes and sleep. 'I have no control over Varik,' she managed weakly. 'I did not ask him to want me. I made no effort to seduce him.'

As if she could seduce a man of such splendid power even if she wanted!

'All whores say the same thing,' he declared, his organ poking her face. 'Which is why we must remind him what you truly are.'

'I – I do not understand,' she said, her voice conveying the simple truth.

'Varik thinks you are a gift of the gods, a treasure sent to him, a wonder of the heavens. By lying with you he thinks to find his bliss, to forget the woes of his office.

Were he to see in you something else, he would abandon this childish idea. Here then is my plan, my little queen. Tell me when I am done if you do not agree – bearing in mind, of course, that your agreement will markedly increase your people's chance of survival in my eyes.'

She nodded, admitting ahead of time her inevitable acquiescence.

Senelek smiled smugly, his eyes glowing with love for his own deviousness. 'You will be returned to Varik, evidence of your lying with others thick upon your person,' he explained, wasting no time on niceties. 'He will see you in this state, and will find himself unable to bear the sight of you. You will then be returned to your castle.'

'Evidence?' Caralissa singled out the word, so glibly issued from his tongue, yet so crucial to her own life. 'What evidence do you mean?'

He grinned, exchanging glances with the men behind her. 'Use your imagination,' he said, 'your majesty.'

'I see. So I shall lie to him and say I have been with others, and by my own will?'

Senelek laughed, encouraging the others to do the same. 'You will not have to lie, my dear,' he said to her at last. 'You will tell him quite honestly.'

Caralissa stiffened. 'The men that do this thing,' she said. 'Varik would have them killed, would he not?'

'Not if I intervene, to conceal their identity. And if they are men I trust there will be no chance at all of their discovery.'

'How convenient,' she conceded. 'For those particular men.'

Senelek meant he and his deputies, of course. Though there was no point in mentioning the fact.

'There is one more thing you should consider,' Senelek

offered, stroking her hair, his thick member at the verge of entering her tightened lips. 'Your prompt removal from this camp and Varik's equally prompt return to his duty protects him as well. Consider it a guarantee for him, against insurrection.'

Caralissa felt the blood drain from her face. The man was threatening his brother, warning her that if she did not cooperate, Varik himself might be eliminated. Was there no limit to Senelek's ambition, to his outrageous evil?

'Varik will never be beaten by you,' she declared, retracting her face as far from his imperiously outthrust crotch as possible, given her kneeling position. 'You are not his equal, and that is why you hate him so much.'

Senelek's eyes glowed a little more hotly. 'Perhaps I am his equal,' he crooned suggestively, his hands thick in her hair. 'In at least one area.'

Caralissa clenched her fists. 'I yield my body to you, Senelek,' she said proudly. 'But my desire is something you will never have.'

'Ah,' he said, feeding himself between her lips in a manner most satisfying to himself. 'But with the taking of your body shall come the possession of your heart, and even your very soul.'

There was no way to respond, the thick manhood of the priest having already pressed itself deep to the back of her throat. As if to enforce the men's dominance over her, hands came down now from behind, one upon each of her naked shoulders. Not forcefully pressing, but resting, possessively, as though enjoying her vicariously.

Despite his claims the priest appeared to yield little to his passion. His motions were efficient, designed to conquer, to subdue and to control, not to engender his own lust. Caralissa absorbed him, her eyes closed as she imagined Varik in the man's place, holding her, teaching her, taking her in the fullness of his lust. Varik alone, branding her, heart and soul, spoiling her for any other, ever again.

Senelek shuddered only slightly as he achieved his climax. Methodically, almost dispassionately, he released himself, as if discharging some ritual required by his gods. Caralissa served him well, her mouth forming a tender, resilient pouch. His eyes showed neither gratefulness nor passion as he pulled himself free, his now shrivelled organ hanging lifelessly in front of him.

'You may take your turns,' he said to the others. 'Make her squirm well,' he added, almost as an afterthought. 'Leave copious evidence and send for me when you are done.'

Caralissa watched as he donned his robe and walked to the entrance. One of the men – the one she now knew as Garat – opened the tent flap for him, allowing him to leave. How strange, she thought: a cruel despot who did not even stay to see his victim plundered.

'You heard the high priest,' said Garat to the others. 'Let us use this slut in the service of the gods.'

'In the name of the gods,' agreed Voorash, grasping her left arm.

'Glory be to the gods of the Rashal,' Birat added, taking her right arm.

Caralissa allowed herself to be raised to her feet. It was Garat who made the first move, pulling her into his arms, delivering a kiss, deep and soulful. A piteous moan escaped her throat, her resolve already crumbling. It was true then, what Senelek said – where her body went, so went her soul. The convulsions of a second orgasm passed through her, her untouched sex spasming as Garat's tongue plundered her open mouth, reclaiming the channel already wrought by the high priest.

'We shall put her on all fours,' said Garat, the apparent leader of the group. 'We shall have her two at a time. Remember, regardless of the orifice you stimulate yourself in, you are to ejaculate externally, on her body.'

'May our semen be well seen and may it give glory to the gods of the Rashal,' said Voorash.

'Their names be everlasting,' echoed Birat.

She did not know whether to laugh or cry; so absurd were their words, their wooden manners. And yet she needed them, more than she could ever say. Needed their maleness, their harsh ways and attentions.

Caralissa did not wait to be placed, but assumed herself the desired position at their feet. It was for the best, she told herself as the priests unsheathed themselves, forming a semicircle about her. With her degradation would come redemption for Varik, the needed impetus to return him to the ways of his people. And she in turn would be freed of him, freed of a potential life of slavery, as the foreign whore of a warlord, hated by all, held in contempt even by her own people.

It truly was for the best, she repeated, her body on all fours in a foreign camp awaiting her despoilment. It was for the good of all.

'Didn't I tell you?' crooned Garat, guiding himself into her mouth. 'That you should save your breath for me?'

Yes, she nodded, sucking him deeply even as another, either Birat or Voorash mounted her from behind; it was true, she did remember.

'Hurry,' she heard a voice complain. 'I want my turn, too.'

'There's plenty to go around,' Garat said, grasping her hair. 'You needn't worry on that score. Isn't that right, Orencian slut?'

A deep groan issued as her pinioned loins succumbed

to another thrust, the greatest one yet. She was going to come again, come like the slut they were calling her. Eagerly she redoubled her ministrations to Garat, though whether to speed the process up to get it over with or else to sweeten it for her own pleasure, she knew not. Such understanding of her own behaviour was beyond her now, as was all form of reason.

'Arrggh!' groaned the man at her rear as he withdrew to spurt upon her back. 'By the gods, I cannot wait!'

'Please,' she heard herself wail as Garat withdrew to spray upon her face. 'Do not leave me like this!'

All at once a new organ was inside her, and she began to weep with joy and shame commingled.

Forgive me, her heart cried, silent and unexpectedly. Forgive me, my Lord Varik.

Caralissa heard the clash of steel just outside Varik's tent. The warlord was practicing at swords, his bare chest pouring sweat as he parried blow after blow from a pair of blond adversaries, their faces wild with bloodlust. She did not dare look up at him, but kept her head down, her eyes on the ground as the two priests Garat and Birat held her firm. Senelek was talking with his brother, trying to get his attention to tell him of the treachery of the captured queen, the foreign whore now naked before them, her body thick and glistening with the semen of Senelek and his priests.

'I will not deal with this now,' she heard Varik say, his voice flat, devoid of emotion. 'I tend to the affairs of men now, not those of females.'

'I shall have her put in your tent,' Senelek replied, bowing quite low before him. 'Your Lordship.'

Senelek signalled to the two men, who dragged Caralissa inside Varik's tent, placing her against one of the corner poles. The high priest handed them a long coil of rope, which they wound round and round her reddened flesh, securing her to the centre pole. The faces of Garat and Birat were flush as they worked, flush from their having of her. She imagined their cocks now beneath their holy robes, drained and limp between their legs from their numerous spurtings upon her supple flesh.

They did their work in silence, just as in Senelek's tent. She'd been a dream of pleasure for them, willing and unresisting, her body leaping before their every touch, pouring forth its passions as though they were her devoted lovers, men to whom she owed her heart. In truth she was a slut, a woman of no shame, no honour.

Each of the priests had taken several turns, trying out all her orifices in a rotational style. Until today Caralissa didn't know that a man could wish to use her narrower passage, but this too was most thoroughly explored. The priests were enthusiastic and most thorough. They seemed to lose little of their vitality with each passing climax, but managed successively to squeeze forth ever-larger amounts of thick white fluid. Though she suffered much they showed mercy at various points, allowing her to come upon their fingers, as their frequent withdrawals from her starved nether opening tended to leave her frustrated.

On and on it went, and like a whore she gasped, begging their rough attentions. In the end it was she who wore them down, till they were compelled to hold her fast, two of them keeping her still while the third sent for Senelek. It was the priest who finished her off, climbing atop her and bringing her thrice to orgasm as he delved her depths, his turgid pole reanimated, as always in the name of the Rashal gods. Expressionless, eyes closed in an attitude of prayer, he filled her with his fluid, being twice over the only one of the four to climax inside her. Rank has its privileges, she'd thought as he removed himself, not deigning even to look her in the face.

'Guard the entrance,' said Senelek to the two when they were finished with the rope. 'I will wait upon my brother.'

'Yes, Lord Senelek,' they said in unison, turning on their heels as if she were not there.

Senelek approached her, touching his finger to her cheek. 'We will meet again,' he promised, 'your highness.'

Caralissa turned her head away from his sneering glare. Fighting back the tears, she tried to think of Varik. How splendid she imagined him looking as he sported with his fellow warriors, their huge swords clashing like lightning, sparkling in the sun as they impacted, one upon the other, over and over, a deafening barrage and yet not one drop of blood drawn.

She heard Senelek laugh and then he was gone. A shiver passed down her spine. By now she ought to be used to this, to being naked and bound, used to having her body abused and left to chill in the crisp daylight air. Upon the battering ram, for example, where she hung like a scarecrow, a figure to be ridiculed by her own people, by the despicable Telos and her own arrogant and sullen sister. And now there were these new ropes to braze her skin as she stood wrapped like a mummy. They could have gagged her too, but there seemed no point. Her own shame kept her silent now. No doubt her well-rested tongue would come in handy when Senelek spilt his lies, demanding her confirmation of them before his unwitting brother.

She was supposed to confirm whatever the high priest might say. No matter what, she was to concur, to agree with Senelek so as to override and destroy Varik's natural inclination to protect her.

But what exactly was it that would happen to her along

the way – once she succeeded in convincing Varik that she was guilty? Senelek had refused to say; his only promise being that by nightfall she would be free, never to be troubled by the Rashal lord again. Senelek was tricking her, she was fairly certain. And yet she did not care. Her life meant little. As for her people, she sensed their best hope lay in Varik, in his maintaining of power over Senelek. It was the leadership of Senelek she feared most, and this, she was certain, could best be avoided by her own despoilment and removal from the camp.

Caralissa's aching body came to sudden attention, her weary heart soaring as she heard his voice. It was Varik, outside the tent, exchanging words as he so often did with his brother.

'I wish to hear nothing further from you,' Varik declared, cutting off the man's initial explanations. 'I desire none of your reports or explanations, with regard to this or anything else. I wish only to be left alone.'

Senelek could be heard to dismiss his men. He then began arguing the point for his own involvement, for a proper interrogation of the prisoner, but Varik cut him off now, his voice menacing. 'I said I wish to be left alone,' he repeated. 'Even by you, my brother.'

'Very well,' Senelek replied, his voice sounding slightly brittle. 'I shall await your pleasure.'

Her eyes beheld him as he entered his tent. Varik seemed careful to avoid looking at her as he scooped a towel from off one of the wooden chests and began to dab at the tiny pools of sweat on his chest. He was holding his sword and scabbard in hand, and he laid it down beside the axe. The man's every motion seemed carefully circumscribed, designed to diffuse the possibility of emotional reaction. Donning a tunic, one of scarlet red that slipped easily over his head, he knelt briefly in the corner, in an attitude of prayer.

After a long time he rose and walked to a place directly in front of her. His face moulded into a most unreadable expression, his eyes lit with a small but discernible glow, he beheld her. Whether it was the prayer or the time with the swords she could not tell, but it was something real and palpable, surely, that possessed him.

How she longed to reach out to him, to understand his pain. He'd refused to hear his brother's accusations. And yet it must be clear to him by her presence, her condition, that something terrible had occurred. Why was he not screaming? Why was he not demanding explanations, or barring that, seeking to comfort her?

'I owe my life to my brother,' Varik began, his eyes connecting with hers, drawing her to that common place, that place beyond pain, beyond explanation. 'Without him we would not be a people. He has his darkness, deep within, but he serves the people. As you serve yours in your darkness, and I in mine. That is what matters. It is the people that have life above us, you and I and he. We are nothing without our people.'

Caralissa nodded, determined to hold within her, still and unspoken, the truth of the day's events.

Varik noted her reaction. Running his hands through his hair he looked to the ground. 'My brother would tell me lies,' he said. 'Lies that are truth in the eyes of our gods. In the final scheme, what is a lie and what is truth?' he asked, beholding the ground.

Caralissa longed to hold him. Curse the ropes that kept her from his arms, which kept her from comforting him.

Varik clenched his fists. 'The ways of the gods are strange. And yet we mortals cannot oppose them.' He looked once again into her eyes, his own consumed with unearthly fire. 'Senelek would tell me that you have betrayed me, and yet I can guess the truth. It was he who violated you – he and his men, was it not? Do not answer me, only listen. There is a deeper truth. Even Senelek is not responsible, but only me. It is I who did this to you. You must learn to hate me, Caralissa. I insist upon it.'

She shook her head violently. 'I cannot do that,' she said, finding her dormant tongue.

'You shall,' he countered. 'I will leave you no choice. In a moment I will call Senelek in here and I shall ask him as high priest to mete out your sentence, for betraying my honour. He shall propose to have you flogged and publicly humiliated, in front of the entire army. I shall agree, and allow him personally to carry out the sentence. From that time on I shall not speak to you, will not heed your cries, nor will I even bid you goodbye afterwards when you are returned to your people. From that time on you will never see me again.' He paused to stroke her cheek with the flat of his hand. 'Thus will you come to hate me,' he said, very softly.

'No!' she cried, straining against her bonds. 'I shall never hate you, no matter what you do to me.'

Varik considered her, his lips at last curling into a smile, both sad and ironic. 'And that,' he told her, 'shall be *my* punishment, Little Flame.'

Turning his head towards the entrance to the tent he called for his brother, whom they both knew was close at hand. 'Senelek!' he cried. 'Come quickly, and bring the gods with you. It is time for them to feed once more on human misery!'

Chapter Five

Caralissa was secured to the platform, her arms stretched above her head, her breasts proud in the twilight air, her flat stomach vibrating ever so slightly with her soft breath. She was naked, her body glistening from the cleansing oils applied following her bath. There were also powders, perfumes and chanted prayers, this being a ritual event, her flogging before the assembled troops of the Rashal Empire.

Discipline was high in the ranks and there were no leering eyes this time, no slanted smiles, no licking of lips. In their ranks they stood, eyes forward, in full battle uniform. Rows a hundred soldiers wide and twenty deep stretching across the plains. Mounted on horseback the cavalry enjoyed a better view, a full panorama of the queen, her arms taut, her calves stretched, standing on tiptoe, doing her best to equalise the pressure on her bound wrists. There was no concealing her predicament, the hardened nipples, swelled with fear and anticipation, the oily smell of her crotch, the seemingly unstoppable flow of her juices.

Only a slut, or worse, a slave, could be so aroused by the prospect of being beaten by a mortal enemy, a man who'd defiled her and then assaulted her character in the bargain. Only a slut would moisten in front of ten thousand men as they prepared to watch her writhe beneath a whip. And not merely a single stick of leather, but a thick-handled braided device, with five thongs, long and devious.

Senelek's boots could be heard behind her as he ascended the platform. He would do the whipping, as Varik predicted. All of this, in fact, was precisely as Varik said it would be. True to his promise he had abandoned her and done nothing to prevent her sentence. Caralissa raised her head towards the crowd. She did not wish the men to see her face, her emotions, but she needed to find him. Needed to scan their ranks, the need and loneliness written across her face as she searched in vain for their heartbroken ruler.

Where was Varik? Nowhere to be seen, and yet it was made clear by Senelek that he would watch, that in fact he must watch by Rashal law. The boots were coming closer, narrowing the distance. His every step seemed to take hours. Her heart, more bared than her flesh seemed flayed by every second, by the truth of time's unfurling. Varik did not care. He could not, would not put any feelings for her above his duty. He would let her be whipped, and for a crime she did not commit, all for the good of his people. Her people, too.

She drew a sharp breath, tried to conceal her naked terror. Senelek was directly behind her. His shadow across her, his breath perilously close to her ear.

'You are mine now,' he told her. 'Queen Caralissa. And not only for the next twenty minutes, but forever. For what I am going to do to you will brand you. I will mark you, and not only on your pretty skin, but in deeper places. Places a man like Varik, with all his ideals and sense of honour could never dream of touching. You see, my dear, I am like you. *Civilised.*'

Senelek nibbled her ear, subtly and for only the briefest of seconds. At the same time, insolently, almost casually, he let the many-stranded whip brush her hip.

'Please,' she breathed, her every thought of defiance

111

dissolving before her eyes, 'I beg mercy.'

Senelek grabbed her hair. He was standing in front of her now, forcing her to look him in the eye.

'No,' he smiled thinly, thrusting the handle of the whip quite unexpectedly between her legs. 'You shall have no mercy.'

Caralissa jolted as though struck already. Helpless in her bonds she received the leather, her vagina filled completely. Gasping audibly she felt the spasms beginning to mount.

'Do not look away from me,' Senelek ordered, his face inches from hers as he began to play with her sex, manoeuvring the whip handle as though it were his shaft. 'Tell me now that you will obey.'

Caralissa looked at him in awe, her earlier fear mingled with a dreaded desire to submit to this hatefully cruel man. 'I – I will obey,' she said, her voice weak with desire.

'I will obey, my lord,' he corrected, administering a slight alteration in the angle of her penetration, enough to make her throw back her head and cry out.

'I – I – will obey, my lord,' she panted as soon as she regained her power of speech.

Senelek closed the narrow gap between them so that his lips nearly touched her trembling mouth. 'With this whip I will own you. Because of what I am going to do to you, you will never again see such a device without becoming heated. You will curse my name again and again because you will yearn to submit to it each and every time, to tear the very clothes from your body and fall at the feet of the man who wields it, begging for him to lash you, to brand you with it, publicly and absolutely.'

Senelek froze his pumping hand, holding her fast at the brink of her orgasm. Her fists clenching and unclenching uselessly, Caralissa moaned, knowing herself at this moment to be naught but a tied and exhibited slut, begging with her ripe body to be used, to be taken, to be lashed, to be dominated.

She nearly screamed as he pulled forth the whip handle, leaving her unfulfilled.

'May I whip you now, your majesty?' he asked with a flourish, his smile full of one-sided mirth.

Caralissa was in no place to appreciate either humour or irony. 'Y-yes, my lord,' she mouthed, not knowing for what she was asking. 'I beg you to use me as it pleases you.'

Senelek thrust the whip handle to her lips. 'Clean yourself from it and I will use it on you.'

Caralissa parted her lips, inviting the leather shaft to pierce that opening. The leather was musky, mingled as it was with her juices. She did her best to purify it, judiciously swallowing her sweetened spit. Somewhere in the back of her mind she was aware of the degradation, the way he was manipulating her in front of Varik's men, and yet she could not at this moment separate herself out enough to know how to resist.

'Such an obedient little thing,' he observed, plucking a nipple between his thumb and forefinger, massaging it idly.

Unable to help herself, feeling her face cloud with shame, she thrust her breasts to him and redoubled her efforts at the whip handle, caressing it in a most blatant manner.

'Mmmm,' she moaned when he pulled the whip away, denying her.

'Varik is a child,' he said to her, flicking the whip across her hip so as to awaken her every nerve. 'I am a man. Now you shall learn the difference.'

He gave her a few moments to contemplate these

ominous words as he strode to a place behind her, within range of her back. Throwing her long hair forward over her shoulder, removing thusly for himself the only obstacle to her flesh, he bared her, from neck to knee. After a couple of light runs down her spine, the whip cords trailing delicately, teasingly, he reared back his arm and struck her.

Caralissa cried out from the shock, the pain, the sudden burning sensation, not to mention the dramatic change in her status. She, Caralissa, daughter of Lysanis, queen of Orencia, was being whipped.

Senelek paused to replace her hair, which in her writhing had fallen once more over her back. Caralissa moaned as he touched her, igniting the fire that seared across her flesh and would not go away.

'Your back takes the lash well, majesty, as well as any slave,' he observed. 'Would you like the next in the same general vicinity?'

'No,' she wept frantically. 'Not there, please.'

'I see. Perhaps your lovely arse cheeks instead?'

Caralissa voiced her protest, but it came too late as Senelek landed a blow across her straining buttocks. Her cry of pain was audible, she was quite sure, even to the very last ranks.

'Had enough, majesty?' he asked, his voice smug with condescension.

'Yes, yes, oh please stop,' she wept, the last of her pride evaporated.

'Very well, no more lashes. For the time being, at any rate.'

Senelek took her from behind this time, the thick whip handle fitting all too easily into her wet opening. Manipulating her breast with his free hand, and seizing her earlobe with gnawing teeth, he pushed through her flimsy defences working her to a frenzy. In a matter of seconds he broke her open entirely.

Shuddering against him, bound and beaten, she yielded. Her buttocks straining she thrust herself against the whip, against his hand and against his hips in a final thrust, the last of her energy dissipating till she hung limply, like a rag doll in front of Varik's troops.

'Now,' he told her, his voice triumphant as he wiped the stained whip across her belly. 'We will continue.'

Caralissa twisted in futility as the whip singed her left side, cruelly striping her hip. Senelek countered quickly with a blow to the right hip, so that she knew not in which direction to attempt to turn her rigidly held body. She knew her motions could do little to ease her predicament, and that they likely served only to titillate her exclusively male audience, and yet she could not bring herself to stay still.

Senelek was both thorough and unrelenting, his next blow landing across her thighs, blazing a trail across her soft interior. Now it was her legs, and then her breasts, a vicious slice coming just below her nipples. Like a lover, hard and demanding, the leather braids had their way with her, taking from her all she gave and more, much more.

When at last he stepped back she was a maddening portrait of submissive beauty. Surrendered woman flesh, peaked in its desirability. He let her hang this way, awaiting the final, inevitable surrender.

'Please…' she croaked, the word dying upon her open lips.

Seizing his opportunity the wily priest inserted the whip handle back into her mouth, compelling her to take it fully even as he worked her sex with his hand, the fingers contorted into a claw, deceptively gentle and probing. Caralissa groaned, biting the whip then sucking it with ferocious passion, arching her back as she did, begging his touch upon her stinging breasts. It was the cold metal of his breastplate she encountered. Lewdly, shamelessly, she rubbed her whip-seared chest against him. She was a bitch in heat now, a beaten slut whose legs would spread for any man strong enough to claim her.

'Save your ardour,' Senelek told her, denying her further pleasure with the removal of his hand. 'For the captains. Respond to them passionately and you will be spared another round of lashes. Show them disrespect by reacting coldly and you and I shall go at it again. Do we have an understanding?'

Caralissa nodded numbly. As if she could refuse him anything!

Senelek continued his iron willed appraisal of her soul. His hard gaze slashed through her, as though it were a second whip. Why was he saying or doing nothing? To be whipped or penetrated would be far preferable to this contest of stares. Any form of force in fact, any action to remove the pretence of her will was what was called for in her mind. He'd conquered her already – why did he not seal his victory? Why was he making her take the initiative, forcing her to declare her status in as shameful a way as possible? Agonising seconds dragged by, until inevitably Caralissa lowered her eyes, her gaze falling upon his crotch and finally settling on his feet, on his black boots.

'Yes,' she acknowledged, fathoming what was required. 'We have an understanding.'

Senelek's eyes glowed momentarily brighter. A thin smile crossed his lips. 'Beg for it, your majesty. Beg for your unworthy body to be used by the Rashal, beg to be the receptacle of Rashal seed.'

Her head swam as it dawned on her what was happening. Senelek was breaking her will, trying to turn her into a

116

creature of cringing obedience, like a dog who might be made to lick its master's hand or lie at his feet, an animal that might be controlled with simple rewards and punishments – the palm of a hand, the blow of a switch or lash. Angrily now, she jerked her head back up, her eyes welling with tears as she sought to convey to him how wrong this was – that she was a person, a free woman with rights to be honoured. To surrender to Varik, the man she loved was one thing, but to be humiliated by this man to whom she owed nothing was a violation of everything sacred.

Senelek's jaw tensed. Moving his lips almost imperceptibly he met the challenge, meeting her glare with a look of his own, cunning, infinitely patient, like that of an untamed tiger. She swallowed hard as he conveyed to her in a single heartbeat the unbridled truth: that in him she had found a man who would not be swayed, would not allow himself to be controlled by any woman, least of all a pretty little barbarian plaything who so plainly belonged at his feet.

Lips trembling, Caralissa conceded, her head dropping of its own accord, her dreams of resistance dissolving once again before the iron will of the high priest, brother of the man whom she adored. 'I beg to be used by the Rashal,' she began, a wave of shameful pleasure overtaking her. 'I beg for my unworthy body to be the receptacle of Rashal seed.'

Senelek seized her chin between his fingers, forcing her head back. 'Speak up.'

Thrice more Caralissa repeated the formula, the third time shouting the words so that a cheer rose from the ranks.

'That's better,' he nodded. 'Now tell me, what are you?'

A tear formed in the corner of her eye. She knew what

117

he wanted from her now and though she fought it with every fibre of her being she could not hold back the words. 'I am your slave,' she told him.

It was a decisive event, the marking of a permanent change in their relationship. Never again would she look Senelek in the eye, never again would she dare presume herself the man's equal. Caralissa's skin flushed crimson as she stood before him, in the fullness of what she had become: his conquered female property.

'Kiss me,' Senelek commanded, his body firm against her.

Caralissa's lips parted obediently. There was nothing Senelek could demand now that she would not give freely. It was not love, but lust, or rather her own stolen passion, wrenched from her and placed upon parade, as enticement to the men, the aforementioned captains who were going to have her and also to those who would merely watch. How she wished her hands were free from above her head so that she might collapse, falling appropriately to Senelek's feet upon her knees, or better still, upon her belly. Let her be hidden in this way, let her disappear inside his orbit; let her be truly a toy, only a toy.

Senelek pressed his still sheathed cock against her. 'Listen closely, Caralissa, to what I am to say,' he warned. 'Much depends upon it.'

'Yes,' she whispered, eyes begging for another kiss. 'Master.'

'You will orgasm for them,' Senelek instructed, specifying more fully his earlier demand. 'For each one who has you. You will show them that you are honoured to be had. You will show them that you are tamed, humbled, and appreciative. Within your bonds, you will writhe and show your gratitude for your usage at the hands of true men, at the hands of the Rashal. Consider

118

each cock to be a godhead, which you serve with your miserable flesh.'

He leaned down to clench her nipple with his teeth. 'Do not trifle with me or fail me, Queen Caralissa,' he said when he had taken his fill or her teat. 'I am not as my brother; your tears will not sway me. You are to me a means to an end, a sacrifice. What is done to you – your plundering, your abject submission shall symbolise your people's conquest. Give me enough here and now, and they will be spared. Attempt to withhold any scrap of dignity, of your own identity, and I will transfer my wrath to them.'

Caralissa lunged with her hips. She begged with her body to be taken, by him, by anyone. 'I am ready,' she breathed. 'Let them take me, master.'

'Begin with the First Horde,' Senelek proclaimed, to some unknown listener or listeners. 'And work through to the last.'

The chosen soldiers were not permitted the whip. Nor were they allowed to unbind Caralissa, to reposition her in any way. There sole option, given her placement, was to take her from behind. The first few were content to limit themselves to the more natural hole, spilling themselves prodigiously as they squeezed her breasts, grunting and drooling, their hands clenched painfully on her breasts.

At first, Caralissa feared she might fail in her need to orgasm with each of them, especially given their utter lack of concern for her pleasure. And yet it was this very disregard, this total contempt for her well-being that proved the most erotic stimulant of all. To be reduced to an object of pleasure, to be a mere body to use and spill into was the most delicious of sensations, one that created in her a savage flood of submissive juicing. The men seemed almost amazed, as though they'd never experienced such before. Even in her bonded state, the marks of Senelek's whip fresh upon her skin, she was a free offering unto them, a fully cooperative vessel, as if she were their own mate or at very least a hired prostitute.

Although in truth, not even a whore would betray herself to abuse, begging for kisses, rubbing herself heatedly and wildly at their slightest touches. She'd no idea it could feel so sweet! There was a rhythm, it seemed, and she was nearly lulled into a routine when she heard, somewhere between the eighth and ninth man, a question quite novel to the proceedings.

'Are we permitted the use of the narrower channel?' she heard a new man say, even as the old one was finishing noisily, his sweat dripping down her back, stinging the lacerations.

'Yes,' replied the chief priest, his voice discretely unemotional. 'You may use the slut as you wish.'

Caralissa nearly forgot to come as she heard the words. At the last second, their implications still ringing in her ears, she gave the man the orgasm due him.

The new man grunted his thanks to Senelek as he positioned himself behind the hapless queen. By his voice he was a big man, and his ham-like hands upon her hips only confirmed the matter. Caralissa was not a large girl, and it took him several huge thrusts, with frequent rests between, during which she hung there, her partially filled rectum throbbing.

There seemed to be no time limit, as he was allowed to bury himself at leisure. She occupied herself looking for Varik, and then when she could not find him, imagining among the faces she saw which ones might make the best lovers. Or rather, masters, for who would have her now as anything but the slave she was?

In the end the presence of the man's shaft inside her tight and tender bottom was less invasive than the smell of him, the feel of his hairy chest on her whip-bitten back. Worse still, he was speaking to her as well, or perhaps to his gods, coaxing them to aid in his ploughing of her captive body. The thrusts grew heavier and faster and a line of drool rained upon her shoulders, ebbing from his fetid mouth as he readied himself. Her body shook with his, cascading towards climax. Her untouched womb burning, she yielded herself, shuddering and crumpling under the assault. The flow of his seed went deep, up into that opening so unsuited by nature for the function.

The man's ejaculation extended for what felt like forever, until finally he began to affect his withdrawal. This too took several stages, his shaft having been nearly fused to her tunnel. Caralissa gasped audibly as she was vacated, the man's seed dribbling out behind the retreating organ.

She'd barely recovered when she heard Senelek call for the next man to come and to be quick about it, thus indicating that the use of her must not be allowed to falter in any way. And so it went, on and on. The men presenting themselves in all shapes and sizes. Small and large, some hard and fast pumping, others slower, their breath issuing in terse contractions. Some sought only to make nether contact, others allowed their hands to linger upon her, straying over her belly, gripping her aching breasts, clutching her undulating hips. Not one, though, was denied the fruit of her surrender. She came for each, under penalty of Senelek's whip. No doubt the priest would be pleased at his exercise of power, and yet the truth was, it was Varik to whom she yielded, Varik to whom she gave her every thought.

She squirmed, accustoming herself to a new man. Where

121

was he? She had yet to see him, nor could she even imagine where he might be. Was he practicing with swords again? Meditating in his tent, cross-legged as she'd seen him do between sessions of lovemaking, the tiny image of the raven god held between his outstretched fingers as he uttered the ancient chants of the Rashal? These were for her, moments of great tenderness, instances when she'd seen into his soul. Pretending to be asleep, lying in whatever position of ravishment he'd left her, she'd watched, wondering at his infinitely serious yet strangely playful expressions.

It made her jealous of that raven, and of the divinity behind it that so held his rapture. For a man with no use for gods, she thought, he'd seemed strangely pietistic. Ironically, it was a look of devotion she'd seen neither on Senelek's face nor those of his men. Their passion was of quite a different order, their god, pain and suffering. Most particularly that of suffering, captive females. It was the whip that Senelek adored, not the raven. And who was to say that the whip was not the supreme power in the heavens? Could even the sweet goddess endure its sting – more to the point would she not, having been once bitten, come to crave it again and again, to beg for it upon her knees, or even on her belly? Could there be a place even in heaven for masters and slaves?

Now there was a thought most blasphemous and wonderful! Could that lovely, too-sweet-to-be-named female Orencian deity, the one so often depicted with red hair like hers, yearn even in her immortal soul to yield to the raven or the dragon or perhaps the monster gods of the Forest of Night? Did they conspire for her possession, manipulating events and working towards some final end in which she would be brought before them to be humbled? Would she then dance for them, under the rain of golden cords, unbreakable, swift as lightning? Would thunder be crashed upon her back, like the blow of a whip? Would she be knelt and mounted by the beasts of the stars, her silent tears falling forth as prodigiously as the drenching rains, the birth flood of spring?

Were such myths true but somehow lost in the shrouded origins of time? And did the gods and goddesses themselves lie to conceal such things and did they even now play upon the raw lusts of men and women to recapitulate such stories of surrender and betrayal?

Was that why Varik claimed to have no use for the family of heaven? Did he see writ large the same corruption as on earth? Did he find religion as tedious then as the politics that forced him ever onward, towards greater and greater conquests?

Would he change his mind? Would he stop the proceedings, as he did in the tent, after the Dance of Cords? Would he risk the loss of his office, unleashing the fury of his men against him? Would he surrender his life's work, the honour of his tribe or even his very life? Could she have come to mean so much to him, in so short a time? Could there be anything between them, or was it merely the seductive charm of her temporary slavery, the indelible link of captor to captive?

Caralissa groaned to the sky, throwing back her head. It was her own sky, her people's sky and yet she was no longer free – would never again be free, in fact, so long as he walked the earth: Varik, the lonely chieftain owned her now. Varik with the haunting eyes and the thousand subtle smiles and his boundless imagination, with the thousand upon thousand promises and threats behind his clouded brow.

She shifted accommodatingly as another expelled himself, relinquishing his place to the leader of the next lower unit. There was a cloying stickiness between her thighs now. Almost certainly she was dripping not only her juices, but those of her lovers as well. If such a term might be employed for the parade of stiff shafts that came for her, penetrating her under orders, draining themselves as a martial exercise. It was almost enough to make her laugh to think what certain others would think of her current predicament. How many at home, she speculated, would line themselves up to administer their own form of discipline upon her available hindquarters? Telos, to be certain, and others besides, Alinor, slim waist, sweet golden curls and Remik, the brooding swordsman with his straight line of black hair and harsh cheeks whom she'd once bested at fencing, embarrassing him publicly then spurning him.

And what of Romila? Would she raise a finger to help or would she turn away, smugly shaking her head, hiding her cowardice, her jealousy from the world? Only her father would have saved her, the great king, that man of a bygone era when heroes defended the honour of ladies, when tyrants dared not raise their heads to men, when swords were wielded by the just and a maiden's honour was a thing to be treasured, a trust inviolate. In her father's day the very earth would have cried out were a virgin despoiled, let alone one who was queen. The sound of that injustice would have grated on every ear, like a knife blade dragged across an iron shield.

'It is done,' she heard Senelek say as this latest man withdrew himself, a feeble, thin fellow, apparently he of the lowest ranking horde. 'She has shown obedience to our gods. Her punishment is complete. We shall leave her now, till her ransom arrives.'

'Forgive me, Lord Senelek,' said a man, hastily arrived upon the platform, bowing low before the high priest. 'But Lord Varik has commanded that she is to be taken down now.'

'Indeed. And does the chieftain no longer deign to speak directly to the high priest of our gods?'

'Forgive me, Lord Senelek,' he repeated, bowing all the lower for his continued effrontery. 'But Lord Varik has ordered the prisoner to be cleansed and wrapped in a robe so that she might be sent home, as is.'

'As is?' Senelek was clearly playing to the listening crowd now. 'But what of the great treasure of gold which we were to receive for all our trouble?'

'Lord Varik will take no gold. She is to be released without price, to symbolise her complete lack of value to the Rashal. It is to be a symbol of our conquest.'

'A symbol, you say? But surely my brother has ordered us to ride down upon the Orencians and achieve the actual victory for which we have worked so hard?'

Caralissa longed to slap the man for his snide, manipulative remarks. It was obvious that Varik would not order the attack, and Senelek knew that. He was trying to make his brother look weak and selfish; that was the only purpose.

'No, sir,' the man explained, any irony in the situation apparently exceeding his comprehension. 'We are to leave Orencia, never to return. It is never to be entered, or even spoken of again. At first break of dawn we march from the Valley of Seven Kingdoms, returning across the plains to our home.'

'I see,' Senelek seethed. 'Well, there you have it then; our victory is complete.'

'We are to blindfold her, sir,' the man continued, ignoring the remarks. 'No man who has possessed her may tend to her bathing. When she is cleaned she is to be wrapped in a robe of state and taken by horseback within sight of the walls of the Orencian castle by a single rider. She will then ride the last portion of the journey herself. I am to tell this rider whom Lord Varik will designate, that when he has turned your back upon her, this will be the last gaze he will have of this accursed valley. For we Rashal shall inhabit it no longer. All these things, the Lord Varik has told me to tell you are the products of a vision, bestowed upon him by the raven god.'

'Of course,' Senelek said acidly. 'My brother is well known for his visions, and for his devotion to the worship of our gods.'

Caralissa wanted to spit upon the man for his cowardly assault upon his brother. What hurt far worse than this thinly veiled contempt for Varik, however, was the chieftain's own failure to deal with her face to face, as a human being. It was true then, how he intended for her to hate him, and how he would not ever see her again, even to say goodbye. Such was the discipline of a warrior, she supposed. She herself, she imagined, would be no less stubborn were she a man. And perhaps they were not so different as it was. He would return to his kingdom, she to hers; duty before pleasure, all personal good sacrificed to the good of the state. Even now she was contemplating her own return, and the sweet revenge, the great victory over her enemies she would enjoy. It was enough to take the sting out of her whipped flesh, and the soreness from her well ploughed loins and hindquarters. Only her heart remained an open wound, but it too would be resealed in time.

The blindfold the man brought was a welcome cloak, a protector of her senses. Dimly now she recalled how as a child she would hide her eyes and imagine herself to be invisible. The pretence amused her father greatly and he would often command the servants to play along with her, to the dereliction of their regular duties. Romila, who was forced to study all day, held this game against her baby sister, along with a host of other supposed favouritisms of her father. As if she could have helped matters, as if she or anyone else could have done a thing to change the mind or opinions of Lysanis, the Lion of Orencia.

Caralissa was conveyed to a stream. She knew it by its sounds, and by the feel of the water upon her skin. Like a baby she was led into the depths, up to her waist. A magic cleansing was taking place, a delicious embrace of wrapping wetness. Her guides were silent as stones and rigorously gentle. She was quite certain she did not know them. Without her vision she was free to imagine these new men as she wished. Strong and noble warriors, men of great honour or saintly old men, priests of some more enlightened god.

What alone she could not conjure was any feminine image. Not only because she was quite certain there were no women in the Rashal camp, but also because it would not have seemed right after all she'd been through for any female to behold her current state. Better for a thousand hostile warriors to see her degradation than a single woman, especially not one she knew. This would be true shame, she realised, of a sort she'd never want to face.

When the bath was done there were ointments, similar to the ones Varik first used on her, along with other kinds as well. They were stolen, no doubt from exotic lands, plunder of the Rashal juggernaut. The smells were mixed: peppermint and jasmine, the extract of the *leet* plant, subtle and musky. With each application she felt the aromas blend, till there was about her a delicious enveloping sweetness.

This was a strangely refined art for barbarians, she

thought. Perhaps these men were slaves, captured from some fallen city to the south. With infinitely gentle hands, reverently attentive, they completed the work, combing her hair and readying her for the robe. It felt rich and warm upon her skin. Its magnificent size cloaked her fully, and she imagined that it belonged to him, perhaps having been worn by him only recently.

Still barefoot and with no actual covering beneath the thick material, Caralissa was conveyed across the grass to a silent, open place. She heard only the most distant of echoes, the laughter of soldiers, the omnipresent clash of practice steel. They must be awaiting here for her escort, she realised. It would be late afternoon by now. Would she arrive home before dark? It might be preferable if she didn't, given her state of dress. As a captive she could hardly be expected to arrive by state chariot in full regalia, and yet it was hardly in keeping with her position to be naked, in a foreigner's robe.

'I shall take her from here,' came the voice, punctuated with the nasal whine of a horse. She cocked her head, thinking it must be her imagination. This man, the one who'd galloped up to fetch her unexpectedly – it could not be him.

'Go now,' the voice insisted. 'Your work is done.'

The men must have been hesitating. Something appeared to have been altered from the original plan.

'Take my hand,' said the voice, placing an arm close enough for her to touch it. She clenched onto him for dear life, her heart beating wildly. It was Varik, lifting her upon his horse! Was he taking her, then, to some secret place, to live forever? The Forest of Night, perhaps, that one place where no one would dare follow – Orencian or Rashal?

'Say nothing,' Varik told her, swinging her behind him,

allowing her to tuck her arms around his waist. 'I am your escort, nothing more.'

His words, his presence confused her, but she held on fiercely nonetheless, tears of joy staining the inside of her blindfold. His horse was swift as the wind, the hoof beats like thunder. Her pulse was racing wildly; she was aroused again, the result being unavoidable, sitting as she was, her naked loins pressed to the hide of the horse, the cloak warmly cocooning her wet thighs, her throbbing breasts. Her pains and sorrows forgotten, she let herself fly and dream. There must be some way, some possible hope for them to be together.

The road was bumpy and he did not relinquish his speed. He seemed hell bent on getting her home as fast as possible. Was it too much to bear for him to be so close; was it too great a temptation after all? Why then was he doing this, violating his own word, his promise never to see her again? Or had he found a compromise, a way to keep his word by sealing her own eyes? Impulsively she reached round his shoulders, to feel his face.

It was as she suspected. The Rashal chieftain wore a mask, a cloth across his face to hide him from his own warriors.

They were climbing a hill now, an incline that Caralissa did not recognise as part of the royal highway. The ground was softer too, dirt and grass having replaced the smooth cobblestones. Here and there, too, he was having them duck for tree branches. She was certain of it now; they were no longer on the road. What trick did he have up his sleeve this time, this man of seemingly endless surprises?

'Whoa!' she heard him cry as he pulled back the reins. They were stopping. Surely he wasn't thinking of...

Her thoughts were curtailed by his sudden tugging at her waist. He'd dismounted and was pulling her down. In a moment she was in his arms, her bare feet upon soft earth. Without a word he pressed his lips to hers, his face still masked by her blindfold and his cloak of cloth. She moaned a soft invitation, bidding him drink more deeply of her lips and of her mouth within. His hands were firm but softly caressing as he slid them down her shoulders to the small of her back. She was in danger of collapsing, and it was up to him to hold them both up.

The kiss was like a dream, a sacred union of two persons at such a tiny point of contact as to seem scarcely real. A gasp of wonder escaped her enraptured mouth as the cloak slid from her shoulders. She was naked before him, naked against him, utterly vulnerable and yet protected, safe and secure in the grip of his maleness.

Very gently he lowered her to the ground, his own body following seamlessly. Their mouths coupled once again, he pulled away the mask but not her blindfold as he began to work at the fastening of his own clothes till he too was naked. Her own unseeing hands conspired, desperately and ineffectively tearing at the complicated layers of mail and cloth and leather. He smelled of musk and sweat, the sweet draught of honest struggle, of a king labouring for his people.

Would her father have liked him? she wondered idly, even as he parted her thighs, pouring himself into her in a single fluid motion. She hoped he would. They were much alike. Strong, proud, stubborn. Intractable, complicated, their greatest strengths being easily twisted into weakness. The ground was like a pillow beneath her. She felt the imprint of grass and of flowers. As if by magic she felt no pain from her lashings, nor did her insides yearn in any way to reject this latest suitor.

Varik was different, that was the only possible explanation. Different in himself and different in her mind, in the way she knew him and touched him and loved him. Yes, she did love him. She'd said it to herself often enough, and her body now confirmed it. She loved Varik. In as much as any one person could love another, she supposed. As far as it could go between a man and a woman in a world such as this. A world of swords and whips and of dark, forbidden forests full of monsters.

Varik's lovemaking was like a healing, from the inside out. She'd never see him again, she knew that, and yet this would be enough, would have to be enough. Actually, she wasn't seeing him even now, but was only feeling him, making a memory with every part of her, burning the lines of his flesh into hers at every point so that they would never be apart again, not truly. It would be a secret thing, that none would ever speak of. Even they themselves would likely never utter the words or think the thoughts to go with these sensations. It would have to stay that way, a secret within secrets, the deepest guarded treasure of the hearts of two lonely monarchs.

Would he ever marry? Bitterly she prayed he would not. For herself she wished the same thing. A cry escaped her lips – her unguarded lips as he increased his pace moving up and down with a familiarity that startled her. How did their bodies come to work so well together, as if they were only one flesh, as if the whole of their prior existences were mere preliminary whose whole purpose was to lead them to their real birth together at this moment?

Varik was breathing heavily. His possession of her seemed to be taking something out of him this time, something painful. How she longed to see his face, to read the emotions she knew were writ there now, uncovered from their stony depths. And yet she knew the very reason he was showing forth his feelings was because she could not see him. Just as the sounds he made were falling upon ears which would never hear his voice again, so too were his features safe from betrayal by her eyes.

Such a sad notion: that she would never hear his voice again. How much more devastating in its particularity than the more general notion of separation. She loved his voice, loved its richness, the many tones and pitches, the growls and grumbles, the laughter, the sound he made when he'd won an argument, the smug cackle accompanying his getting the best of her. How could it be they'd been together only a few days? Was this some trick being played on her mind? Did she lie sleeping still in her own bed, all of this being only a dream?

Varik released himself, and as he did so she followed suit, matching his razor-sharp dance with oblivion. Let them perish together, she thought. Let the gods discover them, slain in the moment of ecstasy, shattered upon the ground as though cast down from the very pinnacle of passion. Perhaps it would even be the gods themselves who would throw them down, for daring to linger in that place of immortality that no mortal should ever touch. It wasn't mere earthly lust between them – that was for certain. No, this was much more: something ancient, inexplicable. As though they'd always been together in different guises, perhaps, clothed in different skin, and yet the same two people over and over.

Caralissa held him wordlessly, doing nothing to denounce his action; neither his name nor his person would be revealed. His secret was safe with her; safe as the deposit of his essence he'd left deep in her womb. Besides, what could mere words do now, except destroy the moment, revealing its absurdity in the larger scheme of things? Better to lie low, to evade the world as long as possible, even if only for a few more minutes, a glorious hour, perhaps.

Anyhow, they said their goodbyes already, such as they might be – him with his ultimatums, her with the softness of her surrender to his soldiers.

Varik seemed content with the arrangement as well – this conspiracy of silence. Rolling himself onto his back he allowed her to lay upon his chest, her fingers twisted comfortably in the thick mat of hair. How warm his body felt, how full of promise. She could easily fall asleep like this, and dream perhaps of never having to wake again. Meanwhile, his hand trailed idly up and down her spine, touching, skimming, but never fully resting. Was his mind already otherwise engaged? Was he moving on in his mind to new conquests, yet unclaimed? Or was it something else – some part of him holding back, some strong emotion in himself he could not yet face?

'The hour grows late,' he said at last, as though this were the answer to everything, the solution to the puzzle of her life and his.

She felt him shift beneath her, and knew it was her signal to rise, to break the bond of intimacy. The pain she now felt was far greater than anything done to her with the whip, much more cruel than all of Senelek's heartless words combined. There was in him no sign of similar anguish, though she'd learned from certain quarters that men were like this, given to sudden shifts and proclamations of readiness for cataclysmic change.

Best to bear up, then. Varik was right, the hour was late and there was much to be done at home. By her calculations, if she guessed correctly the time they'd travelled so far, the ride would be a short one, a half hour at most. The only difficulty would be in having to touch him, to feel his heat against her, as though they were still lovers. Anxiously she waited while he dressed, so he could lift her back upon the horse.

It occurred to her now that the animal would have seen everything between them. What an odd thing to think! Although everything seemed odd now to her still benighted eyes: the buzzing of the mosquitoes, the call of a hawk in the sky. Real, and yet somehow not real. Varik dug his booted heels into the sides of the horse and they were off again. The wind was picking up and it blew her hair, tugging the roots from her scalp ever so slightly.

Clamping her eyes shut, guarding against the risk of even a tiny bit of light which might break into her dark horizon spoiling her reverie, she willed herself home, not relying upon the steed, but upon her own wits. Under her own power, unto her own fate she would go. Alone. Strong. Invincible, in fact.

The cobblestones were tinier, sharper now. By the clomping of the horse she knew she was quite close, in full view of the castle. Varik slowed accordingly. It was an act of tremendous daring for him to come so close to an enemy, a people as yet un-subdued. And to do so alone, that enemy's queen upon the back of his horse was even more amazing. Was it bravery or foolishness? Perhaps even some mad death wish? It chilled her when ideas of this sort popped into her head. Almost as if she could read things in him no one else knew, things he himself would prefer not to view in the light of day.

The horse stopped, giving a wary nay. Perhaps her guards were surrounding them by now. If there were trouble she would issue the order for him to be released. He'd conducted her safely thus far and she would return the favour, insuring his security back across her frontiers. The hands that helped her down this time were not Varik's. They were armoured hands, and the chinks of the riveted links sent tingles up and down her spine. It was not till she was on her feet, her hand clutching the cloak tightly, possessively, that her blindfold was removed.

Varik was behind her, already galloping away. She wanted to turn and call out to him, but she knew that would be a betrayal of what they'd gone through, a betrayal of the carefully orchestrated journey home. Besides, there was another matter in front of her, more pressing.

Caralissa looked at the two men, their unfamiliar uniforms and faces. She frowned. These guards were not her own personal soldiers, nor even those of the kingdom's army. They were foreigners, with the colours of two distinct kingdoms, neighbours in the valley.

'Who are you?' she demanded, straightening confidently even as they drew their swords. 'And why do you bear arms in this land?'

'We are authorised, royal majesty,' said the taller of the two. 'By the League of Seven Kingdoms.'

'What league is this? I know nothing of it.'

The men cast a glance at one another. 'The League exists to secure the peace of the Valley,' said the shorter one. 'We have come to determine the rightful ruler of Orencia.'

Caralissa's jaw locked fiercely, though she dared not show any emotion at this juncture. 'Take me to my sister,' she commanded. 'And we shall see about this. In the meantime, assemble the council.'

'Perhaps her majesty would prefer to bathe first and dress,' suggested the taller of the two, clean-shaven, his disturbing eyes set at cross angles.

'Yes,' agreed the other, relaxing visibly at the possibility of a non-confrontational solution. 'That might be best.'

Caralissa shook out her hair. 'Very well,' she conceded. 'Take me to my room. I shall prepare myself, and then you shall summon my sister. And my guards, as well. I demand to see my own palace guards.'

The taller man bowed, neither confirming nor denying the bulk of her request. 'A bath shall be drawn,' he said. 'At once.'

Chapter Six

Caralissa slammed her fists in fury against the thick oaken door. It was her own door, the portal to her bedroom where she'd just finished her bath and been dressed by one of the servants in a gown of exquisite green silk. At present the fool of a woman – a stranger, like the guards who'd brought her here – was standing behind her, hands clasped at her waist.

'Who has dared to lock my door?' she demanded, whirling around to confront her. 'I shall have their head. And yours, too, if you presume to detain me!'

The woman, who was old enough to be her mother, turned very pale. 'Forgive me,' she said gravely, falling to her knees. 'I only do as I am told.'

Caralissa reddened, realising the brutality of her words. 'Rise,' she said, putting her hand on the woman's shoulder. 'It is not your fault. I too have known what it is like to be under the command of others. Forgive me.'

There were tears in her blue eyes as she stood. 'No one has ever asked my forgiveness,' she marvelled.

Caralissa smiled. 'I am honoured to be the first. So tell me, who is in command here?'

'I do not know, majesty. I am only Deelia, the servant of King Norod of Relacia.'

Norod of Relacia. Of course. Orencia's chief rival in the valley and a miserable old busybody to boot. No doubt he was seeking to capitalise on the turmoil introduced by the now pre-empted Rashal invasion. Perhaps it was he who was behind the most unexpected treason of Romila and the coward Telos, although it was hard to imagine the old fool ever hatching so grand a plot. More likely he was a dupe himself, for Telos or Romila, or some other parties within the nobility.

'I see,' she nodded. 'So it seems my enemies are gathering close at hand. Just as well. Better to have them in plain sight, don't you think?' She winked.

'As you say,' the woman agreed meekly.

Caralissa snapped her fingers, sudden insight flashing into her tired mind. 'The bed sheets! Of course! We can fashion a rope and escape out the window. It's only three stories down. Help me, Deelia; we must gather as many sheets as we can.'

'Yes, majesty,' she bowed, though it was clear she thought the plan folly.

In short order Caralissa made a pile, consisting of nearly a dozen sheets in all, from the bed and from her linen closet. She was thick into the knotting process when a key was heard in the lock. A moment later the door opened revealing Telos, dressed in a gold-buttoned uniform of red and green, a sash across his chest.

Caralissa resisted the urge to lunge at him outright. 'How dare you enter my chambers,' she hissed. 'You sorry excuse for a human being! You despicable cowardly traitor! Leave at once! Leave this room, this castle, this kingdom!'

Telos bent at the waist. 'May I simply say,' he offered glibly, 'that you look most radiant tonight, my dear Caralissa?'

She looked at him with daggers in her eyes. He'd dared to use her name, as though she were a commoner. Recovering from the momentary shock, she searched for a suitable weapon. Quickly she settled upon a fluted vase from off her dresser. Telos ducked, barely avoiding having his skull impacted. 'You may say nothing to me!' she fumed. 'Unless it be an abject apology upon your knees. Although, I promise even that would do nothing to take the edge off my rage!'

Telos sat on the edge of her bed. 'I can see you are upset,' he noted. 'Perhaps if you allowed me to explain?'

'Explain?' she laughed contemptuously. 'What is there to explain? You denounced me to our enemy as a tyrant and you have the nerve to want to explain it?'

'I did it to spare you, Caralissa.' He held up his hands beseechingly. 'Is it not obvious? If the Rashal thought you of great value to us, they would have slain you, or extorted ransom. As it was, they sent you home free of charge. Intact, too – relatively speaking.'

Caralissa smacked him across his sallow, pockmarked face, leaving a bright red palm mark. 'Do not cast innuendoes, Telos, nor should you presume to speak to the details of my captivity. Not now, not ever.'

Telos touched his cheek, a sickly smile on his face. 'Of course,' he agreed, 'Caralissa.'

'And stop using my name!' she cried. 'Address me properly or not at all!'

He pursed his lips, saying nothing.

'Give me the key,' she demanded, grabbing him by the collar with her clenched fists. 'I will get out of here now!'

'I haven't a key,' he said, offering no resistance. 'The guards let me in.'

She released him. There was no point in dealing with this man, or even acknowledging his existence for that matter. He was a worm, and that was that. She thought of throwing him to the floor, but that would only give him the satisfaction of revealing how disgusted she was to have him on her very bed, and that was something she would never allow him. Leaving him be, she turned to her pile of sheets.

'Help me with these,' she bid Deelia, tossing the cowering maid several of the silk sheets.

As Caralissa worked she tried to ignore the interloper. Unfortunately Telos could still be heard breathing – a sound that filled her with nearly as much disgust as the hoof beats of foreign troops that she could hear even now outside her window.

'Telos, is there some reason you are still here?' she demanded at last, not bothering to look up from her accumulated pile of knots.

'Not really,' he sighed, reclining his miserable body on her bed as though he were her lover. 'It merely occurred to me, *your majesty*, that you might wish to share with someone the story of what you have been through. With the Rashal, I mean.' He folded his hands behind his head, crushing her pillows beneath him. 'Surely it was quite an ordeal.'

'No, Telos,' she snapped, 'it was a jolly picnic.'

'They tell me you have marks,' he said, crossing his legs, his head turning towards her nightstand from which he picked up a glass ornament, a swan. 'Were you whipped, then?' he enquired, turning the object over and over in his hands.

'I was a prisoner, Telos. What do you think? And stop touching my things.'

He examined the swan a minute longer. 'Sorry,' he said, putting it back, 'highness.'

Caralissa left off her growing rope of sheets to consider the face of her tormentor. With each mention of her title Telos seemed to be employing still higher levels of sarcasm. 'If you are that curious about whips, *Lord* Telos, I can arrange for you to experience one for yourself.'

He laughed politely. 'Oh, I don't think so.' A moment

later he added, 'Did it hurt very much, to be whipped? I would assume you were naked at the time.'

She chose to ignore him. The far corner of her four-poster bed seemed like the best anchor for her escape rope. Taking one end of the collection of sheets, she affixed it with a triple knot.

'Is it true, then,' he went on as though they were having an actual conversation, 'that you were in no way compromised?'

'Do you mean raped, Telos?' she shot back. 'Is that the word you cannot bring yourself to say, for all your obvious manliness?'

He covered his hands over his ears. 'I shall not hear such language, your majesty. Not in the royal bedchambers.'

With almost gleeful spite, Caralissa strode to the side of the bed and said the word again and again, shouting it into his ears. When she was satisfied she'd made an ass of him, she said, 'There. Now that wasn't so bad, was it? And to answer your question, little man, I wasn't raped at all. Everything that happened was consensual. How does that sound in your prim and proper little ears?'

She was pulling on his sleeve, forcing him to look into her eyes. Leaning over him, her silk-covered breasts dangling in his face, she let him have it with full force, unleashing the sum of her turgid emotions – the despair, the misery of losing the man she loved, of finding traitors in her own castle, of being sentenced to a life of loneliness without the impetuous Rashal chieftain by her side.

'Do you want to hear more, Telos? You'd like the sordid details, is that it? Would you like a vicarious thrill from someone else's sex life to make up for your own pathetic lack of even an iota of manhood? Very well, Lord Telos, I shall tell you what you are dying to know. To begin with,

I laid for them. For their leader and a large number of his officers. They compelled me to, though not by force. They are men, Telos, which is something you will never understand. They needed only to lay hands upon me, to command me with their stern voices, to fix me in their searing gazes and I was left no option but to surrender. They made me wet and helpless between my legs with their merest glances, Telos. Can you imagine such a thing? I, a queen, reduced to naked servitude like a common slave, and at the hands of barbarians, no less. And I would probably do so again if forced to choose between them or some of our own men; for the ugliest most pathetic of their warriors possessed twice the masculinity of anyone in our land.

'What's the matter, Telos? Too much information for you? Then I guess I shouldn't tell you the rest – what it felt like to be tied naked between two poles and beaten in front of thousands of soldiers, the stripes of the whip being interspersed with unspeakable intrusions into my intimate openings with the thick leather handle. Nor should I share with you the story of how your queen danced naked for a barbarian warlord, touching herself under the influence of stinging cords while the men whipping her competed to have her body. No, Telos, have no fear. I shall spare you those things, for they represent experiences of me which you shall never have, nor will you ever even have the courage to dream of them.'

Telos' bland face contorted into a smirk. 'Don't be so sure,' he said, looking up at her, her breath ragged from her long harangue. 'Don't be so sure.'

Caralissa bared her teeth. He'd managed to push her over the edge. Leaping onto the bed she straddled him, commencing to pummel him with her balled fists. Keeping to his character Telos did not fight back, but only sought to cover his face.

Her fists fell like rain, doing little damage but easing her tensions nonetheless. She was on the verge of releasing him when she heard the door opening for a second time. It was her sister Romila with several guards, along with none other than King Norod, who looked much more feeble than ever, with his long beard and stooped shoulders, his robes covering him like a scarecrow. It was just five years since she'd seen him, yet the man seemed to have aged fifty.

'Caralissa, what on earth?' Romila cried, even as the guards moved unbidden to seize her by both arms, pulling her off the passive Telos.

'This isn't what it seems,' Caralissa said, unable to comprehend how anyone could think this little weasel to be the victim. 'He attacked me.'

'Noble Telos,' King Norod intoned sharply, 'is this true?'

Telos was busying himself attending to non-existent bruises. 'I never laid a finger upon her,' he told them quite truthfully.

Norod looked at Romila, who shook her head. 'I do not understand her current behaviour, King Norod. Nor have I understood much of anything she's done since our father's death. First she put us all in grave danger running off to kill Varik, and then she comes home dressed in his cloak. And now look at these sheets, and look at Telos' face. What are we supposed to think?'

Caralissa protested noisily to her sister, drawing an immediate rebuke from the king. 'Young lady, that is quite enough. This is a matter to be taken up at the trial.'

'What trial?' she demanded, having finally succeeded in shaking the two guards off her.

'An inquiry, I should say,' he corrected himself, gesturing with his withered hand for the guards to leave.

'To determine the true ruler of Orencia.'

'I am the true ruler,' she said, straightening her back and thrusting out her chin. 'I am the one who saved us all from the Rashal.'

'Not all,' Romila said. 'Or have you forgotten the three lost kingdoms?'

'I have not. As a matter of fact, I was present when the Rashal chieftain decided to pull out of the valley entirely, thereby restoring their freedoms.'

'Yes,' Romila observed dryly, stooping to retrieve the tangle of ruined sheets so she could hand them to Norod. 'We are well aware of your presence amongst the Rashal. The question is, are you fit now to be queen.'

Norod took the sheets and looked at them with deep distress, as though her actions were some personal offence against him. 'Caralissa, I do not understand. Why were you trying to escape from your own room?'

'It was the only way I could think of to get out,' she said, feeling like a child being chastised by her elders. 'They locked me in here.'

'For your protection,' Norod said. 'There have been threats against you. Some say you collaborated with the enemy.'

Her eyes flashed. 'Lies, all lies!'

Norod handed Romila the sheets, inclining his head to indicate his desire to speak privately with her. No sooner did the two of them turn their backs on Caralissa then she felt Telos behind her, his hand snaking up the back of her leg, under her dress. When he reached her buttocks he squeezed. Shrieking in horror, Caralissa darted forward.

'Caralissa?' Norod asked, his wrinkled brow even more furrowed than usual. 'What is wrong now?'

'It's Telos,' she complained. 'He – he touched me!'

Telos exchanged a glance with the king, shrugging

helplessly as if to indicate to him Caralissa's instability. From the look on Norod's face, he needed little convincing.

Caralissa scowled, crossing her arms over her chest. Blast these men, and Romila too, she thought. They'd put her in a no-win situation. If she pressed the point she'd sound like a hysterical female, one given to flights of fancy, or maybe even bouts of treason in the bed of her people's enemy. On the other hand, if she let Telos win now, what would stop him from demanding of her more and more till she became little more than the man's slave?

Then again she was still queen, at least in name. Taking a deep breath she reminded herself that the overriding concern was to survive the inquiry, trial or whatever else might be thrown at her. She must keep her wits about her; hold her cards as close as possible to her chest.

'Let us drop the matter,' she decided. 'Perhaps Lord Telos' contact with me was inadvertent,' she suggested, offering the man an easy out.

Telos bowed his head, smiling that sickening smile of his. 'My apologies,' he offered, 'for any offence, majesty.'

She managed a forced smile. 'Your true intentions are well known to me, Telos,' she said to him pointedly. 'Of that you may rest assured.'

'The matter is settled then,' declared Norod, obviously relieved to be free of any responsibility in the matter. 'Come, let us go down and enjoy a feast. To welcome home the queen.'

'Yes,' agreed Caralissa. 'I shall join you presently.'

'I will wait with you,' declared a new man, stepping in from the doorway.

Caralissa regarded him. Her eyes widened at once; her heart increased its speed. He was tall and broad-shouldered, dressed in silver breastplate and dark leather breeches, tight and rough. His boots were thick and high, his hair

145

wild and blond. He looked for all the world like a Rashal warrior with his calm, deadly eyes and his confident swagger. There was no way such a man was born of the valley.

'Who is this?' she demanded of her sister, lacking the patience to enter into yet another discussion with the befuddled Norod.

'He is your new bodyguard,' Telos said, answering for Romila, taking obviously glee in bearing irritating news. 'We have entrusted your royal safety to his person.' He paused for effect. 'Not to mention your virtue.'

The words hung in the air until Caralissa could bear it no more. Foreign troops, Telos on her bed, and now a barbarian for a jailor – it was more than she could stand. 'I want the lot of you out of my room at once!' she cried. 'Out of my room and out of my castle, too!'

'But our banquet,' Norod protested.

She poked a finger at his shrunken chest. 'You may take your banquet, King Norod, and you may stick it where the sun will not shine.'

Norod looked at Telos, then at Romila.

'We only have your best interest at heart,' Telos said, demonstrating his utter lack of shame. 'If you present yourself well tonight it will surely look better come tomorrow.'

'For the inquiry, yes,' Norod agreed.

'For the trial, don't you mean, majesty?' prompted Telos.

Sweat appeared on Norod's brow. He cleared his throat, clearly at a loss for words.

'It does not matter what you call it, Norod. I will present myself tomorrow, and not before,' Caralissa declared, putting her hands to her hips. 'And that is final.'

'Leave her now,' said Romila. 'Let her be alone with her wounded pride.'

'My wounded pride?' she laughed. 'How about my character – which you and your little fool of a boyfriend have assassinated? Really, Romila, wasn't it enough you betrayed me to the Rashal; must you now do so to our own neighbours as well?'

Romila's eyes flashed. 'You speak high and mighty words, Caralissa, as always. How quick you are to judge. Consider this though, my sister. Your actions have consequences for others, which you never consider. You run off on a whim to steal all the glory, but it is I who must maintain our livelihood. You win easy favour among the peasants but who is it that must scrape together the gold to run our country? It hurts to be called a tyrant, doesn't it? Well now you know how I feel – now you know what it is like to bear nothing but wrath for your best efforts. Who do you think it was, Caralissa, who kept our affairs in order the last years of father's life, hmm? Who do you think covered for him when the treasury was bare; who collected the taxes, and levied the troops?'

Caralissa stared in open-mouthed shock.

'Cat got your tongue, sister? Let me help you then. It was I, all alone. Just me. And now Telos helps me because I need him. Not everyone can play the hero like you do – some of us have to walk and not fly, some of us have to do the dirty work. So don't come back now on your high horse and accuse me. Not till you've walked the path I have, not till you've faced what I have. You want your precious kingdom back? Fine by me. I don't want it any more!'

Caralissa watched dumbfounded as her sister stormed from the room. Quiet, ever dependable Romila. Could it be there was something to her words? Did Romila really suffer so much all these years?

'Perhaps we should go,' Telos declared, showing his penchant for perceiving the obvious. 'Her majesty seems fatigued.'

She did not like the way he said that word, fatigued; then again, every word from the mouth of the man was anathema to her. Could it be that Romila really needed help so badly as to turn to such a man, a cruel and treacherous lout? It was a sobering thought, a troubling one for all its many implications, not least of which was admitting negligence on her own part and that of their father, the one and only man she ever dared to love.

Before she met Varik, that is.

'Yes,' Norod concurred, smiling stupidly. 'We should leave our royal colleague, the gracious Queen of Orencia. Till tomorrow then, good Caralissa?'

She inclined her head, doing her best to imitate his prattle. 'Good night, my royal colleague, and sleep you well in my castle as a guest this night.'

'I shall remain outside the door,' declared the blond giant, to no one in particular.

'We shall send food,' Norod offered as the door was opened for their departure.

'I shall not eat it,' she replied, wanting nothing more than to be left alone for the night.

'Shall I stay?' Deelia asked softly, having emerged from the background.

She turned and touched her hand to the woman's shoulder. 'No, thank you. You may go and get some sleep for yourself.'

Deelia bowed and walked to the door. The blond warrior let her out then shut it behind him, giving Caralissa one last glance as he did.

Caralissa stood firm under his gaze, determined to show no emotion. It was only when the door was closed and locked again from the outside that she fell upon her bed, balling her fists and throwing her face into her pillows. Her voice sufficiently muffled to avoid outside detection, she yielded herself to the flood of tears that had been building just behind her eyes, kept at bay by dint of tremendous effort these past long minutes.

It was like a hot rain, cleansing her cheeks; the release of so much emotion, so many feelings, all of it pent-up in her heart for days, months even, ever since her father's death and maybe long before that as well. She never meant to hurt Romila, never thought it possible she could hurt her stoic older sister. And yet what if Romila was right? What if she and her father both pushed her too far, eventually making her into a humourless shrew, a scheming penny pincher?

It did no good to speculate, she knew that. But how could she help but feel these things? If nothing else it was a response to the stress, to her capture, to the brutality she'd endured in Rashal custody.

Brutality. Was that the proper word? She hardly knew what to think any more. For the first little while after coming home she fooled herself into thinking she could lock away her painful memories of the last few days. And then she'd seen the blond barbarian, a man who could easily have been one of Varik's lieutenants.

Was it her imagination, or did the fellow look straight through her, past her queenly garb, her stately demeanour, straight into her heart, reading her memories, her emotions? What if the fellow pressed that advantage? What if he appealed to the part of her that still dwelt in the Rashal camp; what if he sought to stake a claim on that part of her, bending her to his will? They'd obviously given him power over her, and perhaps it was even a trap, concocted by Telos or Romila or both. At any rate, she regarded Telos as her real enemy. For while her sister despised her, she was not certain the woman would ever commit treason on her own. As for the little man with all the new uniforms, he was like a vicious dog at her heels. She'd have to be careful with him. He would use her emotions against her; perhaps try to convince Norod and his court of fools that she was unfit, that she was a slut in royal guise. She'd have to be crafty with that one. No more emotion in his presence, no more tears, no more weakness.

Caralissa said a prayer to the nameless red-haired goddess, silent and precious, designed to give her courage and resolve in the face of male aggression. At once she felt a flood of peace, as if the dear lady were caressing her temples with her fingertips, soothing her wounds, commiserating with her female heart. She was on the verge of believing the prayer was actually working when she heard the voice at her window ledge, hushed and packed with emotion.

'Caralissa, help me up!'

She cocked her head. It sounded so familiar, and yet there was no way it could be him. Could it?

'Caralissa, help me! It is I, Alinor, from days of yore.'

She gasped. It really was Alinor; there was no mistaking the voice, the intonations. But how could he climb so high, a thin and sparsely muscled poet such as he?

Caralissa ran to the ledge, planted her hands on the cold marble. 'Alinor, how on earth did you get up here?'

'A ladder,' he huffed. 'I spirited myself to the ledge below, then grappled myself ever higher with this metal hook.'

She noted the curved piece of metal, hooked to the edge of the balcony. It looked to have been swung from below. It was improbable Alinor should have the athletic prowess for such a feat, not to mention the gumption to sneak into the courtyard in the presence of foreign guards, but she was not in the state of mind to ask such questions. She was lonely and curious, which seemed at the moment enough reason to let him in.

'Grab my hand,' she told him, extending her reach.

'My thanks, dear lady,' Alinor grunted as she pulled him to safety. 'That was a close call indeed.'

She put her hands to her hips, observing him as he swung his legs over the ledge to stand before her. The immediate crisis passed, she felt her natural suspicions rising, preparing to equal or surpass her desperate need for male companionship. 'Why have you come here?' she demanded. 'Have you not heard I am under house arrest? Don't you care if you are caught with an accused traitor?'

'I have feelings for you,' he said, shaking out his long pale locks, far lighter than the barbarian's, more white than yellow. 'Is that not enough?'

She studied his soft lips, the very ones from which rolled the most seductive of poems. 'No,' she declared. 'It is not enough. Either you have developed some scheme to capitalise on my condition, or else someone has put you up to this.'

His sea-green eyes twinkled merrily. 'And why would anyone do that?' he offered, his voice betraying not a trace of guile. 'What could possibly be gained?'

She ran her eyes up and down his lean body, revealingly covered in a leotard of black. 'You could seduce me,' she speculated. 'Then testify against me, denounce my lack of morals. Affirming thereby my unfitness to govern.'

Alinor moved towards her, gliding like a cat. She clenched her fists, mad at herself for the appeal he still held in her eyes. An appeal, that seemed to be all the more intense, for her recent emotional opening at the hands of the Rashal.

'That is the first time I have ever heard you admit that I might one day be able to seduce you,' Alinor said, his delicate fingers reaching for her cheek.

'Don't touch me,' she said unconvincingly, her breath quickening.

'I have written you a new poem,' he said, his voice a sweet whisper directed at her left earlobe, which had magically found its way between his gently nibbling lips.

She smiled, in spite of herself. 'Is it something I shall have to spank you for?'

He brushed a finger across her lips, stilling any future argument, both literally and symbolically. 'I was hoping this new poem might induce you to allow yourself to be spanked by me for a change.'

Caralissa felt a warm tingle up and down her arms. As it travelled to her belly it attained a deeper power, transcribing itself into a kind of weakness, so that as she beheld him she felt as if she were looking through someone else's eyes, as if she herself were some supernatural servant, awaiting his commands, ready to do to her own body whatever he might command. 'I am not the same woman,' she said, the words ringing hollow in her own ears. 'I think it would be best if you left now, quickly, before you get yourself into trouble. I have a guard, you know, at the door.'

Alinor moved swiftly, placing the kiss upon her lips before she could even begin to think of resisting. He always was a splendid lover, at least to the point he allowed her to progress. With a small moan she allowed him access to her mouth, her jaw yielding before his tongue.

'I wish to read you my poem, Caralissa,' he breathed into her ear, his hand laying claim to her left breast through the fabric of her dress. 'Won't you sit at my feet and hear it?'

'Yes,' she heard herself say, her voice a soft surrender as she let herself be led to the bed so that he might sit upon the edge and pull her to him, down to the floor. 'Read it to me, Alinor, please.'

He gave her a moment to settle, her legs tucked underneath her. When she was comfortable, her chin resting on his knee, her eyes looking expectantly into his, he pulled from the pouch at his waist a single piece of parchment on which were scrawled in letters tight and narrow a large number of lines, straight and closely spaced, like the furrows of a farmer's spring field.

Heart pounding, wicked thoughts cramming her skull, she waited, hot and fevered, her every reserve cast aside. 'What is it called, Alinor?' she asked him impatiently. 'Tell me now.'

'I call it *The She-Beast*,' he said.

'That is a good title, Alinor.'

'It begins like so: "Come, croons the overseer, the keeper of beasts; come unto me, she-beast, crawling low upon your belly, come and beg for the lash. Wicked little thing, tits tempting, crotch teasing, licking, begging, jaws snapping at the weak, the unsuspecting; come unto me, and feel the discipline of fire. Born to my lash, your sex shaped for my hardness, my endless demands that echo through the long cold night of your captivity. Come".'

Alinor looked over the top of the parchment. 'I am not done,' he told her. 'It is but halfway. Strip off your clothes for me, Caralissa, and I will tell you the rest.'

She shook her head, though she was breathing heavily. 'I cannot do that. I am your queen.'

He rose to his feet. 'Then I shall go.'

She clutched at his ankles, prostrating herself. 'Please,'

she said, scarcely believing the words were coming from her throat, 'do not leave me. I am so alone. You do not know what it is like – what it has been like for me since I got home. I need you, I need your words of comfort.'

Alinor looked down at his feet, making no immediate effort to dislodge her. 'As I have needed you, many times before, and yet always you refused me. My queen.'

'Forgive me,' she trembled. 'I did not know what I was doing.'

'Oh, I think you knew very well. But I am not an entirely cruel man. If you wish so badly to hear the rest of my poem, you may do so. But you will listen to me naked, or not at all.'

Caralissa sighed. 'Oh, Alinor, must you ask this of me? Have you no pity?'

'Poets can't afford pity,' he declared, stepping over her.

'Wait!' she cried, forgetting for a moment the guard at the door who might overhear them. 'I will do as you say.'

He watched her scramble to her feet, her fingers commencing to fly over the buttons and hooks, nearly two dozen of them held her green velvet dress together, both at her bosom and at her waist. 'Do not open those,' he commanded. 'I would have it that you are never again able to wear this dress. Approach me and I will tear it from your skin, and your undergarments as well, till you are naked before me, naked and shamed.'

'This is one of my favourites,' she protested, though she was already on her way to him. 'I could not bear to be without it.'

'Put out your arms,' said the slender Alinor, 'and still your tongue.'

Caralissa obeyed. To her horror she discovered he was

not bluffing. The dress was difficult to remove, but he was persistent. To begin he pulled from the collar straight down the middle. The laces that covered the white silk bodice yielded first then the green velvet below. He continued to tear and pull till she was bared to the waist. Yanking the now useless sleeves from her hands, he completed the first part of his work.

Next he put his hands at her waist, tugging the narrow waistline down over her hips, so that the material was free to slide down her legs. When he'd finished this task, her dress and silk slip lying round her ankles like a pool of material, he told her to step from it, so that she was totally naked.

'Put your hands behind you,' he said, his eyes glowing as he began to feel himself growing drunk with his own power. 'Caress your arse. Flex your knees, thrust out your sex to me.'

She did her best to comply; the acrobatics involved being rather new to her. It was a difficult pose and humiliating, but its effect on Alinor seemed profound.

'That's it,' he said, his hand reaching for his swollen leotard-covered crotch. 'Now put your hands to your nipples. Pinch them hard. Harder.'

Caralissa winced, a teardrop forming in the corner of her eye. It was like being her own torturer, all for his pleasure.

'Keep one hand on your nipple,' he said, his voice thickening audibly. 'Squeeze it. Slap your arse with the other. Again. Harder.'

Caralissa felt the sting, doubly sharp as it reverberated from her soft buttocks to her equally soft palm. 'Alinor, please, that's enough.'

He slapped her face; lazily, just hard enough to get her attention. 'Did I say to stop?'

'N-no,' she stammered. 'You didn't.'

'Alternate the cheeks of your arse with your right hand,' he instructed, giving her no quarter. 'At the same time, with your left, pass back and forth continuously between your nipples and with every third stroke work yourself between your legs.'

She looked at him pitifully.

'Go on,' he said harshly. 'Do it or I shall scream for your gaolers. What will they do, seeing you like this, your majesty? Will they do to you what you deserve – making you a slave?'

Caralissa struck herself, the sound of her palm coming like the crack of a tree branch. Lurching forward she pressed her breast into her own cruelly pinching fingers. She could not allow him to denounce her because they would get the wrong idea. They would think her less than a queen, less even than a woman.

'How does this feel, little Caralissa?' he taunted, his eyes moving hungrily back and forth as she persisted in her self-abuse. 'Is it as enjoyable for you as torturing me with your teasing, unavailable little body, giving me little glimpses and sighs, making me hard and throbbing and leaving me with nothing but a sore arse for my troubles?'

Caralissa bit her lip. 'Mercy,' she begged. 'Please.'

'Mercy?' he snickered. 'For a naked slut? That is what you are, isn't it?'

She made no response. Quite honestly, at this juncture she did not know what she was or who.

'Tell me you're a naked slut,' he coaxed. 'Say the words.'

'I am,' she said, her voice coming in hot stabs, 'a naked slut.'

'Open your eyes, naked slut. Read the rest of my poem. Though under no circumstances will you leave off what

I have commanded of you. Do you understand?'

'Yes,' she nodded, twisting her nipple till she yelped, 'I understand.'

'Call me master.'

She squeezed her eyes shut, hoping it would pass, this latest assault, this most impossible of demands. 'Alinor, you don't know what you're asking,' she said to him when she realised he was serious.

He pinched her cheeks, compelling her to make eye contact. 'Do not disobey me again,' he warned, 'slave.'

She beheld the fire in his eyes. Where did it come from, this sudden power to make her do things, to make her lose her will so easily? And how did it come to be that he and nearly everyone else was treating her so differently? Was there something in her appearance now, in her manner of speech that gave them the clues to her new identity?

'I'm sorry,' she heard herself say, her eyes lowering before his, 'master.'

Caralissa told herself this was a mere expression, a temporary glitch in her life, that it could have no meaning in the light of day, not for her or him or anyone else. It would pass, just as when she'd said the word to Senelek on the whipping platform. It meant nothing. She continued to tell herself that as she maintained her ongoing response to his gruff command to touch and strike herself, all the while attending to the task of reading the rest of his wicked words.

'"Come and beg",' she recited, her voice cracking under the strain, the syllables echoing with the sound of her self-flagellation. '"Borrow and steal; pieces of your broken pride, your co-opted womanhood which I will give back to thee on loan at terms I set myself. Come, my she-beast, to be caged and tamed. Come, my she-beast, to be whipped and named. What do I call thee? Whore, temptress, animal, willing slut to my whims; it is my desires you live for, bend for, spread for; Come to me, come and come and come".'

The words were an invitation as she moved against her own hand, nipples screaming, vagina trembling. There was no holding back now. Letting the poem flutter from her hand she clenched her thighs, riding to her own climax, her own self-abasement, blatant and sordid under the cynical gaze of the poet.

'Go and fetch me a hairbrush, slave,' he commanded when she subsided. 'And be quick about it.'

Caralissa ran to her dresser. She could not help herself; the need to obey was too strong now. Finding the brush among her bottles of perfume she gave a little sigh of joy. 'Here, master,' she cried, placing the rounded silver device in his hands, blithely oblivious to the intentions he might have for it upon her person.

'Bend over, slave. Grasp your ankles, your arse facing me.'

Caralissa put herself as he ordered. It was a position of maximum exposure and humiliation, and therefore one of great arousal – or at least she found it to be such in her current state of abandon.

Alinor touched the cold metal to her posterior, initiating a deep shiver of sexual need. 'You will count the blows, slave. And after each you will beg for the next. This is to be your punishment for the times you dared strike me, making me abase myself to you, my arse bare to your wicked spankings.'

The first blow nearly knocked her from her feet. It was not so terribly harsh as the whip but she'd been unprepared and the impact nearly cost her balance with its sensuous impact. 'One,' she pronounced. 'May I have another?'

Alinor obliged, choosing a place slightly above and to the right.

'Two,' she asserted. 'May I have another?'

The third made her cry out, though she'd promised herself she would not do so in front of such an insignificant man. What Alinor did not know and could never understand, was that after being dominated by powerful men such as the Rashal it was a distinct disgrace, a sign of her overwhelming weakness that she could now be controlled by men who possessed not even a tenth of their strength. It would be as if a lioness, having expected to be tamed by a huge whip-wielding man, his hand wrapped round an outstretched chair, found herself instead about to be trained by a circus clown.

'Six,' she said now, absorbing the newest impact. 'May I have another?'

'You may,' he said magnanimously. 'And afterward, when I am done, you may take my cock inside you, hard between your reddened buttock cheeks.'

Caralissa groaned, the words crashing into her like the brush. 'Yes, master,' she replied, counting the seventh. 'May I have another?'

'You will remember this night, won't you, my queen? The night I tore the clothes from your body and did with you exactly as I pleased. The night I made you my slave, a title you shall bear in your heart forever, for my sake, whether or not you regain your throne.'

'Yes, master. Eight. I will remember. May I have another?'

'No,' he declared, tossing the brush to the floor and pawing at the opening of his leotards. 'You may not.'

Caralissa felt his prick poking at her anal opening. Bracing herself as best she could she endured his assault, bittersweet on account of his fingers, which were tantalising her sex, producing juice enough to provide him lubrication. With only moderate effort Alinor managed to sheath himself, stuffing her fully with his throbbing member.

Clasping her ankles as tightly as she could she yielded to his incessant pumping, allowing him to thrust freely as if he were in her other opening, the more common one. Alinor was breathing fast, his breath coming in low hisses. She was expecting his imminent release but at the last second he pulled out so he could spurt across her back and bottom. His jism was surprisingly thick and abundant, as much as a Rashal warrior's, in fact.

Denying her permission to rise, Alinor attended to his cleansing needs, using her torn dress to wipe his glistening organ. When he was finished he took the green velvet, thrusting as much of it as he could manage into Caralissa's mouth.

'Do not move from this position,' he told her as he tucked himself back into his leotards. 'Till you have counted to a thousand. And in case you are interested, that number is an approximation of the number of times I took myself in hand seeking my own pleasure in lieu of what you steadfastly refused me all those months.'

Caralissa glared at her own feet. She was drooling through the makeshift gag, feeling nauseous from the smell of his semen. It wasn't that it was so malodorous as much as that it represented for her the flavour of her own abasement, the scent of her domination.

One thousand proved to be a very large number. More than large enough for her to think through in her mind all the nasty implications of her being there, exposed and used, a waiting victim, ready to be caught by the spying eyes of her gaoler. Or maybe it would not only be his eyes he laid upon her, but other things as well, other experiences.

Alinor was devious, that was for certain. To make a queen do such things, to take her in so bestial a manner, giving her shameful pleasure in the bargain, this was an evil thing, a thing that could lead only to their mutual ruin. And yet she sensed in her heart that this was only the beginning; that a road was opening for her, a way unto submission that would take her both to the depths of her dark desires and to the soaring heights of her fantasies.

It was a road few dared travel and yet one that she could not now avoid. In many ways she'd traversed a line, a line of decency and order upon which all kingdoms and cities rested. Her name would soon be a curse to her people; of this much she was certain. Keeping herself as quiet as possible, whispering her endless count, she persisted, proving to herself and to the long gone Alinor that she was his slave, if not in perpetuity, at least for the time being.

Let us hope he keeps his silence, she thought, not daring to face the implications of having the events of this night made known to all, known to those men who might exploit the fact, making her their permanent prisoner, their abject slave. Let us hope Alinor has at least some small scrap of loyalty, some sense of discretion, she told herself.

When at last Caralissa crawled wearily into bed, the sheets were cool, though the leftover knots from her earlier escape attempt rode across her flesh in disturbing ways. She collapsed at once upon the pillows, her mind taking her to a place of deep and instant numbness. Her final prayer to the goddess was that she would have no dreams, no disturbing fantasies. She needed her reason; she needed to have her wits about her. In the morning she must awaken as a picture of a sober, chaste queen, a disciplined monarch prepared to deal with her detractors, her critics and her enemies.

Giving a small sigh, barely conscious, she turned, one of the knots gripping between her legs. Inadvertently, as she sought to free herself another coil wrapped round her ankle. It felt like a bond, and that made her think once more of Alinor and his poorly written yet potent poem. Moaning softly, seeking her release, she plunged her hands to her tortured sex then fell asleep.

Chapter Seven

The dreams came to Caralissa like storms, the thunder crashing over the peace of her fragile sleep, lightning flashing over the horizon of her sanity. And rains, drenching and arousing, saturating her carefully preserved consciousness.

Caralissa was moaning. Calling out the name of Varik, running to find him but unable to reach him on account of crowds of men. Senelek and his priests were there along with the soldiers of Varik's army. And Romila was there too, and Telos and Norod. The scene became a banquet hall. She was to be welcomed home by her people. But when she entered the vast room she saw upon the faces of her subjects expressions of horror and contempt. Looking down, she realised she was naked, though she'd been dressed just a moment before.

They were laughing at her and her only impulse was to find Varik, to seek comfort in his arms. For she knew he alone would not laugh. Alinor could be heard, in the centre of a huge crowd, noisily explaining his part in the night's joke, how he convinced the queen to dress in a garment of his own invention, one designed to disappear from the wearer's skin as soon as she donned it. They were congratulating him, Senelek and Telos and the barbarian guard too, the new one whose name she did not even know.

Romila, meanwhile, was telling Caralissa it was all her fault and that what she needed to do was to run as fast as she could from the room, out of the castle and across the moat. As soon as the words were spoken they became reality, and she really was running. In an instant she was all the way to the Forest of Night, having covered hundreds of miles of ground. Thinking she would be safe from her pursuers there – the mocking crowds still hot on her trail – she plunged into its murky depths.

Through the forest she went, though to her great distress she saw that at every turn they were already ahead of her, the laughing pointing people. Faster and faster she went. Her heart was pounding; she was becoming afraid. Behind her she heard heavy breathing, snarling. Over her shoulder she saw a tiger, white and grey, eyes bright red, teeth bared. She tried to call to it, thinking it was Ahzur, but it did not recognise her.

A few feet further into the forest she stumbled over a branch. There was more laughter as she fell at the feet of Norod and several of the councillors. Telos was there, giving inane descriptions of her wild appearance, her sweat-stained body, the scratches that covered her head to foot. The ground was made of marble and she realised she was back in the castle, in the banquet room. Somehow the tiger was still behind her. From all sides people were gathering, talking to one another, ignoring her. There were too many of them; she couldn't run away. Everyone was oblivious as she screamed. The tiger was lunging at her, coming straight for her, its claws slashing through the air. Caralissa cried out one last time, shutting her eyes as its weight crushed down upon her.

She assumed she was dead, but when she opened her dream eyes she was unhurt. The beast was gone and in its place was Telos, a ridiculous mask on his face, that of a purple tiger. Looking at her with a smirk he made a growling sound, in a sarcastic imitation of the animal. She saw she was lying on the floor and above her the conversation was continuing. No one seemed to notice even as Telos unsheathed himself and entered her. When she moved to protest he clamped his hand over her mouth and proceeded to take her by force. To her disgust she found herself aroused, more powerfully than she'd ever before been. Telos was enjoying her predicament, laughing harder and harder. Meanwhile, behind Telos she could see men lining up to take their turns, it was endless, consisting of every man she'd ever known or even laid eyes on.

'What's the matter?' Telos sneered. 'Does the queen not wish to serve her subjects?'

The scene began to dissolve and as Telos' dream words faded into a dim echo she heard another sound – female, a cry of distress. It was Deelia standing over her, a look of grave concern on her face. She did not know what was wrong, but when she followed Deelia's eyes and looked down to her own person, she realised what it was. She was awake in her own bed and Deelia was looking at her actual self, in utter disbelief.

Caralissa's hand was between her legs. In her sleep, unwittingly, she had been pleasuring herself. Quickly she sought to hide the evidence, pulling the damp sheets up around her. It was of course no crime to masturbate oneself, but it was hardly proper for a queen to do so, least of all on the morning of her trial to determine her moral fitness to rule.

'It's all right, Deelia,' she reassured, but as she looked beyond the woman's shoulder she realised it was not all right, for Deelia was not alone. In her company was the stone-faced warrior, the blond fellow with the silver breastplate and the penetrating eyes. How long had he been watching?

It was the warrior who spoke next. 'Leave us,' he said

165

to the already harried maid. 'I shall tend to the queen's preparations this morning.'

Deelia cast a worried look to Caralissa.

'You may go, Deelia,' she said, gathering the sheet at her throat and sitting up to face her new opponent. 'I will be fine.'

After the maid left she addressed the warrior directly. 'What is the meaning of this intrusion?' she demanded, seeking to put him in his place.

Saying nothing the man stepped forward, grabbed the sheet and pulled it from her, leaving her naked on the bed.

'How dare you!' she cried, covering herself as best she could with her hands.

'You were not alone last night, were you?' he said, phrasing his words as a statement and not a question.

Caralissa's cheeks reddened. 'That is none of your business!'

'It is when I am charged with your protection.'

'Protection?' she snorted. 'How is this protecting me? I am locked in my room. I have no privacy. My own throne is taken from me.'

'That is not my concern,' he said. 'I do as I am charged to do.'

'Oh?' she challenged, tossing her dishevelled curls indignantly. 'And what are you charged to do with me now, oh brave and fearless warrior?'

'I am to bathe you, dress you and bring you to breakfast.'

Caralissa shrieked as he scooped her from the bed, gathering her in his arms.

'Let go of me!' she wailed, trying to squirm free. 'You beast!'

'My name is Trajor,' he said, carrying her to the waiting bath and depositing her unceremoniously into the warm water.

'I do not care what your name is,' she told him as she tried to climb out again. 'As far as I am concerned you are a beast and nothing more.'

Trajor shoved her back down. 'You will clean yourself,' he said, handing her the dry sponge. 'Or I will do it for you.'

'Touch me and die,' she hissed, snatching the crusty brown object and plunging it into the water.

Petulantly she dabbed at her skin. Hugging her breasts, which rose just above the line of the water, and clamping her legs, she decided to make it as unpleasant as possible for the warrior. There was no way she'd allow the man to dominate her. If he thought himself her equal he was sorely mistaken.

Trajor folded his arms. 'At this rate we shall be here till the winter feast. You will go faster and at my direction. Begin at your neck.'

Caralissa muttered a curse, but did as he instructed.

'Your shoulders next.'

She bit her lip in fury. The rough sponge was tingly on her skin, like a warrior's touch; it was awakening her in the secret places of her body. As infuriating as it was to have to bathe in front of this arrogant man, it was also becoming exciting, for he was commanding her now, taking from her the control of her own body.

'Slide the sponge down now. Down your arm, then across your stomach.'

Caralissa shivered, wondering how far he would make her go and if she would be able to resist him at any point.

'Arch your back and sit forward so that your breasts are above the water. Now cup them, one in each hand.'

Caralissa flashed a challenging glare. 'I fail to see how this is part of my bath, warrior.'

Trajor folded his arms, regarding her with a look of

167

steel. She tried to guess his intent. Would he denounce her for her tryst with Alinor? Or would he simply force her to obey him? 'Why do you not speak?' she demanded.

Again he said nothing.

With a look of pure hatred Caralissa sat forward, exposing herself. Taking her breasts in hand she proffered them as though she were the man's whore.

Trajor reached down, retrieving a jar of lotion, which he commenced to pour over her aching breasts. The lotion was cool and creamy.

'Rub it in,' he commanded. 'Very slowly.'

Even without touching them, her breasts felt full and hot. She could see the arousal, how her nipples were taut and ready, the cream running over them and down her stomach into the water like the sperm of a thousand warriors. Licking her lips she opened her mouth, very slightly. She did not want to do this thing, and yet what choice did she have? Trajor was a real man – she could see that now. He wished to put her through her paces; he wished to be aroused by her, to draw pleasure from her exploitation.

She gasped at the touch of her own fingers. How she hated being a female and yet how she loved it at the same time!

'Take up the sponge again,' she heard him say, uttering the words she both dreaded and needed at the same time. 'Caress your belly with it.'

Caralissa moaned. The sponge was like dozens of tiny fingers, sending waves of undulating sensation over her soft stomach.

'Part your legs,' he continued matte. 'Place the sponge inside yourself. Show me how you come.'

Caralissa opened her half-closed eyes, his latest command awakening her lulled sense of propriety. 'I will never do that,' she said firmly. 'Not for you or any man. I would die first.'

His eyes continued to probe. She prayed he would not see through her clumsy lie.

'If you do not oblige me,' Trajor said, 'I will reveal to the court how you had a man in your quarters last night, and how you allowed him to mistreat you as though you were a common pleasure-house wench.'

'I did no such thing!'

Trajor wheeled round on his heels. 'It makes no difference to me who they believe. I will simply report what I have discovered.'

'Do that and you will have to explain why you did not intervene to stop it!'

Trajor turned back to face her. 'There are many who wish to see you convicted,' he shrugged. 'They will not give much thought to the circumstances of my testimony.'

Caralissa frowned. More than likely he was right. 'I will do it,' she said, thrusting the sponge beneath the water. It amazed her how much easier it was becoming to abase herself, to capitulate to blackmail of even the most tenuous nature.

'Raise your hips,' Trajor commanded. 'Reveal yourself to me.'

Caralissa arched her back, doing her best to expose herself above the line of the water. Pressing deep she let the sponge take her, rough and prickly, hard and demanding. Biting her lip she fought back the immediate shudders. A voice in her head told her this was slave behaviour, something she'd noted on may occasions in the pleasure-houses, but she was not ready to hear this.

Evan as the orgasm prepared to overtake her, Caralissa tried desperately to think of herself as mistress of her own pleasure, as the captain of her own ship. Simply because she was more passionate now did not mean she was becoming some pleasure pet whose very existence was to fulfil male desires. It was her own hands that touched her – the control should be hers, should it not?

No. This was not true. It was not her will that moved her, much as she might wish it to be. Opening her left eye briefly, seeing Trajor implacably observing, she surrendered herself, writhing and melting under his dispassionate gaze as though she really were a slave, or worse, an animal. It was a discomforting place to be, a terrifying one. How far this surrendering might yet go she did not know, nor did she know the true extent of the danger to her person, her very kingdom.

In the back of her mind questions raged, not least of which was how exactly Trajor knew about Alinor. Perhaps he'd viewed everything through some spy hole; but there was another possibility too, a far more disturbing one.

What if Alinor had told him directly, down to the details about his 'abuse' of her body? Worse still, what if someone had put Alinor up to the whole thing, someone like Telos? What if there were a conspiracy operating around her, designed to force her submission?

But she could think no more at this moment. She was a she-beast, in need of release. Under the eyes of her gaoler she must orgasm. Holding nothing back she gave him what he required. Dimly, shamefully she wondered if he found her pleasing, if she might be the sort of girl he would wish to possess. Pretending the sponge and fingers were his she tried to show him now what he might have, how she might move for him, lay for him. It was a whore's act, a slave's act, and yet it was coming by reflex, just as did the climax, earth shattering, overpowering.

'Take me,' she whispered, her arms raised to him, the words issuing forth as a confession, a terrible and damning revelation.

'No,' he replied, tossing her a towel. 'You will dry yourself and then you will dress.'

Lowering her eyes, shamed and spurned, she caught the fabric, thrusting it against herself in a last ditch effort to protect her honour. It was too late, of course. Numbly she stepped from the bath. She did not know if her legs would hold her, carrying her even as far as the wardrobe where he was already awaiting her, picking out the clothes she would wear.

'This will do,' he said, presenting the dress, made of red velvet with a tight bodice that would reveal her cleavage.

Caralissa clothed herself wordlessly. Today was the most important of her life, a day when every little gesture, each detail could be crucial, and yet here she was donning a suggestive dress at the behest of a stranger, a man who just a few short moments ago compelled her to compromise her virtue in his presence. In her rational mind she knew it was foolhardy trusting such a man, yielding to him in this way. Where would it end – would she become his slave, too? She must fight back, and quickly!

'You will wear your hair down,' Trajor decided when she presented herself for inspection.

'Yes,' she said, walking to her dresser to pick up the brush, the one Alinor had used, inflaming her buttocks to the point of flaming passion, 'I will.'

It was as though she were watching someone else, observing a play about a queen who resembled her but whose personality was completely different. Over and over, she stroked her hair, making it silky and pretty. Again and again she looked to Trajor, confirming that he was seeing, approving.

'One more thing,' he announced as they were nearly at

the door.

She watched in horror as he drew a dagger from his belt and held it at her waist. 'A small adjustment,' he explained, piercing the fabric and drawing the knife down in a straight line. Though he did not so much as prick her skin, she shrieked to see what he was doing.

'How dare you?' she cried.

Trajor shrugged. 'I do as I am commanded.'

Caralissa beheld the slit, cut from hip to ankle. The dress was no longer decent! She would barely be able to walk without exposing herself.

'We will be late,' he said, ushering her into the hallway.

Caralissa did her best to keep up, all the while seeking to keep her hand clenched on the sides of her gown to keep it together.

'We must go,' Trajor declared, his hand guiding her elbow, directing her upon invisible chains down the stairs.

It was Telos whom they encountered first in the banquet hall. 'Your majesty!' he cried, his voice exuberant with joy. 'You must sit beside me; it's all been arranged.'

Caralissa turned white as she beheld the faces at the table. There was Alinor! And Remik, as sombre as ever. And others too, spurned suitors, former councillors removed for impropriety. Conspicuously absent however was Romila, along with any other female who might balance out the obvious sexual inequality.

'We have prepared all this for you,' Telos beamed, spreading his arms.

The long wooden table was elaborately decorated, far more so than was usual for breakfast. There were candelabras, a silk tablecloth, bowls of colourful fruit and trays of sweetmeats and other delicacies, the food piled high upon the silver surfaces. From the look of things they'd been dining for some time. This fact was highly unusual – unheard of, actually, since she as monarch and hostess should have been given the right to begin the festivities at her command.

'I see you began without me,' she observed icily, eyeing King Norod who was seated at the head of the table.

The old king rose hastily to his feet, the others following suit. Their eyes were intent on her as she prayed that she was concealing the tear in her dress sufficiently.

'Forgive us,' the king muttered, his mouth stuffed with delicate stewed eggs. 'I took the liberty of commencing.'

'I do not think introductions will be required,' Telos announced as the men resumed their places and continued eating as though she were some common wench instead of the reigning queen, 'as we all seem to know one another. Caralissa, won't you take your seat?'

Without waiting for her assent he directed her to an empty place directly to the right of his own seat. As he sat her Caralissa felt herself sinking quite low. It was only when she went to put her hands on the edge of the table that she realised what had been done. Her seat was lowered somehow so that she sat several inches below the others, including Telos. It was a petty thing and she could scarcely imagine any man going to the trouble of sawing off the legs of a chair to embarrass a queen, but then again, Telos was far from being a man.

'I hope her majesty is hungry,' Telos said, snapping his fingers for a nearby servant.

'I will have some fruit,' she told the serving maiden.

'I am sorry, majesty,' the woman said, a pained expression on her face. 'But I am not allowed.'

Caralissa watched in shock as the servant snatched her plate and silverware away. The action seemed to startle no one and as she looked about, her neck straining to see over the piles of food, Caralissa was beginning to feel as if she'd landed once more into a nightmare. Were a tiger to show itself she could scarcely be any more surprised, or mortified than she was at this moment.

'There were concerns, majesty,' Telos explained, spearing a chunk of fried meat from his heaped plate, 'that someone might seek to poison you, given the, um, resentment felt by many over your relationship – alleged, of course – with the Rashal chieftain. I shared these concerns, naturally, and even went so far as to volunteer to serve as royal food taster.'

She watched as he took the meat from his fork, took a bite out of it and then put it in front of her face. 'This piece is quite safe,' he assured her as he chewed noisily.

Caralissa blinked. 'And what exactly am I supposed to do with that, Telos?'

He looked to some of the others for support, his eyes telegraphing his bemusement, as though it were she and not he who was behaving so absurdly. 'Why, I assumed you would eat it,' he chuckled.

'I will starve first,' she informed him, rising to her feet. 'I wish you all good day.'

She looked behind her, expecting Trajor to block her exit. Amazingly enough, however, he was not even in the room.

'Caralissa, I am disappointed,' she heard Norod say. The old man's words froze her as effectively as would the intervention of a warrior.

'I am tired,' she lied. 'I would like to lay down.'

Norod pinched his brow, sighing deeply. 'Honestly, Caralissa, I have not wanted to believe the things being said about you, but when I see with my own eyes the way you behave so erratically, what am I to think? Anyhow, I am tired myself and do not wish to host alone today.'

Caralissa sat down heavily. As befuddled and ultimately

untrustworthy as he might be, Norod was the closest thing she had right now to an ally. She needed him, and if that meant enduring a little more misery at the hands of this bunch of overgrown babies, she'd put up with it. 'Forgive me, Norod,' she smiled. 'I would be delighted to help you host.'

'Wise choice,' Telos said, leaning over to whisper in her ear. 'You won't regret it.'

She let out a gasp of air as she felt Telos' hand on her calf under the table, sliding upwards like a snake, tracing the line of the cut in her gown. Before she could draw another breath he reached the bridge of her thighs. So this was why Trajor cut her dress, she thought miserably.

'I propose a toast,' Telos announced, raising his goblet. 'To the safe return of our queen.'

The men looked at one another, then to Norod.

'Yes,' agreed Norod, even as Telos worked his way under Caralissa's undergarments, worming a finger into her sex, 'to the queen.'

Goblets were raised, clinking. Caralissa shuddered as the first drops of moisture began to form inside her. It was absurd that this was happening and a part of her simply did not want to believe it. Either way, she was paralysed and with each passing second it was harder and harder to imagine extracting herself from the situation. Telos seemed to bank on this: on her complicity, her inability to protest.

'To your safe return,' Telos told her, holding his own goblet to her lips.

Caralissa put her mouth to the cold silver, allowing Telos to pour a tiny bit of the sweet cider onto her tongue. Obediently she swallowed.

'Spread your legs wider,' he whispered in her ear, taking the opportunity to cement his power over her.

The words were like a fire, liquid and melting. Unbidden she felt her thighs parting, the point of resistance long since passed. Henceforth she would not be able to deny the man anything. As wretched and hateful as he was, he'd found access to her submissive nature.

Telos watched her carefully as he worked his secret magic. Eyes blank, she stared straight ahead, doing her best to conceal the emotions, the arousal. She could no longer meet his gaze, for if she tried she would have no option but to lower her eyes in deference and surrender. Clenching the edge of the table with her trembling fingers she listened as he poured into her ears his dark promises. The things he would do to her. The things she would be made to do for him.

'Open,' he commanded.

Caralissa accepted the juicy bit of fruit, swimming in the creamy sauce. Whether on purpose or by accident Telos turned the spoon slightly as she sought to take it in, releasing thereby a tiny trail of juice which dribbled down her chin and between her breasts.

'Leave it,' he said simply when she moved to clean herself.

She chewed the segment of fruit, feeling the wet stickiness in her cleavage. Twice more Telos fed her, and each time she was soiled. Breasts heaving she pressed her thighs together, the sensation of the juice only heightening what his fingers were doing to her insides.

He couldn't make her come this way, she thought miserably. He wouldn't dare.

'We are pleased you are joining us, Caralissa,' said Norod. 'In fact, it is our hope to dispense with this trial formality quite quickly and allow you to resume your place on the throne. Frankly,' he shrugged, 'I thought it a bit silly but certain elements of my own council insisted, and of course several of our neighbour countries. Rest assured, the trial commissioners – whom you see before you today – have been chosen with the most judicious care.'

Caralissa felt faint. These were her judges? A roomful of jilted lovers and jealous fools with axes to grind against her? How could this be?

'What's the matter?' asked Telos, his voice hushed and intimate. 'Cat get your tongue – or should I say, Rashal cock get your tongue?'

Caralissa whirled on him in fury. Too late she remembered that though her mouth was free to speak another part of her was not. At the very moment she opened her mouth Telos twisted his finger expertly, reducing her to a mass of female quivering. Shamed, broken, powerless to resist, she moved fiercely against him, opening herself to the mechanically induced orgasm.

No one seemed to notice, presumably the long tablecloth shielded her from prying eyes, but still she was being made to surrender herself at a table full of hostile men, all the while having to pretend nothing was happening – how could this not upset her?

Let it end quickly, she prayed. Let it pass soon.

Finally it did, and she nearly convinced herself that she'd gotten past the worst when Telos started again, faster, harder. 'No,' she whimpered under her breath. 'No more.'

'Very well,' he concurred, giving in far too easily for Caralissa's liking. 'No more.'

He took his hand away, allowing her to relax. Eyes peeled like a hawk, she watched as he engaged himself in conversation with his neighbour, concerning trade deficits. It was the hand that she was worried about, and sure enough he was using it to pick a piece of fruit from a bowl. A moment later the fruit was inside her, absorbing her overflowing wetness.

The strong female odour was obvious as he presented it to her, as was the glistening wetness. How could the others not notice? Or were they merely pretending not to, allowing themselves to be used in some larger scheme of humiliation directed against her person?

'Please,' she whispered when he put the tiny green morsel to her mouth. 'Don't make me.'

Not even bothering to look in her direction, he thrust the juice-soaked fruit to her lips, forcing her to open, to take it in. Her lips trembled as she chewed, the flavour reminding her of the whip handle in Senelek's hand. It was a sensation that belonged to another world and yet here she was at her own table tasting herself like a slave at the command of a cruel and stupid man.

'Lick them,' he said, extending his wet fingers. One by one she did, slowly and sensually, feeling like a wanton whore, not caring which of the men were watching or even if all of them were. At this very moment it did not matter, for were Telos to command it she would, without hesitation, strip off her red dress and fall to her knees, naked. To each man, then, she would crawl allowing him to fill her mouth with his hot hardness, and ultimately with his salty jism.

'So tell us, your majesty,' she heard Remik say, the man's voice every bit as acerbic as she remembered it. 'It must have been difficult, to say the least, being in the captivity of the Rashal. It is said they abuse their female prisoners, treating them like animals.'

Telos leaned close to her, adding an injunction of his own just as she was on the verge of answering. 'Place this inside yourself,' he whispered, pressing the small cube of ice against her belly under the table. As if in a dream Caralissa took the frozen chunk, her hand trembling as she slid it under her clothes, moving it steadily to her pulsating sex.

'The Rashal are not civilised,' she replied, the ice having reached her throbbing lips. 'Their ways are not ours.'

'All the way in,' Telos coaxed, as he thrust the goblet to her lips.

Caralissa slurped greedily. Still the fluid came too fast, running in rivulets down her front.

'Forgive me,' cried Telos, as though mortally wounded. 'You,' he bellowed to a nearby servant, 'take the queen at once and help her to clean herself.'

'No,' Caralissa protested, not daring to move in her current state. 'I am fine.'

'Are you certain?' he asked, his face a picture of deep concern. 'But won't you at least allow me to dry you off?'

'No,' she hissed, even as the ice bit her with teeth of commingled pleasure and pain. 'Do not touch me.'

'Is something the matter?' she heard Norod call out, the man obviously having no clue as to the real nature of this 'breakfast'.

Telos eyed her, his gaze conveying the nature of his latest blackmail. If he were to open his mouth there was no telling what he might say, or what Norod might believe.

She flushed red. It was another trap. 'No,' she said, knowing herself beaten once more. 'It is only a small stain. Telos is going to help me.'

Telos was smiling smugly, like a boy about to pull the head off of an insect. The servant handed him a rag, the thin scrap of cloth being a simple pretence to molest her in yet another form, this time upon her bosom.

Telos' hands beneath the rag were vulgar and coarse. Running them over her bared upper chest he took his time, lingering at her breasts, working her nipples into painful readiness. That the men were saying nothing even at this juncture indicated she was already beaten, her case lost before it could be even argued. In their eyes she must already be something less than a queen, and perhaps only a little more than the sort of female one finds under one's table begging for scraps in a pleasure-house.

Her only question was why they were persisting with this charade. Couldn't Telos simply have possessed her upon her return, declaring her to be his slave? Or was it true that his power was limited and that he needed Norod, needed the legitimacy of his ruling? What Romila's role was up to this point, Caralissa could not say. Did her absence bespeak complicity, or did it indicate that she too, like her sister, was under some form of duress?

So many questions. Straining against the melting ice and roaming hand, she fought to keep her concentration. The line of pleasure and pain was on the verge of disappearing again just as it did in the Rashal camp under the distinct yet equally potent influence of Varik and Senelek.

'I for one, say the queen should be commended!' Norod exclaimed, having begun some conversation in his own head. 'She survived the Rashal and managed even to remove them from our lands.'

'Indeed,' muttered Remik, 'she did survive. Though I can't help asking what she did to earn that survival.'

Caralissa shuddered. She could not believe this was happening to her, that she could find herself in such a state in her own dining hall, in the middle of her own castle. She wanted to tear their eyes out, yet at the same time she was fighting the urge to tear off her clothes and beg the men to use her.

'One does what one must,' she said proudly, determined not to sink to the man's level, 'to make a stand for the honour of one's country.'

Remik gulped the rest of his cider, throwing back his head. 'To making a stand,' he pronounced, holding up the empty goblet. 'Even if it means doing so on your back.'

'I agree,' said Norod. 'It is good to have Caralissa back.'

'I think I speak for us all,' interjected Telos, 'when I say that no one thinks ill of our lovely queen. But we must know the truth, mustn't we?'

All eyes were on Caralissa, who at present was allowing Telos to place a carrot stick in her mouth. The ice was melted by now and she was praying that he would not compel her to take another cube of it between her tortured legs.

'Lick it,' he said, moving the shaft-like object in and out of her softly inviting mouth.

Caralissa sucked the carrot like a slut. Would they find her sufficiently arousing to make her lay for them – right here on the marble floor? Or would she be found wanting? In that case they might well punish her, in the Rashal way. Telos would not be above spanking her or even whipping her. The others would happily join in, most especially Remik.

'Stand up, now,' Telos told her. 'Tell us what you have become. Tell us in your heart what you are.'

Caralissa rose to her feet. She could not deny the man, nor could she hide what was inside, what she felt at this moment. For despite her indignation she was wanting to submit, needing to, in fact.

'Tell us, Caralissa,' Telos pressed, the smell of victory in his nostrils. 'Take off your clothes and tell us. Strip yourself and make yourself free.'

Her mouth was dry. Fingers weak and trembling she

moved to grasp the end of the crisscrossed string that tied across the bodice of her dress. She was going to do this, she really was.

'Caralissa, why are you standing up again?'

It was Norod, trying in vain to grasp the implications of what was about to happen. His doddering voice and nasal whine were all the impetus she needed to return her to her senses. She must get away! It was her only chance. Pushing back her chair, fending off Telos' flailing grabs, she made for the doorway. None of the guards moved to stop her. She would go to the stables, get a horse and ride. It was not a logical plan, but the time for logic was no more. It was about survival now.

No one followed her, though she knew he would come for her. Trajor.

'Leave her to me,' she heard him say as she fled the room, no trace of bragging in his voice. 'I will bring her back.'

Caralissa was adept at riding. Since she was old enough to walk she'd ridden her father's horses, both with and without saddles. She knew a way into the stables through a loose board. She also knew the fastest horses, and the ones that knew her best. She chose a grey mare with a thick mane and hoofs that struck the earth like thunder. The horse responded to her commands at once, accepting her presence as she leaped on its back. There was no time for a saddle or even a bridle and reins. Kicking off her leather shoes, tearing away the hem of her long dress, she dug in her heels, readying herself for the ride of her life.

Using the horse's mane for steerage and calling her name, Grey Cloud, she shouted the animal into fighting frenzy. The handful of groomsmen scattered like insects as Caralissa and her mount burst out of the front of the barn, none of them were equipped to follow. Capitalising on the element of surprise, leaping over three fences in rapid succession, she soon found herself alone on the main road. Caralissa did not know where she intended to go, only that she would ride with the wind, her hair flying and her freedom intact for as long as she could manage.

To the border perhaps, and from there across to one of the nearby kingdoms. Or else she might try to get beyond the valley entirely by escaping into the Forest of Night. Yes, that would be the one place she could go where no one would dare follow, least of all the coward Telos. A pang of guilt struck her as she thought of her sister. What if Romila were in trouble? Oughtn't she try to help? Then again, if she were recaptured what good would that do anyone?

Childishly, she thought now of Varik. What if she could ride to him and beg him to help her? Would he not champion her cause, swooping down into the valley with the host of his army, striking terror into her enemies, magically solving all her problems? Caralissa shook the foolish notion from her brain. Varik did not want her. Why couldn't she grasp that? How clear did he have to make it? Would she be in this predicament now, a fugitive in her own land, if he cared for her even one iota?

Caralissa heard the sound of the rider behind her almost as quickly as did Grey Cloud. No sooner did the horse's ears prick up than she herself was turning to look over her shoulder. It was a black mount, bearing down, it's rider low to the saddle, kicking its side like a man possessed. Like a demon from the mythical pit of fire into which the wicked are cast after death. There was no need to see the glint of silver or the spray of golden hair to know who it was. It was Trajor, coming for her.

Her heart pounded in her chest. She was quarry,

vulnerable to the swifter more powerful male. It was only a matter of time till she was caught unless she did something to even the odds. Pulling from the main road she took one last desperate gamble. If she could lose him in the woods, in the royal hunting reserve, she might yet win her freedom. She retained the advantage, having ridden in these woods all her life. There were hidden trails, places to hide, places a large man could not go.

Caralissa ducked to avoid the low branches. Grey Cloud was nervous and needed reassurance. 'Hold steady, girl,' she promised, 'and we will find you the biggest bucket of oats in the Forest.'

Or whatever passed for oats in the Forest of Night.

It was said the Forest was full of demons, and that no one who crossed its borders lived to tell the tale. Maybe demons were what she needed, though. Maybe they were the ones who would champion her cause, find her sister and rid the valley of the interlopers who dared sit at her table, drink her fruit wine, eat her food and mock her honour.

Twice the horse nearly lost its footing. They were going down the side of a hill, the path crisscrossed with exposed roots and twisted underbrush. If she could get below the canopy of umbrella trees at the bottom of the old streambed she could ride for hours, virtually undetected. She could not hear Trajor behind her any more. He followed her as far as the first trees, but appeared to have lost his way at one of the many double-back turns she'd made. Her trail would be unreadable now and in a just a few short minutes she would be out of reach of any of them. Allowing herself a small smile of satisfaction, congratulating herself prematurely, she tucked her head to the horse's mane, evading thereby a branch, a foot thick and craggy with aged bark.

There was no way the larger, bulkier warrior on his huge steed could follow this path!

'Good girl,' she told the horse, even as Trajor dropped on her without warning.

He'd been hiding in the tree above her, having somehow anticipated and cut off her escape path. He landed behind her, his chest pressing her back, his thighs gripping the horse's flanks. With one hand he clamped her waist while with the other he compelled Grey Cloud to an immediate stop. This accomplished he kicked hard into the horse's side, issuing a single command, imperious and harsh, compelling the hapless mare to turn around.

Silently they re-ascended the hill. Caralissa voiced not an utterance of complaint, not even when he made Grey Cloud stop in front of a large oak in a grassy clearing at the edge of the woods. For several moments he looked at the tree, then dismounted, having satisfied himself on some score. Pulling Caralissa down after him he tossed her over her shoulder, carrying her effortlessly to the base of the tree.

'Put your arms above your head,' he ordered, as soon as he deposited her on the ground.

Caralissa gripped the black earth with her bare toes. The wispy grass tickled her calves. After a second's hesitation and no more she did as she was told. There was in his eyes a harshness, a glint of steel not unlike that which she'd seen in the eyes of many a Rashal. It was almost a relief as he removed her dress, leaving her naked in the open air. He regarded her, her place and his now clear. She was woman and he was man, she was captive, he was captor.

At his belt he carried rope in a long coil. Tossing one end of it overhead he looped the rough and fibrous coil over a high branch. Fashioning a slipknot he tied it off then used the free end to secure her hands. In a matter of seconds he had her bound, on tiptoes, her body stretched humiliatingly, enticingly.

Unable to move a muscle she watched as he searched among the smaller branches lying about the ground. Discarding several, having tested them first by slashing the air to and fro, he finally settled on a medium-sized one. Employing a knife he stripped away the bark till it was smooth and bare.

All this he did in plain sight, taking his time, allowing her to know that she was in his power absolutely.

'You were a prisoner of the Rashal,' he said, placing the stick beneath her chin, raising it to eye level.

'Yes,' she replied defiantly.

There was, of course, no need for her to have answered. The fact of her captivity was well known by both of them.

'I, too, was their captive,' he said soberly.

The revelation shocked Caralissa more greatly than the surprise of having Trajor leap upon the back of her horse. 'You?' she managed. 'Were a prisoner?'

Trajor nodded. 'My people were neighbours of the Rashal,' he told her, tracing a line with the tip of the switch in the valley of her breasts. 'We were conquered. Most of our men were killed. I was still a boy. I was allowed to live. When I came of age I devised a plan. I escaped into the mountains and became a mercenary. My skills and my knowledge proved quite valuable in the service of those opposing the Rashal. Most recently I have served Norod.'

Caralissa enquired no further. From his tone it was clear no more would be said of the matter – particularly with regard to the details of his escape and prior to this the means of his survival among brutal foes. It was enough to know they shared something in common once, but that now their positions were in opposition. It was nothing personal. He was doing a job. For gold.

The switch played freely over her curves. Trajor was playing with her body, and yet with each touch, light as it was, she shuddered, for she knew what the switch might do to her. She suspected that Trajor, too, had felt such pain. That the experience would somehow weaken him or cause him to cower from his duty to punish her was, however, an impossibility.

Trajor was a warrior. A man of codes, a man of honours.

'I do not permit the escape of those I am entrusted to guard,' he told her, the tip of the freshly carved wood resting at the juncture of her thighs. 'Were you male I would slay you for the attempt, though the act might cost me my own life at the hands of my employers.'

Caralissa's breath was heavy. 'I deserve punishment,' she declared, allowing the device to graze her clitoris. 'I beg you to punish me, Trajor. I beg you to whip my bottom.'

Trajor slashed instead across the flesh of her breasts. 'Do not presume to tell me what to do,' he warned.

Caralissa lowered her tear-filled eyes, the pain stinging her consciousness. 'Forgive me.'

'Were you my woman,' Trajor informed her, compelling her to raise her lowered eyes yet again. 'You would be taught obedience. As it stands now, you seek to command your masters, dictating the terms of your usage.' He looked at her more deeply, a puzzled expression on his face. 'I find that surprising, given where you have been of late.'

Caralissa could not resist the opportunity to brag. 'Varik, the Rashal chief, loves me,' she told him. 'Beware that you do not invoke his wrath when he returns for me...'

Caralissa's arrogant words melted into a scream as

Trajor struck two blows to her belly, savage and efficient, one upon the other. Horrified and shocked she looked at him, then at the angry marks across her flesh. For an instant she contemplated opening her mouth to protest, but when she saw him poised, implacable, ready to do it again, she stifled herself, opting instead to lower her head in silence.

He regarded her. 'This time,' he told her, 'you are denied permission to scream.'

The Orencian queen bit her lip, bracing herself. She'd seen it coming, his arm moving, slowly, deliberately as he positioned himself with perfection. She prayed he would not strike her sensitive sex lips. He did not, opting instead to level a slice on the tender skin across the front of her thighs. Throwing her head back she choked on her own agony, killing thereby the impulse to cry out. Long painful breaths came instead, and a low groan followed by a submissive whimper, but not one scream did she emit.

Though he said nothing by way of encouragement, Caralissa was proud of herself. She was obeying him and – she hoped – pleasing him in the process. She blushed at the implications of her thoughts. She was sounding like a beaten cur, an animal that lived for its master's approval. Where was her fire, her indignation? Had she suffered so much abuse, and at so many different hands that she no longer grasped her own identity? If so, how would she ever prove to her subjects, let alone her enemies, that she was rightfully queen, fit to govern?

'Trajor?' she heard herself ask, her voice sounding hollow and distant. 'I am hungry. Will you please feed me?'

It seemed a strange request, irrelevant at best, and yet it was only now she'd felt the sharp hunger pangs, the result of not having eaten in over a day.

Trajor gave no response except to whistle, the high-pitched sound carrying far across the meadow on the light breeze. To her amazement a few moments later his horse appeared, happily chomping on a mouthful of grass. Patting the horse in praise, he reached into one of the twin saddlebags.

In it were sugar cubes and a thick slab of bread. Taking the bread for himself, biting off a large chunk, he thrust several of the cubes up to the mouth of the horse. As the animal devoured them noisily, Trajor withdrew his sword and scabbard, which was tied to the side of his saddle. Baring the blade he thrust it cleanly overhead, severing the rope that held her, cleaving it midway between her wrists and the branch.

Caralissa's release was unexpected. Hands still bound she lost her balance, falling forward onto her knees. Instead of offering her help Trajor snapped his fingers, pointing to a place at his feet. Remembering what he'd said, about how a woman of his should behave, she did not rise but lowered herself onto her hands so that she could crawl to him. For a reward she was given two of the sweetened cubes, nearly as many as he gave his horse. Weak and hungry, dizzy and exhilarated, she took them from his hand, using only her lips and teeth. The sugar was good, and when she was done she felt grateful. Unbidden she pressed her head to his crotch, kissing him gently, emitting as she did so a soft sigh. It was all a dream; it must be. At any moment she'd awaken and be somewhere else – back in her room or in the tournament field or upon her throne. This was not her: this cringing girl, willing to take her place at a warrior's feet, her status lower than that of his mount.

Caralissa rubbed her cheek over his throbbing cock, its outline clear now through the rough material of his britches. She wanted him, needed him badly. For a long time he let her beg, with her body, her kisses. At last, having been satisfied with her self-abasement, he opened his belt, allowing her to take him deep inside her hungry mouth. If only she could love him well enough, she told herself, he would keep her safe, spare her from her trials.

'Trajor,' she breathed, releasing his unspent shaft, 'will you not take me away and make me yours? I will live even as your slave.'

Trajor put her mouth back on him. 'I must take you back to the castle,' he said. 'It will be the dungeon for you now. A stone cell and heavy chains. You will be released each day for your trial, so long as it lasts. Whether you are freed ultimately will depend upon the verdict.'

Caralissa arched her neck, parting her lips as wide as they could go. The dungeon would be dark and lonely. She would need this memory, this final act of passion to sustain her. Trajor grunted once, twice, his tones modulated, regulated, like those of a true soldier. He flooded her then, giving her his essence to drink. Obediently she continued her motions, pulling out every last drop, not daring to move until he commanded it, not daring to release his sweet cock again until he withdrew.

'Good girl,' he offered softly, rubbing her head with the flat of his hand. Then, more wistfully, 'I do believe I shall miss you.'

He gave her no opportunity to ask what he meant, for no sooner did he speak the words than he was lifting her to her feet, raising her arms and dressing her as though she were a child. Silently, passively she waited as he helped her into her torn dress, lacing it tightly.

'You must be bound now,' he explained, holding up the long coil of rope. Caralissa put her arms to her side, sensing his intent. The twist of his design was cunning, the rope being wrapped tightly over and across her velvet-covered breasts and down between her legs. Her dress was rucked up to her waist in the process. To conclude, he used the end of the rope to secure her arms to her body. Pursing his lips he paused to admire his work. The intent of it, clearly, was not merely to secure her but to sexually bind her, in ways that both flaunted and tamed her womanhood. Caralissa blushed at her arousal, flushing all the more completely to have him notice.

A tiny gasp escaped her lips as he rubbed her hard nipples, pinched efficiently between two layers of the cord. She gasped again when he tugged at the rope invading her crotch. Were he to check with his hand he would find her shamelessly wetting her dress with the juices of her submission.

Having accomplished this initial layer of bondage upon his fair prisoner Trajor hoisted Caralissa over his saddle, on her belly. Pulling a second coil of rope from his saddlebag he secured her, wrapping the cord tight about her so that she could move neither hand nor foot. Checking the ropes and finding them satisfactory, Trajor administered a sound smack to her upturned buttock cheeks before hoisting himself on the saddle.

What an arrogant brute he was! How like Varik, and how unlike the men of the valley, with their sneaking ways and their deceitful cunning. Barbarians, by contrast, took what they wanted and made no effort to hide their desires and lusts. They were men of few words and when they spoke it was to an end. To the end of achieving victory.

The whole way back to the castle, her own mount in tow, she thought more fully of what it would be like to yield to such a man as this mercenary Trajor. It was a frivolous thought, wicked and traitorous, but real nonetheless, reflective of desires that she feared no amount of self-denial would eliminate.

The question was what would become of her if she were made to admit those female desires before Telos and before Norod and his court. Would they use them as pretext to strip her of the throne, turning her rightful place of power over to Romila? Or was Caralissa's sister in danger too? Certainly there was no cause to trust the likes of Telos or to assume that he would serve anyone's interest but his own. It was not impossible and perhaps even likely that he himself fancied the throne of Orencia.

Caralissa struggled, testing the limits of her bondage. Trajor was clearly skilled, having affixed upon her bonds that were both secure and maddening.

Upon their arrival at the castle, Trajor rode directly across the moat and into the courtyard. The dungeon keepers were already waiting for them. Caralissa identified them immediately by their sallow colouring and by their stained grey tunics. It was nearly enough to make her wretch. She had never once set foot in the dungeon, nor did she ever desire to do so. It was one of her goals, in fact, to eliminate the place entirely.

Two of the dungeon men carried her, still bound in the ropes, as though she were a rolled carpet, they lumbered down the dank narrow stairway. The stairs were circular and they seemed to go on forever. Were it not for the steady drop in temperature and corresponding rise in dampness, she might almost believe they were taking her to the very pits of fire.

Caralissa did not like it. Her tender skin, made even more sensitive by the ropes, prickled with every step. There were rumours about the dungeon and the horrors that supposedly took place down here. Stories of rats the size of cats and of brutal instruments of torture used on criminals too wicked to see the light of day.

Surely they would not subject her to such things! She was only a temporary prisoner, a defendant being held for trial. They would never dare to harm her. In fact, by all rights she should be back in her room, under guard or house arrest, and not the dungeon at all.

Caralissa stiffened, her ears pricking as she heard the mournful sound, a lonely, faraway wail. Was it some kind of bird or was it another sort of cry – a human scream to be precise? How she wished she could be with Trajor now, or even Alinor. Perish the thought, even to be in a room with Telos, his hand in her crotch, being forced to eat from his fork was better than this!

At last the stairs ended and they were on level ground. It was difficult to see, the rough stoned walls being only imperfectly illuminated by the torches, one every twenty feet or so. In between the torches were rows of vertical metal bars. Doors to cells, within which, peering from the dark, she saw eyes. Human eyes, she assumed, though they seemed so lonely and large, so hollow and haunted. Every now and again there came the rustling of chain which made her wonder what sort of men were locked within those terrible cells. She shuddered to think what might happen to her should any of these desperate creatures actually seize hold of her and drag her into its filthy lair.

In one cell she beheld bony knuckles on the bars and deep yellow eyes. As they passed the claw-like hand reached out to graze her tightly bound breast. The fingers made contact with her tender nipple, causing her to scream in horror. A guard came running down the passage and as they passed, he could be seen entering the cell, wielding a large wooden club. From inside came a terrible din as the man surrendered to a beating.

Caralissa felt sorry for him. She hadn't wanted to be

touched but he must be so lonely and she was, after all, only a female. *Only a female*. Had her thinking come to this, that she would so demean herself?

She was grateful when they reached a better lit area, one with newer stone. Here the doors were rounded and wooden, like the ones upstairs in the castle. Before a particular one they stopped, one of the men rapping upon it lightly.

'Enter,' she heard a gruff voice proclaim.

They carried her across the threshold, depositing her on her feet before a wooden platform. Behind it, stooped over, a hammer and spike in his hand, stood an enormous man, both in girth and breadth of shoulders. His eyes were small and red. On his forehead was a birthmark in the shape of a small lake. Caralissa identified him at once as Drendel, the dungeon keeper. He seemed engrossed in breaking some bit of chain and did not even bother to look up at her.

'Welcome, your majesty, to your humble abode.' The voice was all too familiar and she did not have to see the man emerge from the shadows behind Drendel to know it was Telos. 'What's the matter, your majesty – have you nothing to say to your royal food taster?'

She looked at the man, doing her best to conceal her emotions – the revulsion, the shock, the hurt. 'I see the answer is no,' he conceded, his face locked in a superior expression, his gloating barely disguised. 'In that case, perhaps you would like to greet me instead in my new capacity as your defence attorney.'

Caralissa narrowed her gaze. The news of this latest effrontery was serving to jar her from her earlier state of passivity. 'And by whose authority is this?' she demanded.

'King Norod,' he said, folding his arms cockily. 'Apparently he was impressed with how well I took care of you this morning. Naturally, I assured him I would do a splendid job.'

'Naturally,' Caralissa agreed dryly.

Telos sighed, his narrow shoulders vibrating very slightly. 'I daresay you don't seem very excited. Should I take this personally?'

'No, Telos, what you should take personally is your own upcoming execution – you and all the rest of your little cabal. And I assure you, this is an event I intend both to orchestrate and to personally witness, from a front row seat.'

'Still the same old girl, I see.' He shook his head. 'I had so hoped the events of the last few hours in Trajor's company would have, shall we say, altered your disposition towards me?'

She snorted. 'Trajor is a man, Telos. Too bad you aren't one yourself, or you might see for yourself if I've changed.'

'Oh, I think I will see plenty,' he smirked, snapping his fingers to draw Drendel's attention. 'Keeper, remove the prisoner's bonds.'

'I want to see my sister,' she demanded, as Drendel lumbered towards her with a sharp knife, easily stripping her of the cumbersome ropes. 'I want to see Romila.'

'All in good time,' laughed Telos. 'Trust me, you'll find it worth the wait.'

Caralissa didn't like the sound of that, not one bit. 'So will you,' she bluffed, 'because after I get out of here I plan on something special for you and your little friends from breakfast. I won't spoil the surprise, but I will say it involves your losing a bit of weight, from the neck up.'

Telos smiled condescendingly. 'Save your breath,' he advised, striding to a place inches from her face. 'And concentrate on doing what you're told. For starters, we will require the removal of your clothing.'

Caralissa straightened her back. If Telos thought he would play the part of the dominant warrior he was sadly mistaken. 'Go ahead and try,' she told him.

'Really, Highness, do you think you are in a position to resist us?'

A grunt came from Drendel, who was standing close behind her. 'Step aside,' he complained to Telos. 'I have no patience for your prattling. Eyeing Caralissa he growled, 'Girl, strip yourself naked before us. Arms extended and crossed. Now.'

Caralissa complied, unable to meet Telos' gaze. It was as this morning, only worse, for now she was betraying her open and easy submission to the horrid dungeon keeper. She wished to fight the impulse, and yet, how could she help herself? Drendel was ugly and foul, but he was a man, strong, elemental. And she was a female; weak, desirous, needful to obey.

Her knees trembling, her lips soft and open, Caralissa removed her dress. Gracefully, fearfully, she stood hands before her, wrists crossed, quite naked.

Caralissa saw the chains, dangling and gleaming in Drendel's hands as he fetched them from the worktable.

'You will not get away with this,' she promised Telos as the man began to lock her in the merciless bonds of steel.

'I already have,' Telos countered. 'I already have.'

Chapter Eight

For the next several days Caralissa led a double life; split, as it were, between two worlds. During the day, upstairs at her trial she was a politely demure defendant, silently sitting on a comfortable padded oak chair, the ever-leering Telos at her side. Meanwhile, by night she was an abject prisoner in the dank hole of her cell. Each morning, in order to effect the transition, Deelia was permitted to come to the dungeon to help her, cleaning her, perfuming her and helping her on with whatever particular gown Telos might choose for her to wear that day.

Not surprisingly they were all cut low at the bodice and tight at the waist. It was his special pleasure to sit beside her at the defence table gawking, his drool practically pouring onto her creamy breasts. During the trial itself she was not allowed to speak, except when asked questions by her lawyer. Moreover, she was to keep her hands in her lap at all times. This was especially challenging since Telos seemed not to know how to keep his hands off her to save his life.

At first it was infuriating and frustrating, especially as the man was so entirely childish, sneaking tiny opportunities to grope her breasts or rub his leg on hers. After a while she came to look on it as merely pathetic – an obvious sign of the man's weakness.

On two occasions he compelled her to take him in her mouth in a dark hallway during a recess. The first time she performed the act with such dispassion he was unable to complete his ejaculation. The second time she moved so quickly he spilled himself before he could derive any enjoyment. The one time he'd tried to lay with her in the judge's chamber she'd been as a corpse.

Her lack of emotion frustrated the man no end. If he were looking for her to betray herself before him, however, he would find himself sorely disappointed. As for the trial itself, she remained expressionless the entire time, reacting neither positively nor negatively to any of the testimony. Naturally the evidence was quite damning, the prosecution having secured endless bits of evidence of her sexual escapades since returning home.

Alinor was there, to testify to her reaction to the hairbrush on her buttocks and also concerning her wanton desire to be laid by him. Deelia provided her testimony – she sobbed the whole time, begging forgiveness from Caralissa over and over – as to the queen's pleasuring herself in her sleep as well as her erratic behaviour with regard to the bed sheets.

Trajor, in turn, was called to account for his time with her, though to his credit he remained largely closemouthed, despite frequent warnings of proceedings against him if he did not cooperate. After a long barrage of questions, with Telos being as hostile in his inquiries as was the grey-haired prosecutor, the warrior finally rose to his feet and walked out, declaring that they would have to cut him down where he stood to induce him to speak any further on the matter. They let him go and the next day he was gone for good.

There were also the so-called expert witnesses, men claiming to be skilled in the ways of the Rashal, offering to the court outlandish accounts of ritual Rashal sex acts that would abhor any civilised man. It was a farce of course, although she was quite surprised they were being this careful, amassing such a detailed case, albeit a specious one. Personally, she'd expected to be found guilty within the first hour. Norod, however, seemed intent on dragging things out, with endless minutiae.

Frankly she wished it would all end, for there was nothing in the trial or in Telos' behaviour that was so unnerving as the constant going back and forth to the dungeon; each emerging into the light of day for brief periods only to be returned once more to Drendel's dark little world with its thousand miseries. How she dreaded the return each evening to her cell! For starters, she was required to strip in Drendel's presence. The humiliation of undressing, unfortunately, did not diminish with repetition. Nor did the unwanted thrill she felt when the chains would be brought and she would be required to kneel on the cold stone floor to receive them. The routine was unshakable. First her hands would be shackled, the cold steel encircling her wrists as she placed her arms in front of her, head bowed low. Next would be the collar, with interconnecting chains that would fall directly between her breasts and thighs. At the other end of these were the ankle chains.

Her bondage was only the beginning. There were in the dungeon certain rules she must follow, rules that made her status as virtual slave indisputable. Under no circumstances was Caralissa permitted to rise to her feet unless commanded so by a guard. The occasions for standing were twofold. Number one, to be bound for a whipping or beating, and number two, to be bound for sexual usage. Otherwise she was to convey herself on all fours, head lowered, eyes continuously peeled for male boots, which she was required to kiss and lick whenever she encountered them.

Caralissa was always exhausted at the end of a day. Before she would be allowed to go to her cell, however, she must first crawl to Drendel so he might make use of her mouth. The dungeon keeper was fond of this ritual, especially as it contrasted so greatly with her position as queen – a fact that he delighted in reminding her of. Drendel generally expelled himself in her mouth. Afterwards she could not release him without permission. On one occasion he made her linger over him with her servile tongue till he re-hardened and achieved a second ejaculation.

After Caralissa paid obeisance through oral service she would be allowed to make known any needs she might have, assuming there were no other plans for her which might preclude this precious personal time. It was at this point that she could request to use the bathroom or perhaps beg for a small treat. The term 'bathroom', of course, was a euphemism, as she was required to relieve herself over a grate in a large common area full of chained prisoners, all male. There were also the guards who enjoyed watching her as she squatted.

The guards delighted in torturing her on these occasions, requiring her to caress her breasts as she peed. She dared not disobey, for she knew full well it was in their power to decide whether to simply use her themselves or turn her over to the inhabitants of one of the dank cells. Caralissa was quite diligent in seeking to appease the guards and proved to be for them a most arduous lover, for any omissions on her part were corrected with the whip.

If in the end she did not please them enough, or if they simply wished to be cruel, they would allow the prisoners a turn. Caralissa dreaded these times, not only for the horrible stench and the filthiness of these benighted, half-mad creatures, but for the terrible fact that she was helpless to resist these near animals. Even the dirtiest and most pathetic aroused her now and she could be heard to scream in pleasure at their slightest touch. It was as if day by day she was sliding deeper into something dark and irresistible, something in her soul which was less than human, and yet every bit female.

When not in use, Caralissa was kept in a damp cell with barely room for her to lie outstretched. Each night she endured this captivity. Upon her release shortly before dawn she would be required to observe another set of rituals, beginning with her crawling to kiss the feet of the Keeper Drendel. As a signal to rise, a whip would be tapped against the outside of her thigh, inclining her to straighten her back, prettily, obediently.

In this position, her mouth, breasts and sex were all open and available once more to the guards if they so desired, or any early morning visitors who might be present. Alinor made frequent morning stops, as did Remik and several of the council members, the ones she treated most harshly in her rule. Once she pleased the men sufficiently, performing whatever servile acts they might require, she would be allowed food, in the form of scraps for which she begged and licked, having learned quickly that her one bargaining chip was her own helplessly proffered body.

Caralissa sought to earn a good breakfast, for all too soon she would be dressed and returned to court to begin the cycle all over. With the passage of each day it grew harder to distinguish which part of her dual life was more real. At times it was the dungeon that felt like a dream, or rather a nightmare of chains and endless capitulation. And yet more and more this seemed to be her true reality, while her time in the courtroom upstairs, in the light of day, clothed and dignified, the picture of prim royalty, felt like a cruel illusion.

In any event it was with joy that she received the news from Telos towards the end of the second week that there was a 'sudden break' in the case and that, thanks to a plea of mercy on his part, Caralissa was to be allowed to make a full confession, after which she would abdicate the throne and receive her sentence. Telos required only her signature on a document to that effect. Naturally, he'd authored the confession himself.

As the terms were read she was put on her knees on the dungeon floor, Telos' stiff member jammed to the rear of her throat. It made no difference to her now what she might sign or what might happen to her. All she cared about was Romila, and how at last her greatly wronged and mistreated sister would take her rightful place on the throne.

Telos grunted as he expended himself down her gullet. 'There you have it, my dear. You need only scratch upon the dotted line and we shall be done with the matter.' He tossed the parchment paper upon Drendel's worktable.

'I will not oppose you,' she said, under his stalwart gaze.

Telos studied her where she lay exhausted at his feet, then shrugged. 'I must admit,' he confessed, drying his shrivelling member with a thick wad of her hair, 'my disappointment. Have we really broken you so easily?'

'My life is nothing,' she told him. 'I would have signed such a document from the beginning. I only ever wanted one thing in exchange.'

'And what might that be, my sweet?'

'My sister's safety. And the knowledge that she will be made queen, as is her right.'

Telos laughed dryly. 'You underestimate me again, my red-haired slut. Surely you can see I must remove both you and your sister if I am to become king? Guards!' he called out through the open doorway. 'Fetch prisoner number twelve!'

Caralissa felt a sickness in the pit of her stomach. She did not need to see the face to guess the identity of the mysterious number twelve.

'Ah,' Telos chortled as they brought her in. 'The grand reunion.'

Caralissa was allowed to rise, her balance shaky in the heavy chains. It was, of course, her sister who hung limply in the arms of a huge guard. Romila was in rags, wearing the remainder of a sheer undergarment torn at the left hip and at the bodice. Her lustrous black hair was loose, a wild tangle about her shoulders. She was barefoot and dirty.

'Romila,' she gasped, the tears welling in her eyes. 'What have they done to you?'

'Let them embrace,' Telos said, as they sought to keep the two apart. 'I am a sentimentalist at heart.'

Romila was shaking all over. Her eyes were full of fear. Despite her earlier bravado it was clear she lacked her sister's strength and imagination to endure her subjugation. 'Caralissa,' she said, her voice so very tiny. 'What have I done to us?'

'Romila has been our guest nearly as long as you have, my dear,' Telos explained, folding his arms across his chest. 'Though we've not given her the luxury of a cell. She is somewhat more inexperienced than you. I have taken the liberty of breaking her in personally. I keep her chained at the foot of my bed when she is not otherwise occupied.'

Romila lowered her gaze, her cheeks red with shame.

'You son of a bitch!' Caralissa screamed, lunging at Telos. 'I swear I'll kill you with my bare hands!'

She never reached him, having been seized immediately by a guard, her arms pinioned behind her.

'Really, Caralissa,' Telos sneered. 'I expected better

coming from you.'

She spat at him, falling far short of her target. 'And from you I expect nothing – nothing human, at any rate!'

Telos laughed. 'Always on your moral high horse, aren't you? Why don't you ask your sister what she thinks of me and my methods?' Snapping his fingers he called to Romila. 'Come girl, show your sister how affectionate you've become.'

Caralissa squirmed in the guard's grasp. 'No, sister, don't do it!' she cried, seeing how Romila was about to abase herself.

For a moment Romila hesitated, looking both to her sister and then to Telos. Finally, as he snapped his fingers again, calling her name more harshly, she jerked forward, traversing the distance step by step.

'Good girl,' Telos said smoothly, rubbing his hand over her head as she fell to his feet.

Caralissa felt a wave of pure nausea as she watched him put his hand to her sister's mouth, receiving from her a series of wet, servile kisses. Romila closed her eyes and trembled the whole time, as though fighting her own desires. It seemed a conditioned response. A trained reaction.

'Before her enslavement, your sister would never actually touch me. Did you know that, Caralissa?'

'You won't get away with this, Telos. My sister has committed no crime.'

Telos was busy running his pinkie finger over Romila's lips, inducing her to open them. The girl whimpered at first, clearly ashamed, but after a few seconds she opened her mouth and began to suck at his fingers.

'Your sister lacks your skills, Caralissa, and your natural whore's instinct, but she's not bad. And yes, I will get away with it. I told Norod she was kidnapped by your

Rashal friends and the old fool believed me.'

Caralissa would have ripped her own arms off to escape the guard's hold on her. In a heartbeat she would be at Telos' throat, squeezing the life out of him. 'By the goddess,' she vowed, 'you'll pay for this, I swear it!'

If only she possessed a man's strength – even half that of a Rashal warrior. Or for that matter, if she could but borrow a company of Varik's men so they might sweep down upon the castle and burn it to the ground. Better to see it in ruins than under the rule of Telos. As for the crown, she wished it did not exist. What good had it done her or her father or her sister? Let the Rashal destroy everything; let them build again from the ground up.

'Do you hear me, Telos? I curse your name.'

Telos ignored her threats, his lust-filled eyes focused exclusively on his hapless victim. 'She lacks your curvaceous form as well,' he observed, grabbing cruelly at Romila's small breasts. 'Then again, not all women can have the body of a slut.'

'Insult me all you like, Telos. Possess me, whip me, but leave her be. She is innocent. It's me you want.'

'You?' Telos snorted, pulling Romila to her feet and facing her in Caralissa's direction. 'What a vain little whore you are. What do you know of what I want? What do you know of true love? Romila, show your sister how much you love me. Show you sister your belly.'

Romila's eyes were vacant, downcast. Mechanically she lifted the hem of the torn, stained garment. Caralissa nearly cried out as she saw the whip marks, crisscrossing her stomach and breasts. Further down she was wet, her open vagina, primed for use. Like herself, Romila had become a man's plaything, nothing more.

'Oh, sister,' Caralissa wept. 'I'm so sorry. It's all my fault. It should have been me. I should have suffered in your place.'

'No,' said Romila, finding her voice. 'You shouldn't have.' Turning her head towards Telos, she asked, 'Sir, will you please release me, that I may go to my sister?'

The request was so mild, so servile, even Telos seemed taken aback. Wordlessly he complied with her desires.

Romila went to her sister.

'Release her,' Telos ordered Caralissa's guard.

Caralissa fell into her sister's arms. They both wept openly.

'Romila, I'm so sorry. I only wanted to help our kingdom.'

'Oh, Caralissa,' her sister cried. 'I am the one who should be sorry. I should never have allowed this to happen to you. I don't know what came over me.'

'It's all right,' Caralissa said at last. 'Now that I see you, I know it's all right. We love each other, that is all that matters.'

'How touching,' sneered Telos, yanking Romila by the hair and thrusting the blade of a dagger against her throat. 'Now sign the paper, Caralissa, or I will kill you both.'

Numbly, as if walking on air, Caralissa went to the table and picked up the quill pen.

'Good choice,' he told her as she showed him the completed signature. 'Now we can conclude this ridiculous trial and send that senile old fool Norod on his way. Guards, chain these two slaves from the ceiling. We won't be needing them for the time being.' He pointed to the huge man and to one other, a short fellow. 'You and you, do what you want with them for the day. Use your imagination and don't worry about getting in trouble. I sent Drendel on errands for the day.'

'But Telos,' Romila cried, tears in her eyes, 'I thought you loved me!'

Telos laughed cruelly. 'You expected me to waste my time on a skinny little bitch like you? Don't be ridiculous. You were valuable only when you might have become queen. Now you're just a slut like any other.'

'Please!' she cried. 'At least let my sister go! Caralissa won't harm you!'

'Neither of you will harm me, once Norod crowns me king.'

Telos laughed all the way to the stairs. Caralissa was trying desperately to comfort her brave sister but the guard was holding her fast, attaching her to the chain. In the end she could get no closer than a foot from Romila as together, arms pinioned overhead, they were chained on tiptoe, side by side, their bodies stretched wantonly.

'Oh, Caralissa,' Romila wept as her scant covering was torn away,' I am so ashamed. Telos made me do things; he made me want him. I could not help giving him…' Romila's voice trailed off as calloused fingers, thick as bananas, began mauling her breasts. With his other hand the guard flicked a thumb over her dark fleece, casually, insolently.

'We're going to play for a while, princess,' the hulking man croaked, the man who'd brought her in, his stinking alcohol-soaked breath in her ear. 'Doesn't that sound nice?'

She tried to turn her head away to avoid his kissing mouth. 'Please, just leave us alone,' Romila begged. 'What have we ever done to you?'

'Nothing,' he conceded. 'You did nothing, you and your stuck-up sister both, strutting your arses, flashing your tits, making us all hard and not a damned thing we could do about it.'

'Nothing at all,' echoed the second guard, a stocky fellow with a stringy beard who at the moment was occupied with Caralissa's nipples, pinching them between his smaller thumbs and forefingers.

'Just let them have what they want,' Caralissa gasped, her words a ragged string as she fought the mounting sensations. 'Come for them, and they won't hurt you any more.'

'Get away!' Romila shrieked, ignoring her sister as she squirmed to avoid her tormentor's liquor-saturated kisses.

'You have to know how to handle 'em,' the stocky fellow advised. 'Observe my technique.'

Caralissa saw stars. He was ratcheting up the pressure, sending shooting sensations down the front of her.

'Kiss me, queenie,' he told her, leaning in malevolently, one hand at her crotch. Desperately Caralissa gave him her mouth, allowing him to plunder it with his tongue. 'There, you see?' he bragged, releasing Caralissa's throbbing nipples. 'She's nice and easy. Yours will be just the same.'

Caralissa felt herself flood at the casual mention of her subservience, her nonexistent virtue. It shamed her deeply to react this way in front of her own sister.

The big man muttered an oath. 'Why do I always get the frigid bitches?' he complained.

'Why not switch?' the other offered jovially.

'I'd be much obliged,' the giant said.

The stocky fellow hooked his thumb inside Caralissa's vagina and pressed hard enough to get her attention. 'You be nice to my friend, understand, queenie?'

'Yes,' she whispered out of reflex, 'master.'

Caralissa let the new man kiss and fondle her, giving him appreciative little moans as well as the full effect of her curvaceous body, as much of it as she could move in her present bound state.

The man's belly and shoulders heaved. He was red-faced, hard and hot. Scrambling to undo his trousers, he plucked between his legs to expose his member. Puffing and snarling he fed himself inside her. She was wet, of course, and completely open. She thought he might have a heart attack as he rutted at her. Trying to forget her own predicament she looked over to her sister. The stocky fellow, obviously the cleverer of the two, retrieved a leather drink pouch from his pants. Unscrewing the top he put the bottle to Romila's lips.

'Drink,' he said menacingly. 'Or it won't be my cock you'll have to slake, it'll be a bullwhip.'

Romila looked at him wide-eyed, as if waiting for him to tell her it was all a joke. Would that it were! Alas, she knew in her heart it was only the beginning of an intended life of slavery and degradation, one that would reduce the sisters to cringing beasts, scarcely recognisable as human beings. Pinching her eyes shut against the tears she thought of Varik even as she addressed her terrified sister. 'It's okay, Romila,' she lied. 'Just drink, it'll do you good.'

Romila parted her lips, allowing the man to press the mouth of the pouch to them. She sputtered, but managed to take down a large gulp anyway. The stuff seemed to calm her almost immediately, which was just as well, for the man was behind her now, opening his trousers, taking careful aim in the furrow of her cheeks.

Romila cried out briefly, but as he began to thrust his way in and out with increasing vigour she grew strangely silent. How Caralissa wished she knew what was going on in her sister's mind. Was she coping, preparing to yield, or would she succumb to madness?

'Do you like that?' the big man asked Caralissa, having stroked himself back to life. 'You want more?'

Caralissa bit her lip. 'Just be quick about it,' she pleaded. 'For my sister's sake.'

The big man moved behind her. Without preamble he

cleaved her buttocks, forcing himself into the narrower of her two channels.

'Quick is his middle name,' the other man grunted, his own loins being fully immersed in the sweet womanhood of Romila.

'At least I get off in the end,' the big man laughed good-naturedly.

The jibes seemed to spur them both on. A few more minutes of sweating and grunting and they were done, both of them. Without saying another word they turned on their heels and left. The two girls stayed like that for a long time: silent, alone, suspended in chains with nothing to do but wait.

'Just a while longer, Romila,' Caralissa encouraged. 'Just hold on and help will come. Just wait, Romila. Wait and see.'

If her sister heard her, she wasn't sure, but after a long time of sobbing Romila seemed to hang more peacefully in her bonds. Caralissa hoped she'd managed to fall asleep. Chances are it would be the only rest Romila would get for a long time to come. As for herself, she would bide her time. There was nothing Telos could do to her now that would shake her hope in Varik.

'Let him come,' she whispered, 'let him come soon. And if he cannot come then at least allow me to go on believing he will. For if I cannot believe then surely I will die.'

Caralissa knelt, her head to the marble floor, awaiting the arrival of the king. She was naked and it was his intention this morning to share her body with yet another company of his troops. This latest indignity was just one more heaped upon her by the poseur, the fraud Telos. It was three days since the conclusion of the trial. By Norod's verdict, she was now a slave in the castle, while Romila was to be sold at auction to a pleasure-house. Her sister had fainted upon hearing her sentence, much to Telos' delight. Personally, Caralissa would have preferred the pleasure-house; at least then she would be gone from this horrid place, and from the sight of the man she so despised.

The new king, of course, was delighting in his victory. His usage of her body was almost constant and he allowed her only a few hours of rest each day. When not actually beneath him she was forced to endure spankings, whippings and long periods of bondage. In addition he employed castle guards and soldiers whom she was required to pleasure on a regular basis. It was reaching the point where her brief respites chained by the neck to the foot of the man's bed were a comparative diversion, an opportunity for peace and quiet.

Mostly during her ordeals she thought of Romila, distracting herself by trying to convey good thoughts to her sister. The two had been separated since their sentencing, and presumably the stoic Romila was long gone by now. Caralissa could only imagine what it was like for her; prayers on her behalf to the goddess were on her lips almost constantly. The only reassurance she felt – and this was small to be sure – was that her sister shared her blood and would therefore likely find pleasure in her treatment to at least a small degree.

For her own part, she did her best to appear neither pleased nor displeased with what was done to her. Although she could not avoid screaming her pleasure when possessed, she did manage to restrain her temper at his cruelties such that Telos derived little satisfaction from owning her. She knew it was a fight he wanted, and therefore she vowed never to give it to him.

Unable to hide his own emotions, Telos was growing

more and more furious at her lack of defiance. She herself drew great joy seeing him so thoroughly confounded. Having a weak personality to begin with, it must have been eating Telos alive to see her so indifferent. In order to outwit her he devised trials to elicit what he hoped would be uncontrollable responses on her part. This morning, for example, she was to orally please twenty cavalry troops as they stood in a line.

She heard their marching feet before she saw them. The boots tromped past her, each set representing yet another organ she must take between her lips. There was a trumpet's sound, first to signal the closing of their ranks, the second to mark the arrival of the king. It was a great flourish, a cavalcade of nonsense that would have disgusted her father. Leave it to Telos to need to have his ego fed so lavishly.

At long last the order was given and Caralissa went to work. Rising to her knees she went from man to man, inserting each to maximum depth, exerting upon them the sweetest pressure, allowing her mouth to be a dream of pleasure. There was no flavour to the men, no scent, for she blocked out such things now.

It was a matter of sheer mathematics as she counted twenty shafts with their spurting hotness. Twenty times was her mouth breeched, twenty times did she induce a climax and drink it down. Telos observed everything, following her and calling her names the entire time, seeking to compound her shame. Afterwards he put her on her back, pressing his booted heel down on her stomach.

'How much sperm is inside you, your majesty?' he demanded, employing her former title to maximum effect.

She gave no reply. Splayed as she was, her vagina soft and wet, her arousal thick in the air, what could she say? Using only his foot he made her orgasm then, her body spasming upon the floor. It was a degrading way to be had and naturally the sated soldiers were invited to stay on as witnesses.

'Whore,' he snarled at her, spitting upon her face when he was done. 'Go now and kiss the feet of every one of those men. Thank them for using your whore's mouth!'

She considered correcting him, pointing out that she could not be a whore, as prostitutes receive payments for their sexual acts, while she received nothing, save her life and the incidental privilege of sleeping on his floor and eating occasional scraps of food from the hand of one or another of her possessors. There seemed however little point to making this distinction as it would only earn her a beating.

'Yes, master,' she told Telos. Upon hands and knees, crawling from man to man, she kissed and licked the boots of each, thanking them humbly.

'Here, girl,' Telos snapped his fingers when they were gone. Caralissa crawled to him, weak and weary. He told her she would now have to clean the floor, to remove the filth of her sexual antics. That they had sported with her on only a few square feet of space was of no import, Telos said. She would clean the entire floor, if it took her all day. And if she complained, well then there would be no need to give her a scrub brush, would there? Not when she could use her body as a cleaning implement.

Telos waited, clearly hopeful he'd at last raised her unquenchable ire. Alas she disappointed him again. Putting her head to the floor, hair spread out about his feet, she replied, without an ounce of sarcasm, 'If master wishes, this slave will clean the floor with her tongue or with her tits.'

Her response seemed to silence him. Without another word he stormed off. A few moments later the steward arrived to inform her that she was to scrub not the small antechamber, but the very walls of the castle itself. Had she any emotion left she might have cried to see the thirty-foot high wall, craggy and filthy made of huge cut stones, and her alone, naked, in the hot sun, with only a small bucket of suds and a tiny brush. Could there be a more cruel or more futile task?

She worked for the better part of an hour, with no end in sight. She'd done barely a fraction of the surface area by then, and her water was already so filthy she was accomplishing little more than the transport of dirt from one place to another. She was just as filthy, and covered in sweat as well. Clearly she would never make it. She would not, however, give him the satisfaction of abandoning her work. Never would he have an excuse either to punish her or to gloat over having reduced her to total failure. She was better than him and stronger, and she would prove it.

Besides, Telos was a usurper, a tyrant, and such men always got their comeuppance, even though it might be slow in coming, even though it might take years of suffering on the part of their victims. However long, she would wait. And if death came first, then from beyond the grave she would still wait.

'What takes you so long, my queen?'

Caralissa stiffened. Telos was behind her, his sickening voice all too obvious in her ears. 'Forgive me, master. This slave serves as best she is able,' she replied, continuing her work.

Telos placed his booted foot between the backs of her legs, forcing her to separate them. 'You are the picture of obedience as usual,' he observed. 'Forgive me if I am suspicious of your motives.'

'Slaves have no motives. No thoughts, no rights, no feelings either.' She resisted the urge to shudder with revulsion as he poked his gloved finger into her open loins.

'Spoken with true and humble devotion. But we both know better in your case, don't we?'

Caralissa heard the sound of leather slipping through the air. 'I do not understand, master.'

The belt struck her buttocks with surprising force. It was not like the whip, but still it was enough to make her wince.

'Do not stop your work,' Telos commanded.

A second blow followed the first. Caralissa continued to scrub.

'If you wish to,' he offered, 'you may cry out or beg for mercy.'

She stooped to dip the brush in the water. 'Master is generous.'

'I am thinking of selling you, you know.'

Caralissa maintained the rhythm of her scrubbing, rising on tiptoes to reach a particularly troublesome spot. 'Oh?'

'Yes.' He let the belt lightly touch her heated skin, allowing the leather to make contact with her legs and sex. 'Does the prospect frighten you? The idea that some stranger would have total power over you, your very body and life, and that you would have no say even in how he looked or whether he was kind or anything?'

She smiled grimly, knowing he was baiting her. 'As master wishes.'

Telos grabbed her waist. 'I want to know what you think,' he breathed hotly in her ear. 'And I know ways to make you talk that don't involve the whip or belt.'

Caralissa drew a deep breath. It was true there was another way. But what he might obtain by it would mean nothing.

'You have a delicious body, Caralissa,' he observed, piercing her with his exposed cock. 'It is a pleasure to own you.'

'Yes, master,' she sighed, pressing her breasts against the wet stones as he increased his pace.

'Although I find your name a bit long now, a bit unwieldy for a slave. Have you any suggestions for a better one?'

She shivered as he paused, the ridge of his cock pressing her clitoris. 'No, master.'

He shoved himself hard. 'Hmm,' he noted, 'what did the Rashal chief call you? Or didn't he give you a name while he was using you?'

She shook her head. That was a secret. She couldn't be made to reveal such a thing.

'Tell me,' Telos demanded, reaching round to seize her nipples in a way fraught with pleasure and pain. 'Tell me now.'

'Little Flame!' she cried, her voice breaking apart.

Telos snorted. 'Little Flame? Well isn't that sweet. Coming from a Rashal butcher. Personally, I prefer something simpler. Don't you agree?'

'Yes,' she whimpered, miserable and broken, 'master.'

Telos made a suggestion for a name, as vulgar as it was coarse.

Caralissa reddened. After this morning even she had to admit it was appropriate.

'I'll take your silence to be acquiescence. Actually, though, I think just plain 'Cara' might be good. Shorter, easier on the tongue. Yes, Cara it is.'

She pictured him calling her that, shaming her with the diminutive of her own name, employing it as a mere slave appellation. 'Please, master,' she begged, 'may I come?'

Telos withdrew his stabbing shaft. 'May who come?'

'May Cara come,' she corrected. 'Please, master, Cara begs to come.'

He watched her, noted her writhing, the helpless

twitching motions of her back and buttocks. Deciding to torture her further, he said, 'And why should the King of Orencia be bothered giving pleasure to a slave? Do you insult his majesty?'

'No, master,' she thrust her buttocks towards him. 'The slave Cara begs the king to use her unworthy body, to shoot himself deep within her.'

'Will the slave Cara be pleasing to me, then?' he asked, as though she were some person entirely new to him.

'Yes, oh yes. She is hot, majesty, and delicious, by your own words.'

'Do not use my own words against me,' he warned. 'I shall be the judge of your quality. For now I command you to fall naked upon your belly.'

Caralissa, now Cara, obeyed instantaneously, feverishly lowering her smooth stomach down onto the dirt as his feet. The surface of it was cool and gritty on her thighs and breasts and cheek.

Telos fell upon her, reclaiming the channel only recently vacated. 'Now,' he hissed, finally feeling himself to have the upper hand. 'Tell me what you really think of me. No more lies!'

'I hate you,' she wailed, unable to hold back the words. 'I despise you.'

'And yet I am within you; and you yourself begged for me to be there.'

'Yes!' she cried, hating herself far worse than him. 'I have betrayed myself and my people both.'

'But you need to be taken, do you not? Even on your belly, on the ground for all to see, with a man you hate, who makes you scrub your own castle, who reduces you to servitude, a man who prostitutes your body and that of your sister – even from such a one, you still need it.'

217

'I do,' she cried, the confession pouring forth from deep in her soul. 'I am a slut, a woman who has lost her honour!'

'Women have no honour,' he corrected. 'Women exist to please men and for no other purpose.' He pressed her harder, pointedly. 'This is what you are, Cara. For all your beauty and power and privilege, this is what you were made for. Admit it.'

She grit her teeth, wincing. Yes, he was right, but it was not for him, but for Varik that she was made. It was to him she wished to yield; to him she desired to give her body and heart, to submit to his pleasure, his discipline, his incredible love. 'Please,' she gasped. 'Please no more.'

'No more?' he fumed. 'Do you reject your king?'

Telos retracted his hips, making room enough to smack her buttocks with his bare hand. The blow was petty, but under her current circumstances the stinging contact was maddening. Her sweat-covered body filthy on the ground, she groaned low and deep. Twice more Telos repeated the procedure, interspersing the blows with long, mind-churning thrusts.

Caralissa whimpered, mewling for her release, begging all over again for him to finish her off. She was beside herself, beyond reason. There was no limit now to what she'd promise to him, to what she'd offer to make of herself to achieve release. Thankfully Telos too seemed to be on the brink. His endless chatter ceased as he focused on his having of her. Pushing his hands onto the small of her back he positioned himself for his maximum pleasure. Liquid splashed her shoulder blades. She identified it as the man's drool, running in a line from the corner of his mouth. He was muttering obscenities, blithering to some god or other. She could feel him swelling, readying himself to explode.

She nearly fainted when it came, a rushing torrent down into her womb, her soft body cushioning him as he fell onto her, his energy dissipating. Without asking permission she climaxed with him, though hers was an act not of conquest but of utter abasement and submission, a perfect counterpoint to his own selfish grasping. Repulsed and desperate at the same time, Caralissa screamed and cried out, making clear to any in the vicinity that she was indeed Telos' slave now, the slut of his loins.

'You are improving,' he said, with a final grunt, the insulting compliment delivered along with a tongue slobbering of her ear. 'It is too bad I am going to be selling you anyway.'

She heard the words from deep within her cocoon. She could no longer care or react or move. Telos had won. Whatever reserve of strength was left, whatever pride, it was somewhere far away. Somewhere she would have to rediscover. In her dreams, perhaps, whenever they might resurface.

She only prayed that her new master or masters, whoever they might be, would not discover them first and exploit them, chalking them up as part of her purchase price.

'Clean me off,' Telos commanded, compelling Caralissa to lick her own juices from his rapidly diminishing cock. Caralissa obeyed, though she knew it would only serve to arouse him again, thereby insuring her ongoing violation. What choice did she have? She was a slave now, no longer queen, no longer free.

'That's it,' he encouraged as he swelled within her warm mouth. 'Take it down take it all. It will be good practice for your auction tomorrow.'

Caralissa moaned. He was going to sell her in front of strangers, to the highest bidder.

'That's right, my little slut. An auction. You and your sister both. Naked, completely naked.' Telos reached between her legs, found her wet. 'You like that, don't you?' he chortled.

She shook her head vigorously but he only laughed all the harder, smearing the glistening evidence across her cheek.

Caralissa closed her eyes, telling herself for the millionth time it was not her fault. She was not a slut; she was neither enjoying nor desiring her own conquest. She was being forced, being made to respond to mechanical impulses only.

It was a lie, of course, but one she must perpetuate. How else could she endure, except that she pretended to still be a lady? Were she to truly accept the slavery of her heart and live it out there would be no hope left, no chance to ever again see the ones she loved, for Telos would have won, would have eliminated her spirit.

Hope. There was hope. If for no other reason than that Telos had let slip that Romila was still in the castle and that she would see her tomorrow. At their auction.

Chapter Nine

Cara the slave girl knelt naked in her chains watching the makeshift stage, a wooden platform hastily erected in the castle grounds. As this exact moment the naked Romila was being made to spread herself painfully wide upon it. She was on her back, her hips raised as the crowd full of strangers cheered wildly. Sweat covered her body, along with fresh red welts from the auctioneer's whip, the lash having induced her ready cooperation with his commands, lewd and disgraceful as they were.

The need to display her thusly was understandable, of course, considering that Romila was being sold as a pleasure-house girl, a woman whose value would consist solely in her ability to arouse men through her own subjugation and degradation. She must not only know how to submit, but how to arouse men in the process. Could she make them hard by prostrating herself to their whips, by throwing herself to their feet to be beaten and taken? Could she drive them half mad with desire, begging with her bound body and eyes to be abused at their hands in the pleasure rooms?

The auctioneer was most brutal in his appraisal. He told the audience that he felt she was too thin, too frigid and inexperienced. Cheeks red, tears streaming down her face she was made to display herself, in all her imperfections. Twice she was brought to orgasm by hand, and even here her deficiencies were fully noted. Caralissa would have strangled the man if she could. He had no right to wound her pride this way. Then again, Romila was a slave now and as such she had no right to her pride or to any identity at all, save that thrust upon her by a master.

'What am I bid?' the man roared, his head cloaked in black cloth as he slashed across Romila's vulnerable belly.

Caralissa winced, as though struck herself. Were she able she would take all of Romila's pain. But there was nothing she could do, save wait her own turn on the stage, and her own fate.

A number was called out, none too high.

The auctioneer displayed shock. 'But lords and ladies,' he said. 'Surely she is trainable?'

Romila was pulled up onto her knees, the man's hands in her hair. Using the back of his whip as if it were a penis, he thrust it between the lips of the stunned girl, forcing her to take it deep. She gagged, fighting the sensation of the leather. The auctioneer was relentless, moving it in and out. Romila's hands were over his, ineffectively trying to stop the assault.

'Put your hands down,' the man ordered. 'Down, and between your legs.'

Romila went pale, her eyes desperate. She tried to shake her head, to resist, but his gaze was like iron. After a few seconds of feeble protest Romila did as she was told, commencing to masturbate, it shamed her greatly though it proved a boon to the bidding.

Higher and higher numbers were shouted as the girl awkwardly pleasured herself, all the while servicing the whip handle with her soft and gurgling mouth. At the peak of her shuddering a phenomenal price in gold was announced, and the auctioneer drew the bidding to a close. Shaken, stunned, Romila was removed from the stage, her body thrust into the hands of a dark-robed man, his face veiled.

Romila's owner. Or her owner's agent. Either way, she

was now sold, Caralissa thought in amazement. Her sister's body, her person, her very being now belonged to someone else, a stranger. A pleasure-house owner, if Telos' earlier threat were made true. In which case she would be put on display, compelled to serve drinks and to have sex with an endless number of strangers on a nightly basis, earning for herself little more than the amenities one might grant a household pet.

As they dragged Romila away, a heavy chain now secured to her neck, Caralissa despaired of ever seeing her sister again. What good were all her hopes, what good in the face of steel chains and whips and men who paid money for females, bidding on them as if they were horses or dogs? What good when it was now her turn to perform, to be assessed and sold?

'Your sister did better for us than we'd hoped for,' the auctioneer whispered, helping her delicately up the platform steps, her bare feet pressing gingerly on the wood surface. 'Which means we expect all the more from you.'

Caralissa reached the top step. They allowed her to wait a moment there as they hauled up the large contraption. It was quite simple in design. A flat base, covered in some sort of thick material some fifteen feet square, and in the centre a vertical spike-like object, tapering into a rounded knob, smooth and ebonite. There were gales of laughter as the men set it in place. The thing was nearly a foot and a half high and very much the shape of a man's shaft.

Caralissa turned pale. Its purpose was all too obvious.

'Do exactly as I say,' the man commanded, releasing her from the shackles and seizing her left breast. 'And be quick about it. Any trouble from you and I won't be dainty with the lash the way I was with the other little slut. Understand?'

Caralissa nodded, her sensitive nipple cruelly twisting

in the man's grip.

'I hope so,' he growled, pushing her down by the neck till she was on all fours. 'For your sake.'

His first command was for her to crawl upon the base and kiss the shaft. Upon closer inspection she saw it was a perfect representation of a penis, though far longer than any she'd seen in real life, even among the cavalry officers.

'Rub your tits on it,' he barked.

Caralissa put her firm breasts against the cool, seamless material. Closing her eyes she released a tiny moan. She could imagine the things that were coming next, the things she'd have to do before these men. They were sickening things, and yet she was aroused nonetheless. What a slut she was!

'Squeeze your tits around it. Move them up and down. Faster. Faster.'

She wrapped the shaft in her soft flesh, pleasuring it there as though it were inside one of her other openings. In order to get close enough she was required to kneel up and spread her legs on either side of it. It was a hard material, but flexible nonetheless. The feel of it was making her hot, making her need to do things, sexual things. And yet she'd have to await his orders, no matter how long he made her wait.

'Put your cunt to it, now,' he said, punctuating the request with a slash of the whip across her back. 'Juice yourself.'

Caralissa cried out as she thrust herself forward so that her sex was in direct contact, lengthwise. She shuddered as she slid herself up and down, tentatively. The fragrance of her arousal was heavy. Shutting her eyes against the sea of faces, she began to yield.

A bid was called. The number was respectable.

'Remember, gentlemen, lords and ladies, this is the

former queen. Would you not like to own her? To have her body to caress or beat, to put to your every whim?'

More bids; he was prickling their interest.

'Put your mouth down over the top of it,' the man told her, laying a stripe across her buttocks. 'Hands behind your neck.'

Caralissa obeyed, linking herself by mouth to the shaft. She did not need to be whipped another time to know she must suck. She had to put her chin to her chest to take in the top of it, though once achieved it was a wondrous sensation. Dirty, disgusting, and yet very pleasurable. The shaft was like a lover. She was fused to it now, from her face down to her delta. It was a clever device, diabolical yet brilliant. She'd thought the design awkward at first, but she realised its nefarious purpose. For even as she felt the need to rub her clit faster and faster against the side, she found herself drawing the end deeper and deeper into her mouth.

Whimpering and mewling she deep-throated the thing like a demon, desperate to obtain the friction necessary to orgasm. Her motions, and the passion evinced by it, seemed to impress the buyers, for she was now at a hundred and fifty thousand, already ten thousand more than her sister's price.

'Look at her, friends. Have you ever seen such a natural slut? Which of you would not wish to be this lucky piece of *rauxite?*' he joked, naming the particular material from which the shaft was composed. 'Which of you would not like to train her to please you this way?'

Of course they all would; who in their right mind could resist the naked, aroused girl, subjugating herself, reducing herself in all their eyes to little more than a hot, sleek animal?

'What would you do with her?' he pressed, inflaming

their imaginations and libidos alike. 'Would you keep her naked, chain her to your bed, lock her in a cage, flay her each day with your whip? Or would you be more merciful, allowing her clothes, giving her tiny scraps of dignity so that you might have the pleasure of taking them back from her?

'Would you require her, with her mouth and cunt and arse to earn her scraps of food, her rags? Would you compel her to lay for passers-by, for friends and enemies, would you tattoo her skin to mark her forever or is there some other dream of yours, secret and untold?'

Romila's asking price was now doubled. Hands were flying fast in the air, men were wildly applauding and cheering. And it was all for her.

'Enough game playing,' said the auctioneer to Caralissa. It is time they see how well you can screw.'

The word 'screw' seemed apropos, for indeed that is exactly what Caralissa was forced to do, having to go up on tiptoe to fit herself over the end of the elongated shaft. She gasped as the auctioneer commanded her to squat and impale herself. The shaft filled her, making her throb with shame and need.

'You know what to do, slut,' he bellowed, treating her to another taste of the whip, this time across her belly. Caralissa did her best to move upon the thing, though it threatened to tear her apart. Sweat-covered, she began to writhe.

'Surely you would want to have this for yourself?' he proclaimed, shaming her even further by referring to her as an inanimate object. 'The flanks, the arse. The shattered remnants of her will as queen?'

Caralissa touched her hands to her heaving breasts. She was able to push the shaft deep, very deep. She was going to come and there was nothing that could stop her. The bids were rising. Three, four times the value obtained for her unfortunate sister. The man was shouting, touching her, making them laugh and cheer and bid.

On and on it went for what felt like hours, and then finally the man shouted, 'Sold!' and the auction was over. They pulled her from the shaft. A steel collar was put around her neck, connected to a long chain. She was dragged from the platform and across the courtyard to a waiting wagon. It was windowless, made of thick slats of wood. Unknown hands thrust her deep within and the door was locked behind her. A few moments later she heard the sound of a whip, the sound of men ordering horses forward.

The wagon was on the move. Dazed, stunned, in the dark, she lay upon the floor, feeling the vibrations of the road underneath. The reality was only just beginning to sink in. She had been sold. Separated from her sister and sold as if she were a common animal to the highest bidder. Everything she knew and loved was gone; an unknown place awaited her and an unknown life. Her face dotted with tears, the jarring road at last lulling her, she fell into a deep sleep, silent and dreamless.

She was still unconscious as they took her from the wagon many hours later. Taking her in the back way of the arched wooden structure, down the stairs and into the basement, the black-shirted men laid her upon the floor. The surface was rough, made of stone. Caralissa stirred but did not awaken.

'Douse her,' said a female voice, harsh and imperious.

Buckets of water were poured upon the sweat-stained girl, she spluttered at once, sitting up with a start. 'What are you doing?' she cried.

A whip cracked the air between her shoulder blades,

the tip singing her flesh. 'Silence, pleasure-house girl.'

She rubbed her eyes. Where was she? A slave keep, most likely. One of the locked chambers where girls were kept when not in use by customers. But which pleasure-house was it? Was she still in Orencia or had they crossed the border?

'She seems a bit skinny,' she heard the woman say. 'I'm not sure the customers will go for her.'

'She has the mystique of her former office,' said a male voice, deep and gruff. 'And she's passionate. At auction she stiffened every prick. My own included.'

'Spare me, Jolar,' the woman mused. 'A good breeze stiffens your prick.'

Caralissa beheld the pair. The woman was tall with long dark hair, jewel-green eyes and a veil that covered her lower face. She wore silk pantaloons and a vest. The man sported a pointed moustache and a long thin beard, terminating in a braid. He wore silk as well, a suit of green and lavender along with leather boots. The woman was shapely, her healthy bosom accentuated by a tight waist.

'Down, girl,' growled the man, noting Caralissa's gawking attention. 'Pay homage to your mistress, Lady Fira.'

The whip whistled through the air again, this time hitting her full in the back, she fell forward in pain, her palms bracing her as she fell to the stones.

'Crawl to us, slut,' Jolar ordered.

She obeyed, not being anxious to taste the lash any further. When she reached their feet, the man raised his foot, pressing the toes of his boots down upon her shoulder. He did not wish her on all fours but upon her belly. The stone was hard and cold, indenting her from chin to thighs.

'Behold the Lady Fira,' he repeated with great fanfare,

though at the moment Caralissa could see nothing but the floor. 'Proprietress of the Silver Veil. You are her property now, available for her and for her customers, howsoever they may wish to use you.'

Caralissa grunted in pain. The boot was hurting her whip-bitten back.

'Secure her hands behind her back,' said Lady Fira. 'Put her on her knees before me.'

Two of her men performed the task with lightning efficiency.

'Better,' Lady Fira nodded. 'Now we can talk.'

Caralissa strained her hands against the tightly wound leather thong. 'Where am I?' she demanded, determined to regain the upper hand.

Jolar looked at her in fury. Rearing back his palm, he was prepared to hit her with the flat of it.

'No,' Fira said, causing him to freeze instantly. 'I don't want her face marked.'

Jolar grumbled an apology – not to Caralissa but to the Lady Fira.

'I am sure Cara wants to be a good girl,' Fira said, taking a step forward, sliding her pantaloons down over her waist to reveal a glisteningly bare and shaved sex. 'Don't you, Cara?'

Caralissa felt nauseous. Fira was stepping from the pants and putting her crotch inches from her face. It was obvious what she was going to do, and the very idea of it made her sick.

'Have you ever tasted a woman, my dear?' Fira crooned with deceptive sweetness. Caralissa shook her head. Never. Not even in her dreams. 'You will taste me, Cara, or be lashed. The choice is yours.'

Caralissa locked her jaws. She'd never allow herself to do such a thing – never. She would die first.

'How dare you disobey!' cried Jolar, his voice rising an octave in pitch.

From behind came the inevitable, the whip cracking across her buttocks, hard enough to make her scream. Immediately Caralissa thrust her face into the woman's opening. The scent was deep and musky, the aroma almost overpowering. Tears grazed her cheeks as she began to move her tongue to find, as she knew she must, the deepest recesses of the woman's slick opening. Lady Fira shifted her hips, allowing Caralissa deeper access. The juices ran down Caralissa's chin and across the bridge of her nose. The others were watching, which made it all the more disgraceful... and also arousing. For between her own legs Caralissa was aware of the familiar moisture, the strange stirrings. She only hoped they would not notice and think worse of her. She was a civilised woman, a former queen. Even now, on her knees, slavishly servicing another female, licking and caressing her sex as though her mouth were a man's cock, she had her honour.

Honour was everything in a place like this. For so long as they imagined her to have some dignity, some sense of decorum, she could hope to avoid the worst of pleasure-house life. Even so, she knew it would not be easy. The endless parade of men, the acts, relentless and demeaning, night after night. How ironic to think she'd spent so many hours herself in pleasure-houses, watching in dreaded fascination, wondering with a morbid curiosity what it might be like to submit, to be owned and passed from customer to customer.

Caralissa's mistress moaned. It was the self-satisfied sound of a cat, a predator. Using her talon-like nails, Fira pressed Caralissa's face into the desired position. It was the clitoris, of course, that Caralissa knew she must find and pleasure. It was Varik who introduced her to this tiny wonder in her own body and he'd also been the first to exploit it, using its sensitivity to manipulate her into exquisite submissions.

She wished now that she'd had occasion to teach Romila a few things before they'd parted ways. It would be harder on her sister, much harder, if she did not know how to sufficiently please the patrons of her house, not to mention her master or mistress. It would be up to the goddess to keep her safe, she supposed.

'That's it, girl,' Fira croaked. 'My, but you have a gift.'

Although she did not wish to, Caralissa glowed at the compliment. It was a testimony to how far she had declined that such a remark might be taken well by her, as if she were naught but a slave, one whose sole purpose was to give pleasure.

Fira cried out, exclaiming her obvious joy. Holding Caralissa fast against her she began to rock, the juices pouring copiously till the hapless slave began to cough and sputter. Obediently Caralissa continued her ministrations till the woman's orgasm passed, a fiery peak over which she rode with reckless abandon.

At last Caralissa was released. Now if only she could have a little attention herself, she thought, to complete her own dangling climax.

Fira shoved her backwards. 'Place her over the horse,' she ordered. 'And bring me my shaft. I wish to sport with her some more.'

Sport with her some more? What on earth did that mean? And what sort of horse were they planning to bring inside the basement of a pleasure-house?

Jolar snapped his fingers, further delegating the action to two of the waiting men. The pair lifted Caralissa with ease, holding her by her bound arms as they dragged her across to the device. The thing consisted of a kind of horizontal tube with two sets of legs, set at sharp angles. They laid her across it on her stomach, pulling her arms down to cuffs that were attached to two of the legs. Her ankles were secured to the other two legs, also by cuffs. This accomplished, she was now quite exposed, head to the floor, legs spread, buttocks and vaginal opening easily accessible. Her breasts meanwhile were cruelly pressed against the sticky material that covered the tube, inducing her to clammy perspiration.

Caralissa grimaced. With her loins cleaved and her mouth and chin over the horse's front, she felt rather like an exposed tunnel, with two vacant ends.

It was Jolar who attended her first. 'You are no longer a queen, are you, girl?' he demanded, swinging a large wooden paddle against her quivering buttock cheeks.

'No,' she cried pathetically as the paddle slammed at her nerve endings. 'No.'

Jolar struck her again. 'What are you, then?'

It was Fira who provided her the correct answer. 'You are a pleasure-house slut,' she said, having moved to a place directly in front of her, arms at her hips.

Caralissa gasped as she saw what Lady Fira was now wearing, long and terrifying, attached to her waist by means of straps and a leather belt.

'Impressive, isn't it?' Fira asked, noting the horrified look as she beheld the ebonite shaft, fixed prominently as though it were a natural erection. 'We use it for practice. Today we are practicing on you.'

Caralissa began to struggle, trying to free herself. She could get no leverage and the shackles were strong and tight. The best she could hope to accomplish was to rock the entire structure hard enough to topple it over. Alas, it was too heavy even for that.

'What are you?' Jolar repeated, punctuating his repeated

question with another two blows of the paddle.

Caralissa winced. The paddle's sting was not like the pure fire of the whip, nor was it like a man's bare hand, but there was to it a cumulative effect, a kind of building heat that was rapidly approaching the point of flammability. 'I am a pleasure-house slut!' she cried.

'Very good,' Fira told her reassuringly, stretching her hand out to pat her head. Caralissa clamped her mouth shut. The shaft was approaching, and it was in line to ram between her lips.

Fira feigned surprise as the girl's resistant lips rebuffed its tip. 'Oh my, what have we here? Is Cara too much of a lady to sport with us?' Fira clamped Caralissa's nose shut before she knew what was coming. The prisoner whimpered helplessly. It was only a matter of time till she must gasp for breath, thereby leaving her mouth free to be plundered. Fira was patient, and the shaft was ever present. Cara feared she might pass out, but at last she closed her eyes and opened her mouth the tiniest bit, just for a second.

The artificial cock was thrust immediately to the back of her throat. Cara gagged, nearly retching. The thing was bigger than any man she knew, bigger perhaps than any man could be. Putting her hands on both sides of Caralissa's cheeks, Fira pumped herself in and out mercilessly. It seemed madness that she would do this given that the woman couldn't even feel pleasure from it, but apparently it served some purpose she did not understand.

'We need to get it good and lubricated with your spit,' Fira explained, 'so we can fit it in your arse next.'

Caralissa trembled and moaned in agonising despair, her eyes dotted with tears. Was there in this woman no pity at all?

Fira began to laugh, the sound rising like a high cackle. 'Do you smell that, boys?' Caralissa's invaded cheeks reddened, the scent of her arousal thick in the air. 'I think little Cara is enjoying herself,' the woman observed, shoving herself to the back of her mouth yet again. 'Are you not, slut?'

Caralissa tried to shake her pinioned head. No! A thousand times no!

'Don't lie to me,' Fira warned, pulling back on her damp hair. 'You do want it. You want this in your arse. Admit it.'

Fira removed the shaft. Caralissa was weeping. 'Yes,' she heard herself cry, her voice small and possessed, 'I do.'

The words were a fierce utterance, almost unearthly.

'Very well,' Fira said graciously. 'Jolar, you take my place while I accommodate our fine lady.'

Jolar grunted his affirmation, and Caralissa began to swoon as he put himself in place. The last thing she remembered was the dual sensation, a pressing on both openings. The two shafts, one artificial, one natural, wreaking their havoc, piercing her, body and spirit. The orgasms seemed to come at her from all sides, like cascades of water, an overwhelming flood. She thought she would die at that moment, die of pleasure, die of shame.

'Let us switch places,' she heard Fira say at last, and then she passed out.

234

Chapter Ten

Caralissa shrugged the hand from her upper arm – a tricky prospect whilst balancing the frothy tankards. The man was drunk, his attempt to grab her playful. Shouting something to his companion, who lay head down on the table next to him, he let her go, giving her thinly-covered bottom a healthy pat as she scampered past.

She couldn't object of course, as the man had every right to do with her as he pleased for as long as he wished. The customers awaiting their ale might have been annoyed but there was no question of her having any say in the matter. Caralissa was a pleasure-house girl. She belonged to whoever laid coins upon the table for her use.

A few tables down there was a fight. She narrowly avoided a plummeting body as she passed. Her own customers were a pair of merchants. Setting the beverages down she hoped to make a quick exit, but it was clear they had other intentions. Making her turn about they lifted her short silk skirt to examine her nether aperture.

'Are you good and tight, girl?' the one asked, a chubby, bearded fellow with a turban.

'Yes, sir,' she replied, thinking it the safest answer.

The other man, a hook-nosed fellow with thick eyebrows, stuffed his finger up her for good measure. They both laughed when she yelped. Caralissa squirmed on bare feet. She was essentially naked, the covering she wore being a sleeveless low-cut cloth garment with no underclothes.

'What took so long with our orders, slut?' asked the fat

one, caressing her thigh.

'She was probably off flashing her tits to some handsome soldier,' mused the hooknose, taking a large swallow of his ale.

'Sirs, forgive me, I—'

The fat one seized her arm. 'We'll teach you to be insolent,' he interrupted as he threw her across his lap.

'Please,' Caralissa cried in vain as he raised the cloth and began to spank her, 'I didn't do anything!'

'Careful, Minak,' the hooknose countered, 'or she'll juice all over your robes; you know how hard the stains are to remove.'

Minak slammed his hand down, making her cry out. 'Then she'll bloody well be whipped, won't she, Torano?'

Minak continued his relentless assault whilst Torano said nothing. There was in Minak's hand neither sweetness nor love, only punishing blows. Hating herself for her weakness, Caralissa began to cry.

Noting the flow of tears, Minak yanked her to her feet. 'Oh, for pity's sake, if it's not one stain on me it's another! I really will have to beat you now!'

'Later, Minak,' Torano said. 'There's something else she needs to do first.'

Caralissa watched him fumbling at the belt on his robes, feeling herself reddening. The man wouldn't make her do something here, would he, out in the open? She'd only been working three days but to her knowledge sexual acts were allowed only in the pleasure rooms.

'Sir, I don't think this is permitted,' she protested meekly as Torano revealed an enormous member.

Minak shoved her down and forward in the relevant direction. 'Oh, be silent, whore. You are boring us.'

Caralissa landed on her knees, and Torano's slender fingers were at her head at once, positioning her tearstained face. The floor was sticky and the man tasted sour, almost rancid. She doubted he had bathed in weeks.

'Hey, save some for us!' she heard a nearby fellow roar. Others were laughing, too. Tankards were pounding on the table. This was wrong, she thought. Surely someone would stop it before it was too late.

'Suck hard, little slut,' Minak proclaimed, speaking for his friend, whose head was back in slack-eyed ecstasy. 'We have powerful friends. Very powerful. Cross us and we'll send you some place that makes this stinking place look like paradise.'

Caralissa tried to keep her focus, but it was all beginning to blur in her head; the innumerable sex acts since her arrival, the degradation, the cruelties. One man left her chained from the ceiling for five hours while he lay passed out next to her on the floor. Thank the goddess he'd been too drunk to touch her with the wildly flailing whip he took from the rack on the wall.

Another man poured beer over her head so his brother could lick the foam off her breasts. On more than one occasion she'd been made to take customer's orders to the kitchen on her hands and knees so they could enjoy the sight of her wriggling buttocks. Seldom did she keep her clothing on for an entire evening. Some customers would demand she strip even before they would accept her as a waitress.

And of course there were the stares, the leers and endless probing eyes, letting her know in no uncertain terms what they planned to do to her later on. She'd been aching and sore at the end of each night, raw in every orifice. The cream, used to lubricate, was available, but it cost extra and few men desired to waste their money on the comfort of pleasure-house sluts.

'Try to enjoy it,' was Lady Fira's only advice. 'You'll

237

stay wet that way.'

Some of them would let her lubricate her anal passage with juices from her vagina. Even so, at the end of a shift she could barely stand. The mat on the floor in the basement, where she was allowed to sleep, neck chained to the wall, seemed like heaven to her tired body each time she lay down. She seldom stayed awake more than a few seconds after being chained in place. Sometimes the guards would use her in the middle of the night and then she'd have to wake up again.

Her allocated four hours of sleep a night flew by like the wind. How she wished to stay in bed longer each time, but there was no avoiding the predawn call to begin her labours along with the other girls who were responsible for scrubbing, cleaning and preparing the establishment for the next night's revels. Naked, under the eyes of an overseer, the girls would attend to their duties. It was at these times that she thought most often of Romila, wondering what her sister was doing at such an early hour, hoping she was in a better place, sleeping peacefully.

Caralissa felt Torano shudder inside her. It was reflex to draw out the sperm, to take it down into her empty belly. She hoped she pleased him. Customers were allowed to give treats to the girls if they felt they'd earned them. It was the only supper the wenches ever saw.

Lady Fira's theory was that needy girls were more attentive. As her chief aid, Jolar would give lectures to the girls to this effect as they ate their morning bowls of gruel, scooping out the contents with their hands. If they were lucky afterwards, Fira might call one or two of them to her chambers for the rest of the day. They'd be put through paces of course, made to submit to the woman's seemingly endless whims and her even larger supply of strap-on phalluses. Sometimes though, they might be allowed a little sleep too, either before or after, with Lady Fira clutching their leashes as they lay curled at her feet. Caralissa had been so summoned yesterday and when she was granted her turn in the bed – an actual mattress of feathers – she wept openly.

'A little nourishment for you, eh?' Torano winked, as Caralissa was finally allowed to come up for air. 'Good for the digestion, they say.'

Silently she fumed, even as they laughed together at her expense.

'Oh, cheer up,' Torano drawled. 'At least you didn't have to swallow Minak's cock. That thing looks worse than an over-pickled courgette.'

'To the demons with you, Torano,' Minak declared good-naturedly. 'Say, little whore,' he said, turning his attention to Caralissa who was till kneeling in front of them. 'How about a little treat?' Caralissa eyed the bit of shrimp freshly plucked from the heap on the man's plate. It was pink and succulent. Her eyes widened. Minak grinned malevolently. 'Sit up and beg for it, slut.'

Her lower lip began to tremor as she watched him dangle the seafood cruelly. She'd rather die than humiliate herself any further before these two, but she was so hungry. Who knew when she might get another chance to eat? And if she cooperated, she told herself, they might give her more food in the bargain.

Slowly, agonisingly, Caralissa put out her hands, cupping them. 'Please?' she mewed, making her voice as soft as possible. 'Please feed me.'

Minak guffawed. 'Oh, come on, you can do better than that!'

Torano wagged his tongue for her, holding out his hands like paws. 'Try it like this,' he suggested, simulating as he did the panting of a dog. Tears in her eyes, Caralissa imitated the degrading position.

Minak shook his head, still unsatisfied. 'Dogs wear no clothes,' he pointed out. 'Your performance is lacking in that regard.'

They watched as Caralissa lowered her eyes, reaching for the hem of the skimpy covering. In a single motion she pulled it overhead, baring her lithe body. Cheeks red now, her sex throbbing, she repeated the gesture.

Like a pet, she thought – naked and begging for scraps.

Minak sighed, appearing to consider. 'Maybe, but let me see you play with your tits first.'

Caralissa cupped her warm breasts. Her already erect nipples pulsed beneath her palms.

'You'd do anything for this shrimp, wouldn't you, slut?' Minak sneered as she rubbed her hands slowly, helplessly over her firm mounds.

'Yes,' she whispered shamefully.

'Spread your legs, then.'

Caralissa widened her knees, exposing her soft, glistening nether lips.

'Taste yourself,' Minak ordered.

As if in a dream Caralissa lowered her head, her hands and fingers brushing the moist opening, collecting a healthy sample. A moment later she was sucking, her fingers deep in her mouth.

Minak looked at her, eyes glowing. 'Stand up, slut.'

Caralissa did so, her belly at the level of his fat waist. She watched as he took the bit of sea meat, pinched between his thumb and forefinger and held it in front of her. Still grinning, he pressed it deep inside her, between her legs. Slowly, very slowly, he twisted it, allowing it to soak up her juices.

'Use only your mouth,' he said casually as he extracted

the shrimp and threw it to the floor at her feet.

Caralissa hesitated only a moment before getting down on all fours, lowering herself to the ale-soaked wooden surface. Daintily, using her teeth and tongue only, she seized the little piece of meat. It tasted of her own saltiness and the staleness of beer. Greedily she swallowed it down.

She hoped the worst was over now, but as she tried to raise her head she found she could not move. Minak's foot was there, on her fan of hair, pinning her in place. Panic gripped her. She was trapped, cheek to the floor.

'Oh, how clumsy I am!' Minak exclaimed sarcastically as he began to pour his drink slowly and deliberately on the floor next to her. The rivulets of ale were landing a mere inch from her head, the spray splashing up to soak her face and hair. 'Lick it up,' he told her. 'Every drop.'

Caralissa sobbed silently as she extended her tongue, reluctantly, half-heartedly, onto the disgusting surface.

'Harder!' Minak demanded.

'No,' she heard a male voice say. 'That is enough.'

Caralissa's heart jumped. That voice – was her mind playing tricks on her or could it be him?

'Are you addressing me?' Minak asked. 'I certainly hope not, for your sake.'

'Yes,' the man responded, very tall, his face and body disguised behind a black hooded cloak. 'I am addressing you. Let the girl go.'

Minak growled from low in his throat. 'See here,' he said, his voice suddenly agitated, 'you are obviously a stranger and probably from some other world because you obviously do not know that I am Minak, the foremost?'

'I do not need to know who you are,' the man replied as he stepped across Caralissa to grab the huge man by the collar of his robes, 'to know that you are rude and

241

disrespectful.'

'Let me go!' he squealed, feet kicking foolishly in air as the stranger lifted him clean off his feet.

'Now see here,' Torano began, his voice high-pitched and nervous. 'If you think you can just?'

'Get out,' the man said to Torano. 'Both of you.'

Caralissa knelt up, beholding the mysterious, powerful interloper. It was Varik. It had to be. And yet what would he be doing here and alone?

'Never mind, Torano,' Minak said hastily, having been set down on his feet once more. 'We shall deal with this man in our own time.'

A blade was drawn smoothly and cleanly from a scabbard slung across the newcomer's back. The tip of it was brought to rest a millimetre from Minak's throat.

'Do not make threats, merchant,' the man said, 'that you do not intend to keep.'

Minak's eyes popped nearly from his head. Sweat was pouring from his forehead. 'Please,' he whimpered, 'we meant no offence. Let us go about our business and we will trouble you no more.'

'We will never return to this place again,' added Torano. 'We swear it!'

The man's eyes looked deeply into those of Minak, the sword still in place. A second later a puddle appeared on the floor at the huge man's feet. The man blanched red in shame.

'Go,' the stranger repeated, replacing the sword in its scabbard. 'Now.'

Torano and Minak nearly demolished each other in their race for the door.

Caralissa was overwhelmed; she wanted to laugh and cry at the same time. She wanted to embrace this man and thank him. But there was something else she needed to do first. Grabbing his arm, looking up into the darkened shadow of his cloaked face, on tiptoe, she asked, 'Varik, is it you?'

'Be silent, woman. And follow me.'

A wide path was formed for the cloaked man, as girls and men alike stepped warily from his way. Caralissa hoped he might lead her out the front door, but alas he led her directly back to one of the pleasure rooms.

'Wait here,' he said, when she was inside.

She stood there in the dark, heart thumping, trying to discern if she was crazy or if she was really being rescued by the chieftain of the Rashal.

A few moments later he returned with a clean towel, dampened. 'Wash yourself,' he told her, tossing the thick cloth.

Numbly, Caralissa wiped the towel over her stained face. It was a guest towel, a privilege ordinarily denied to pleasure girls. For her part, ever since her arrival, her body had been allowed to touch nothing but rags.

'Who are you?' she asked, as he drew the curtain closed behind him.

'Turn your back to me,' he said. 'And put yourself on all fours.'

Caralissa's knees were so weak it was hard to obey, hard to keep from collapsing at the man's feet. His power was so overwhelming. Who was this man? The voice was right, but the solitary figure so silent and gracious was a mystery. If he wasn't Varik why did she feel so safe and sexy in his presence, even in the middle of this dingy room, with the chains on the wall, the whips, the stone floor?

Gravity itself compelled her downward. The lowness, the solidity of the prone position was what she desperately needed at this moment. She felt so open, so vulnerable.

Terror gripped her briefly as she realised that if he was a stranger he might hurt her, or even kill her. If she was wrong about his identity she might not survive the night.

'Spread,' he ordered, manually widening her calves with the toe of his boot. 'You have a sweet arse,' he told her, kneeling beside her on one knee.

Caralissa cried out as the flat of his hand impacted possessively against her quivering cheeks. It wasn't pain, but recognition she felt. That hand – she'd know it anywhere! 'Varik!' she cried joyfully.

'Silence, wench,' he complained, repositioning himself to fill her opening. 'Do you want the entire house to know our business?'

'No,' she smiled, 'master.'

'Do not call me that,' he chastised. 'I do not own you.'

Caralissa backed against him, taking him inside her to the hilt. 'Yes, you do.'

Varik withdrew halfway only to plunge into her again, more forcefully and with a deep grunt. 'Insolent girl,' he exhaled.

'Yes,' she agreed, 'master.'

They came together in a flooding torrent, powerful enough to wash away the world, even with all its history, all its pain. As she began to regain her powers of thought, she said a silent prayer.

Let this not be a dream. Let it be reality.

Caralissa saw her sister first. She was in a long line of prisoners, marching between two columns of Rashal soldiers.

'Romila!' she screamed from high atop her horse, Grey Cloud.

'Caralissa,' Varik chided, seated beside her on his own mount. 'Show some dignity, will you please?'

244

'Sorry,' she smiled, 'master.'

Romila was running towards them, having broken through the ranks unimpeded. Caralissa dismounted and the two embraced: the elder sister still in rags, the younger in a long green dress, belted with a sash in the Rashal manner.

'Little sister?' Romila wept, beholding the redheaded braids, the feathers and claws on Caralissa's necklace. 'Is it really you? I thought you were dead! Oh, sister,' she cried, throwing herself into Caralissa's arms. 'It was terrible. After the auction I was taken to this horrible pleasure-house. The most unspeakable things were done to me there. I thought I would die there, but then, quite out of the blue, we came under attack and the whole place was in flames. It was the Rashal, we were told, under a new leader, the old one having been deposed.'

'Voluntarily stepped down,' Varik corrected, looking down on the two sisters. 'My brother and I came to a new arrangement. He will run the empire, and I will chart new territories for him.'

Caralissa beamed. 'Varik and I are journeying together. Into the Forest of Night.'

Romila blinked. 'But what of the rest of us – what of Orencia?'

Varik pointed to a body of horsemen, fast approaching. 'Your answer is coming now.'

They watched as Senelek rode proudly towards them at the head of a squad of mounted warriors, behind them on a long chain, a line of naked prisoners, all males.

'Greetings, brother,' said Senelek, as the party came to a halt in front of them.

'Greetings, chieftain,' replied Varik.

'No, Romila!' Caralissa was saying as she tried to hold her sister back from one of the prisoners, a small weasel of a man who held particular interest for her. 'Do not acknowledge his existence. Let him be taken away and executed with the others.'

'Get her off me!' Telos wailed pitifully, unable to raise his chained hands in self-defence against the flailing arms of the princess.

Realising her sister would do little harm to the man she decided to let her have her fun.

'Mercy!' the prisoner begged, falling to his knees as Romila fell on him.

'Mercy!' begged Remik, who was chained to Telos' left.

'Mercy!' parroted Alinor, chained at his right.

'Chieftain,' Varik said, trying to maintain the dignity of the meeting. 'The princess Romila is obviously quite spirited. May I recommend her as administrator in this new region of the empire?'

Senelek inclined his head. 'We take the counsel of our brother with the utmost seriousness. Consider it done.'

Caralissa tried to keep herself from giggling as she noted the scar on Senelek's briefly down-turned forehead. There were similar ones on Varik's chest. According to the former chieftain, the two had hammered out their peace under torchlight, in the dead of night upon a lonely hillside, grappling at one another for the better part of four hours until they finally collapsed together, utterly exhausted.

'The great chieftain is most generous,' Romila spoke up, straightening herself proudly, revealing herself to be a natural born politician and pragmatist. 'We shall humbly serve the Rashal. May we make, to this end, one small request?'

'Name it,' said Senelek. 'Romila, Administrator of the Valley of Seven Kingdoms.'

Romila looked at the chained men, a wicked smile slowly

snaking across her lips. 'Allow me to take these prisoners off your hands, my lord. We can find use for them here, as our slaves.'

The men trembled at the queen's words, particularly the final one. Caralissa allowed herself a smirk. She had no doubt these arrogant fools would pay dearly for their crimes under Romila's new administration.

'So be it.' Senelek raised his hand in a gesture of finality. How splendid he looked in his chief's armour and cloak. 'Deliver these wretches to the castle,' he commanded a nearby officer. 'I must bid you farewell,' he said to his brother. 'There is much work to be done.'

Varik bowed low in his saddle. 'Your presence has honoured me, chieftain. Until we meet again, I shall serve you ceaselessly.'

Senelek's lips moved into a near smile, the closest she'd ever seen the man come to actual mirth. 'I've no doubt of that, Varik.' Pulling up on his reins to commence a turn, he added, 'I fully expect when next we meet that you will have single-handedly subdued the entire Forest of Night.'

Varik pressed his lips together. 'As you command. But as I am no longer alone in the world,' he declared, indicating Caralissa, 'I shall be due only half the credit.'

Sometime later, in a humble tent, a lone traveller reclined upon his side, bare-chested, his head resting on his hand as he regarded the splendid kneeling girl. For the better part of an hour he held her in this position, hands clasped behind her head, knees spread, breasts prominently displayed, as he finished his supper of warm meat chunks and gravy served with thick brown bread. As he beheld her now, his eyes lingered on the most delicious parts of her.

'Have you something to say?' Varik asked with amusement, breaking her enforced silence.

Caralissa's eyes burned with fury. 'Your girl is hungry,' she said, stating the obvious. 'If it pleases her master.'

Varik belched, picking a bit of meat from between his teeth with a toothpick. 'And what concern is that of mine?' he enquired.

'Your girl will starve, master,' she reminded him, 'if master does not feed her.'

'Indeed.' He raised an eyebrow, as though this were some revelation. 'Am I simply to give away my hard earned bread, then?'

'No, master,' she replied, with as much sarcasm as she could still manage. 'Allow your girl to earn her pitiful allotment of food. Allow her to please you as a god.'

He exhaled uneasily, eying the half a loaf of bread and partially filled pot of soup. 'For such a feast,' he said, 'a girl would have to be very pleasing indeed.'

Caralissa cast him a wicked glare, promising much. 'Yes, master,' she replied huskily, lowering herself to her belly on the dirt. 'Your girl understands.'

Caralissa was prostrate, slithering her way to Varik's feet. Her aching nipples chafed on the ground, her tender sex twitched with need.

'I beg permission to kiss your feet,' Caralissa said, her mouth ripe and needful.

'Permission granted.'

Caralissa closed her eyes as she worked her lips over his skin. As far as she was concerned – her present anger aside – every part of Varik really was sacred to her. Gradually he allowed her higher up on his body, compelling her to bathe every inch of his feet and legs with her tongue.

How she longed to rush ahead to his manhood, skipping the rest of the preliminaries. And yet she knew she must earn that right, as she must earn the right even to beg, offering her willing body in exchange for food or beverage.

Varik was a ruthless master. Devious and harsh. He kept the reins tight. Though it was only a few days since they'd reunited, he had already tamed her considerably. Obedient and attentive, she was readily assuming her place as second in the household behind the boisterous Ahzur. To her surprise she was even becoming jealous of Varik's attentions to the beast, the way he petted the animal, allowing it the privilege of lying beside him whenever it wished, the way he allowed it to eat and drink as it desired.

The first night she threw a fit when he revealed to her that if she were thirsty she would take water from Ahzur's dish, lapping it with her tongue. All through the night, feverish and parched, she'd lain, chained in the dirt, too stubborn to move. Finally, shortly before dawn, humbled and desperate, she begged for the opportunity to use the once spurned dish.

'Across my lap, wench,' Varik told her now.

Caralissa shuddered, knowing immediately what he intended. Once again he would feed her under discipline, compelling her to beg for a spanking in order to receive a few measly scraps of bread.

'Is Cara hungry?' he asked, employing the diminutive she so hated.

'Yes, master,' she replied, her buttocks warming under the spread of his caressing fingers, 'Cara is hungry.'

'Bread is five strokes a bite tonight,' he told her.

'The rates have gone up,' she noted. 'Master.'

'Inflation,' he shrugged, applying his hand for the first stroke.

Though she did not wish him to see it, she was grinning. He was such a beast!

Her buttocks red and inflamed, she opened her mouth

at last to receive the piece of bread. She licked his fingers as he fed it to her.

'Are you ready to earn another?' he asked.

'Yes,' she whispered, 'master.'

Bracing herself, she made a vow in her heart. Before the night was done she'd have the whole loaf – and a healthy dose of his semen as well.

'I love you, master,' she told him.

'And I you,' he acknowledged, his hand swatting her yet again. 'And I you.'

More exciting titles available from Chimera

***

Sales and Distribution in the USA and Canada

Client Distribution Services, Inc
193 Edwards Drive
Jackson
TN 38301
USA
(800) 343 4499

***

Sales and Distribution in Australia

Dennis Jones & Associates Pty Ltd
19a Michellan Ct
Bayswater
Victoria
Australia 3153